THE ATLAS
of LOVE

THE ATLAS

of LOVE

Laurie Frankel

St. Martin's Griffin
New York

THE ATLAS OF LOVE. Copyright © 2010 by Laurie Frankel. All rights reserved. Printed in the United States of America. For information, address St. Martin's Press, 175 Fifth Avenue, New York, N.Y. 10010.

www.stmartins.com

The Library of Congress has cataloged the hardcover edition as follows:

Frankel, Laurie.
    The atlas of love / Laurie Frankel.—1st ed.
        p. cm.
    ISBN 978-0-312-59538-8
    1. Graduate students—Fiction.   2. Female friendship—Fiction.
3. Parenting—Fiction.   4. Seattle (Wash.)—Fiction.   I. Title.
    PS3606.R389A94 2010
    813'.6—dc22

                                                    2010036060

ISBN 978-0-312-55270-1 (trade paperback)

First St. Martin's Griffin Edition: November 2011

10 9 8 7 6 5 4 3 2 1

literally for paul

PART I

Before the Wor(l)d

One

WHEN I WAS six years old, I found a baby in the lobby of the Waldorf-Astoria. Wound in a sheet and nestled among the roots of a veritable island of overgrown potted jungle in the corner, it was exactly where no one but a six-year-old would look. You wouldn't go back there unless you were obsessed with *Where the Wild Things Are* and knew a forest hung with vines when you saw one and your grandmother was taking forever to check in and wasn't paying any attention to you anyway. Or unless you were a twenty-year-old front desk clerk, secretly pregnant and scared to death, who had just given birth on your lunch break in a third-floor suite which you knew wouldn't be occupied all week because its carpet was being replaced. Then that potted jungle might look pretty good to you.

I had slipped stealthily away from my grandmother and wandered bravely into that forest in search of wild things. There, I found mostly dust, one heads-up penny I pocketed for good luck, two Rolos stuck to the floor which I ignored because even at six, I wasn't eating Rolos off the floor, and, underneath a caladium, a tiny squirming thing I took at first to be Max in his wolf suit.

I could not, of course, have understood, but on the other hand, I must have understood because I hunkered down with the baby in my lap and leaned against the wall of the potted jungle and, to quiet her, stared into the eyes of my new friend without blinking once, ignoring the frantic cries of my grandmother and the wild rumpus of a lobby full of strangers pitching in to call my name, to peek under bathroom stalls and into the gift shop and out onto the sidewalk and a dozen other places a six-year-old might wander accidentally. It took another kid to rat me out, to poke his grubby face into my forest and cry, "I found her. I found her. *I* did," as if his were the heroic act.

I watched my grandmother's face pass from relief to anger to confusion all in a moment as she tried to work out how her six-year-old granddaughter had managed to slip away from her and give birth in under five minutes. She opened and closed her mouth a couple times before she finally settled on, "Janey, honey, tell me you did not steal somebody's baby."

Later, upstairs in our perfect room with its huge white beds and huge soft towels and huge windows full of a million glowing lights, after we'd escaped the media frenzy that had taken over the lobby when an ashen front desk clerk figured it was time to come clean, my grandmother held me in her arms after I'd changed into pj's and told me she was very proud of me.

"You're not mad?"

"I'm a little mad," she admitted, "so don't ever, ever run and hide from me like that again. But I am also very impressed."

"Why?"

"Because I see the big girl you're going to be when you grow up. And she's lovely."

"Why?"

"Because it was scary but you were brave. You didn't know what would happen if everyone found you, so you stayed put and quiet and didn't leave that baby. Even though you knew I might be mad. Even though you never took care of a baby before. Smart thinking and sweet and gutsy. You have a very full heart," my grandmother told me.

I considered this. "We should take her home to live with us."

"No, my love. That baby belongs to someone else."

"But if she didn't want her . . . ?"

"Not your baby, baby. But tomorrow, we'll go to the toy store and pick out one of your very own."

And later still, much later actually, my grandmother argued that this was where it all began. Traditionally, people like to trace this sort of thing back to eggs and sperms, but it almost always begins well before that. Jill thought it started when Dan saved the student government. Katie thought it started with the cream puffs. But my grandmother argued it was twenty years earlier in the lobby of the Waldorf-Astoria. It's always hard to nail these things down, but I think that's probably a little premature. Myself, I put the no-going-back point with Jill in the cracker aisle. Everything else followed from there. Family may not be blood, but it is destiny. It's not like you get to choose.

Two

I MET JILL among the crackers at the grocery store the night before the start of classes, the night before we started graduate school, the night before we started teaching. I thought some Triskets or something would be nice to snack on while I panicked until dawn. Jill was loading a cart with boxes of saltines.

"Hey, you're that foreign girl," she began when she recognized me from orientation.

"I'm from Vancouver," I said.

"Canada's a foreign country," said Jill reasonably. True enough I suppose. I was feeling perfectly at home though. Seattle is practically Canada.

"That's a lot of saltines," I observed. This wasn't going well so far.

She shrugged. "They're cheap. And I don't like the grocery store."

"So you're punishing it by buying all its saltines?"

"I'm buying as many as I can now so I don't have to come back."

"They'll go stale."

"Saltines already taste stale, so it doesn't matter," said Jill.

"What about vitamins?" I said. She looked at me blankly. "Vitamins? Nutrients? You know, healthy food?"

"What do you know about healthy food?" said Jill, looking in my basket. Pasta, boil-in-bag rice, Triskets. "I don't think that pack of gum is going to help you power through either," she said. Also true I guess.

"I'm going to the farmers' market tomorrow," I said, even though it hadn't been true until just that second. "I'm only here for staples."

"I don't eat vegetables, but you can pick me up after classes," said Jill as if I'd invited her. "Maybe I can absorb some vitamins by walking near yours."

"I'm Janey," I offered, kind of blown away by her forwardness but glad to have a maybe-friend.

"I remember," said Jill. "Janey from Canada."

It didn't take immediately though. We sat together in class usually, but that was about it. Then walking out of seminar one afternoon, I asked, "You don't go home and eat saltines for dinner?"

"Sometimes."

"Just saltines?"

"Or a sandwich."

"A saltine sandwich?"

"Sometimes. What do you eat for dinner?"

"Pasta. Or rice. But with vegetables."

"You cook them?"

"I microwave them. But still. You should come over for dinner."

"I can take care of myself," said Jill.

"Evidently not," I said. It's that statement that was truly true enough. I didn't know that yet. She came for dinner. I microwaved frozen broccoli in cheese sauce and frozen peas in butter sauce and dumped both pouches over pasta. Penne in cheesy butter sauce with broccoli and peas. It contained some vitamins probably, but it was kind of gross.

"This is kind of gross," said Jill.

"It's better than saltines for dinner."

"I'm not sure it is."

I wasn't sure it was either, so I decided we better learn to cook. Faced with the evidence, Jill agreed this was a good idea. How hard could it be? Cookbooks were books, and books were our specialty. I got several, read them, and we ventured back to Pike Place Market that Sunday afternoon. Jill proposed eating first.

"We're here to cook," I protested.

"We're here to shop."

"Then let's shop."

"You should never shop for food on an empty stomach," Jill said sagely.

"The only food you've ever shopped for is saltines."

"Not when I'm hungry."

She brought us to a little hole-in-the-wall deli just up the street from the Market. It had tatty wallpaper and a sticky floor, two rickety tables with mismatched chairs, and a girl behind the counter chewing very grape gum and petting an enormous and impossibly placid (or perhaps catatonic) German shepherd.

"I don't think so," I said.

"The food is great," Jill assured me. "My mom loves this place."

"It's dirty."

"You don't like dogs?"

"I love dogs. But not in my food."

"She's wearing gloves."

"To pet the dog."

"There's nothing on the menu over five dollars," Jill raved.

"I am willing to pay extra for a sandwich without dog hair," I said.

We opted for lattes instead. Afterwards, we wandered through the fruit and vegetable stalls, the fish stands, the cheese counters and bakeries, the nut place. The wine shop. We were a little out of our element, but it was fun looking. We were a little out of our element, but everyone was happy to look at our list and make suggestions. It was dark by the time we got home.

"I'm too tired to learn to cook," Jill declared, collapsing dramatically to the floor.

"You had three coffees," I said. But Jill managed to raise herself only as far as the sofa where she stayed for the rest of the evening, being helpful by copiously sampling the wines and cheeses and determining which ones went best together. I made the most laborious meal in the history of time. It took me thirty minutes to chop three carrots and a head of broccoli. It took an hour of Googling to decide how best to broil a piece of fish. It took two and a half hours to cook the potatoes, and even then they weren't done because I had the oven at 350 because I was baking cookies at the same time (the cookies weren't done either, but they were still fine because raw cookies are better than done ones anyway). It was after midnight by the time we finished dinner. I couldn't imagine doing that even once a month let alone every night.

"Saltine sandwiches are better," said Jill.

"You're too drunk to judge," I said.

"That's true," Jill giggled. "Plus imagine how much worse this would taste if I'd helped."

By Thanksgiving, I had mostly figured out what I was doing with seafood and vegetables, but animals with feet still eluded me. I could not get my head around reaching down a hole in a turkey (made when its head was chopped off), pulling out a bag of its guts, and replacing them with bread crumbs. As a solution, I proposed we be vegetarians. We made a feast without turkey. But it is hard to feast small. I made latkes (it was almost Hanukkah too), homemade applesauce ("Why buy when you can torture yourself?" asked my grandmother in an e-mail passing along her mother's recipe), braised scallops ("Very vegetarian," said Jill), roasted beets, and mini cream puffs with a variety of fillings for dessert. We lit candles and gave thanks—for having made it to the holiday, to the end of our first term, to the end of the year. We said thank you for the miracles of the semester—for learning how to cook, how to teach, how to be grad students, for not having to eat frozen spinach in cream sauce over boil-in-bag rice for dinner every night. For friendship.

You don't get through graduate school without alliances. It's like war, international diplomacy, and middle school—perilous climates untenable without support. For this I had Jill. And also like war, international diplomacy, and middle school, graduate school is rife with archnemeses. Everyone has one. Ours was

Katie Cooke. Always overdressed and over madeup, she knit during seminar, used color-coded pens to take notes, and wore her reading glasses on lanyards which always, always matched her outfits. She sat in the middle of the front row if the chairs were in rows and right next to the professor if the chairs were around a table. She raised her hand to answer every single question posed. She was a Victorianist *and* a Mormon. We spent long evenings over beers that first semester mocking her. It was our stress release.

The Monday after Thanksgiving, we still had lots of leftovers, so we brought mini cream puffs to seminar. Everyone was wildly impressed that I had made them myself, even Katie. She cornered us after class.

"Those cream puffs were amazing," she enthused. "You must be such a great cook."

"I'm learning," I said noncommittally. "Slowly."

"No, those were really good. And healthy. Because they're small so you can eat lots of them and it's still okay."

"Good point," I said, wondering if she were crazy as well as annoying.

"No one cooks in graduate school," Katie added.

"Sure," I managed.

Suddenly she grabbed my arm. "You have to teach me how," she whispered.

"What?"

"You have to teach me how. I can't cook. I should be able to cook. My last name is Cooke."

"You can't cook?" Jill was incredulous. "You're like some kind of domestic goddess. You knit during class. You're wearing a suit."

Katie shrugged. "Yeah, but I can't cook." This was surprising.

Both that she couldn't cook and that she was talking to us. Katie is often surprising. She sneaks up on you in ways you never expect. I didn't know that yet.

I wanted to say, "I don't really know how to cook either. I'm just a beginner." I wanted to say, "It's kind of a busy time of the semester right now. Maybe another time." I wanted to say, "But we don't really like you." Instead, I panicked and said, "I've been practicing on Sundays. Jill helps by tasting and providing commentary. You could join us." Jill glared at me.

"I have church until at least noon," said Katie.

"Okay," I said.

"I could come after though. Do you buy anything?"

"What?"

"Do you buy anything? I can't buy anything on Sundays. But other people can cook for me. As long as I don't pay them."

"Thanks," said Jill.

"I guess you could come after the shopping but before the cooking," I offered.

"I'm so excited," said Katie, clapping her hands. That made one of us.

That Sunday, I grilled mini pizzas and winter vegetables. Jill sat on the sofa, drank wine, and grilled Katie.

"So . . . Victorianism, huh? Kind of tight ass," said Jill.

"Not so much . . . prudish," Katie substituted, "as ordered, restrained, dignified really. Full of contradictions too."

"Is that why you're a Mormon?" Jill pressed.

"Because of the contradictions?"

"That too. And the prudishness."

"We are fifth-generation LDS on my father's side," said Katie. "If you wanted, I could tell you about it."

"No thanks," Jill said. "Coffee's pretty much a deal breaker for me. What's wrong with coffee anyway?"

"Short answer? It's addictive."

"So is wine."

"No alcohol either," said Katie.

"Even wine?" Jill was horrified.

"Even wine."

"But the Bible's all about wine," Jill protested. "Have you even read the Bible?"

"Short answer?" said Katie again. "Modern clarification. It's important for people to be in control of themselves at all times. Important and hard. Wine does not help that endeavor."

Jill rolled her eyes. "Why are you so desperate to learn to cook anyway?"

"For when I'm married," Katie said.

"You're engaged?"

"No."

"Seeing someone seriously?"

"No."

"Have a great feeling about someone you've just met? Falling in love with a friend? Embarking on an arranged marriage?"

"Waiting impatiently," said Katie. "Preparing in the interim."

"I kind of liked her," I admitted sulkily after Katie left.

"She's so weird," said Jill. "She said she wanted to learn to cook, and then she didn't even pay attention."

"So did you," I said.

"Yeah, but I didn't really want to learn to cook. I wanted you to learn to cook for me."

The next Sunday Jill and I shopped for food while Katie tagged along and figured if she didn't pay for anything, it was okay to look. She was becoming an expensive archnemesis. Then we went home and I cooked, and Katie and Jill sat in the living room and chatted. Katie had evidently decided that being sociable was more fun than learning to cook anyway. She held her own against a none-too-gentle Jill. She came and stayed. What could we do? We were down one archnemesis. We were nemesisless.

Later, much later, like my grandmother, he will also wonder how it started. He, who will know us all so intimately, will wonder how such different people came together. And why. That will be his real question. And so I will skip the Waldorf-Astoria and tell him this story instead, for here is where his story really begins, somewhere between the wild things and the cream puffs, with a friendship. Well before the eggs and sperms, I will tell him, there was this at the beginning: brilliant, beautiful, glaringly bright, embarrassingly blind, unspeakable faith.

Three

T. S. ELIOT MUST have been in graduate school when he concluded that April is the cruelest month. In April, I had two twenty-five-page seminar papers to write, roughly a dozen books per paper to read (and not the good kind; the literary criticism kind), and fifty research papers to grade, at about forty-five minutes apiece, for the two Intro to Composition courses I was teaching. It's because, nearly four years on from the cracker aisle and the start of grad school, though I had figured out what I was doing, I had not figured out how to make it doable. On the one hand, I was teaching at Rainier University, an A-list institution if ever there were one, and reading and thinking about literature for a living, however meager. On the other hand, I was distinctly not a professor, never mind the hours and hours every week I spent planning lessons and meeting with students and grading and grading and grading. My professors are teaching at the same school I am, teaching, as I am, two courses per semester, and being paid, as I am, to teach and read books and write about them for a living—except there are two major differences. One, they really are paid enough to qualify as a living. Sometimes they even go out to a nice restaurant for dinner. Two, though they are teachers by profession, their priority is their research not their classrooms. Some of them don't even like to teach. Some of them are very old and have forgotten how. Some of them have ceased to care at all. In contrast, I never go out to a nice restaurant. But I do care quite a lot.

My students sense this. Apart from their English class, most of my students' first year of school is spent in enormous halls with three hundred other people listening to a professor lecture while they furiously scribble it all down. So when these students have a crisis, which is often because they are eighteen, away from home for the first time, and living in a dorm with about five hundred other eighteen-year-olds away from home for the first time, they come see me. During office hours, I usually have a relatively small number of rough drafts but a steady stream of students in crisis.

For instance, on the day from which I will really start telling this story, a day which was another kind of beginning, Isabel Rallings was in my office in tears. Through the snuffling, I came to understand that her boyfriend hadn't been calling (typical), hadn't visited in a few weeks despite promising to do so (typical), didn't sound very excited to hear from her when she called him (typical), and that she thought she might be pregnant (not so typical, but not unusual either; I average about two pregnancy scares a semester). Relatively easy, maybe not for Isabel, but for me. I've had practice. We talked about the importance of communication. We talked about how cycles become irregular by this time of the semester. We concluded with how pregnancy tests are fifteen bucks, a fortune for an undergraduate (and, hell, me) but worth it maybe for her peace of mind. I handed her Kleenex, made kind soft sympathies, and sent her on her way.

"Next," she said, smiling tearfully at James Rains, sitting in the hallway against the wall waiting for her to be done. He slunk ruefully, half ashamed, half already smiling, into my office. James was the third of these that week. I knew what he wanted before he even said anything. "So," he started, "you're gonna think this is really funny." For sure, I was already amused though I doubted this was what he meant. He was grinning but wouldn't look up from his shoes. "We went out last night, but I came home early to start writing my paper, but then my roommates came home, and they were all drunk, and I had just finished my essay, and one of them accidentally sat on my computer, and I lost the whole thing." I mocked him for a little while, so he knew I knew he was full of crap, and then I gave him a one-day extension. It's not like I was going to grade them all in one night anyway. Plus I felt sorry for him. If it was true, it was a very sad story. Imagine doing all that hard work—and giving up a night of partying besides—and losing it all. If it was a lie, I pitied him anyway—I felt sorry he couldn't come up with a better excuse and had to embarrass himself with that one.

At the ends of semesters, there is a steady stream of James Rainses seeking extensions. To me at least, the women come with more involved, sadder excuses (sick roommates, crying little sisters, relationships in need of repair), the guys with a flurry of technical problems (lost flash drives, broken laptops, beers on keyboards—there are endless permutations of these as well). It's not that one or the other of these excuses is more likely to be true—there's no way to tell for sure. And it's not that the guys don't have emotional crises too; it's that I'm less likely to hear about them. These excuses annoy my colleagues, but I don't mind so much. My slacking students make me feel on the ball.

Which I never am. At the ends of semesters, I can't even carry all the grading I have to do let alone all the books I have to read. Faced, as I was that afternoon, with a couple hours of free time, I should have gone home and read. I should have canceled office hours in the first place. I shouldn't even have been allowed out of the house—that was how much reading I had to do. But you don't get through graduate school by plowing through. You get through graduate school by taking breaks. At least that's what I tell myself. Thursdays, after classes, after office hours, before the weekend, I met my breaks for drinks.

"Drinks" is something of a misnomer. Half the time, we couldn't afford drinks. All of the time, we couldn't afford the depressant. The last thing I needed was to go home and fall asleep at a decent hour. I'd never make up that time. Jill likes to get a beer and a coffee and figures they'll balance each other out. Katie just eats pastries. But in Seattle, strange religious tenets notwithstanding, even the Mormons go to coffee shops. As in England, where everyone has their pub, in Seattle, everyone has their coffee shop. Ours is away from campus, minimizing the chance of running into our classmates, or worse, our students, or much worse, our professors. Most coffee shops are kept a bit cool—in part because it's hard to insulate against so much rain and chill but really to encourage you to buy more hot beverages. Joe Bar, however, is warm, dark, and nooky. It also has tables out front for when it gets finally sunny. April is usually not quite spring in spirit in Seattle, but it had stopped raining, and Katie and Jill were outside braving the chill when I arrived. They were sharing an egg salad sandwich. And fighting about eggs. When I sat down, Jill was saying, "It's just exactly like we're eating dead baby chicks on rye."

"No it's not," Katie insisted. "The eggs you eat aren't fertilized."

"Chickens have sex, and then they lay eggs."

"No they don't."

"Of course they do."

"No, it's like fish. She lays the egg and then the rooster comes and fertilizes it. Or, in this case, the farmer grabs it before it gets fertilized. That's why we're not eating dead baby chicks."

"How does he?"

"He just takes it out of the henhouse."

"Not the farmer. The rooster," said Jill. "How could he fertilize an egg that was already out of the hen? Does he have a little drill bit on the tip of his penis?"

"I don't know," said Katie. "Maybe the eggs are soft when they first come out and then he sticks it in and then it hardens up later."

"No, because if it came out soft, it would get hay and shit in there. The whole point of the shell is to protect the baby chick."

"I guess that's true," said Katie, resigned, like she couldn't possibly trump logic that solid. This is a good demonstration of why I don't eat eggs unless they look like something else. Scrambled, quiched, in a cake, or I'm not interested. This is also a good demonstration of why we aren't in graduate school for biology.

"What brought up chicken reproduction?" I asked as if there could really be a satisfactory explanation.

"Katie thinks it's romantic that chickens mate for life," said Jill.

"That's geese," I said.

"Maybe swans," said Katie. "Maybe cranes?"

"Why are you talking about animals who mate for life?" I took a stab at getting back to the point.

"I was thinking about it for my *Great Expectations* paper," said Katie, as if that explained everything.

"How were office hours?" Jill asked. "I can't believe you're still holding them. Classes are over. It's reading period."

"How can they make excuses about late papers if I don't hold office hours? It was fine. One squashed computer, one lost assignment sheet, one actual rough draft to go over, and one pregnancy scare."

"Two," said Jill, her mouth full of egg salad.

"Two what?"

"Two pregnancy scares," said Jill.

"No," I said, just one, just Isabel.

"Also me," said Jill. And because we were both looking at her blankly, not getting it, she added, "I think I'm pregnant."

Katie paled. She had always known, of course, that this is what comes from sex among the unwed. But it seemed a great tragedy to her already. In the couple seconds of silence that followed Jill's bemused announcement, Katie pictured her wretched and wandering the frozen streets of London circa 1850, torn and dirty shawl wrapped around a screaming, malnourished infant, looking for men to whom to prostitute herself in exchange for a desperate scrap of bread. This is the way for Victorianists. A Shakespearean, I took the news better though what flashed briefly through my brain was a montage of after-school specials on how to avoid this very situation.

"What makes you think so?" I asked.

"I'm late," Jill said.

"April stress?" Katie suggested hopefully.

"And we weren't being especially . . . safe," Jill admitted.

"Still . . ." said Katie.

"And I looked at my cervix. It's blue."

I sighed and rolled my eyes. Probably she didn't need this display of annoyance, but I couldn't help it. Foggy though she was on chicken reproduction, Jill had a grossly detailed hold on her own. She thinks she knows when she's ovulating and all that crap, so she doesn't use birth control when she thinks she doesn't need it. Which, obviously, doesn't always work.

In conversations like this one, it's hard to know what to say first. Katie got right to the point, breathing, "What will you do?" at the exact same moment I tried the more practical, "Have you told Dan?"

"I don't know," said Jill, the least fazed of all of us by far. "And not yet. You're the first."

We were pretty well done with Thursday afternoon drinks.

Four

ON THE WAY home, I stopped at the store for snow peas, asparagus, carrots, and a pregnancy test. At times like these, April times, I deal with almost everything by chopping vegetables into tiny, tiny pieces. The best thing about learning how to cook hadn't been the vast improvement in meal quality but the unexpected revelation that cooking is insanity management. During especially stressful days, I close my eyes and reassure myself that if I can make it through the afternoon, I get to go home to red peppers and my paring knife.

Later, while we were waiting in the living room, silent on separate sofas, as Jill limply held a plastic wand she'd just peed on a little bit away from her with a slightly sick expression (Jill, for all her willingness to examine her own cervix regularly, is a bit squeamish about pee, poop, blood, and germs—something she'd probably need to get over if she had a baby), I had a brief, strange flash of wishing it were me. It's conventional wisdom that it's best not to have a baby if you are poor, barely employed, absurdly overworked, without plan or direction, and totally single. But it's also conventional wisdom that you'll never have a baby if you wait until you're ready, in fact, that you'll never do anything if you always wait for conditions to meet ideals, and for me, this wisdom extends to a further important truth—I'll never do anything if I have to decide. Decision making is not my strong suit. But my strange jealousy was not only about its being appealing to have something so monumental just thrust upon me. I thought it would have been comforting, a relief, to know.

We waited.

"Pink," Jill said, three minutes later, holding it up for us to see. "Flaming pink. Magenta. Fuchsia. Crimson."

"It looks pretty sure," Katie admitted.

I stood up, removed the wand from Jill's hand, walked to the kitchen, deposited it unceremoniously in the garbage, washed my hands, started chopping vegetables, and burst into tears. Neither Jill nor Katie was moved by this. Each sat still and stunned. I made dinner while they freaked out alone in their own heads. When half an hour later I returned to the living room with food and nothing had changed, I figured it was my job to bring it up. At a loss, I began this way: "What are the options?" I am a fan of options, of listing them, ruminating over them. Maybe not a fan. More of an addict. I can't help myself. I have to consider everything. The truth is though, as anyone who has ever been or thought about being pregnant in the whole history of time could tell you, there are only ever, at most, three options, and unless you are delighted about the first, they are very, very difficult to talk about.

"This is why abortion is still legal," I said anyway.

"No it's not," Katie snapped.

"Um, yes. It is."

"No, not, no it isn't legal; no this isn't why."

"I know what you meant, and this is exactly why."

"This is a terrible case for abortion."

"She doesn't need to make a case."

"She's not poor; she's educated; she's in a stable relationship—"

"I am poor," Jill broke in.

"—no one forced her. She had sex ed in school."

"Yeah, but I probably wasn't paying attention," said Jill.

"Abortions are tragic and should not be taken lightly."

"Are you running for Congress, Katie? Who's taking this lightly?"

"You guys aren't helping," said Jill.

"I can't believe we're having this conversation," said Katie.

"I can't believe you'd think we wouldn't."

"I can't believe this is even on the table."

"The only reason to have a baby," I said, "is because you want to be a parent. Otherwise, that's why there is abortion."

"Or you could try not having sex."

"I think that ship has sailed," said Jill.

"Right, because a moratorium on sex is totally reasonable."

"You should try it sometime, Janey." Like I have sex all the time. I wish.

"Or even appropriate. It's not like she's twelve."

"Twelve?" said Katie. "That's the cutoff for you? Twelve?"

"I think we're getting off topic," said Jill.

"The reason to have a baby is because you're pregnant. That's what pregnant means," said Katie. "If she didn't want to have a baby, she should have thought of that before she got pregnant."

"Who says I don't want to have a baby?" said Jill.

We stopped and looked at her. We might have forgotten she was there.

"Do you?" we both asked at the same time.

"I don't know," she said.

"Well, do you want to . . . stop it?" Katie asked.

"I don't know."

"Do you want to be a mother?" I tried.

"Someday. I think."

"Now?"

"I don't know."

"Does Dan?"

She just shrugged. We let the "he probably doesn't want to be a mother" joke lie there untouched.

"Can we not talk about this right now?" said Jill. "Can we watch a movie instead? Can we do nothing?"

I thought fleetingly of my so-much-work and realized it was not to be. We watched something stupid. Katie and Jill fell asleep on their separate sofas. I threw blankets over each of them and crawled off to my own bed sometime after midnight.

I don't know how long they'd been up and talking, but by the time I wandered in the next morning, Katie was already on "This is your son or daughter we're talking about." I sighed loudly. It wasn't that I desperately wanted Jill to get an abortion or that I thought she'd make a terrible mother or that I was all about all abortions all the time for everyone. But having a baby because it's against Katie's religion to have sex is a stupid reason. And since no one else was going to say it, it had to be me. In movies, on TV, abortion's usually not even an option, not because of the political implications, simply because if she has an abortion, there's no story, at least not that one. Abortion is a plot hole. Real people have to make the decision.

"It's only your son or daughter if you want it to be," I said, distributing bowls of Cheerios all around. "Only if you let it grow into a baby. Right now, it isn't a baby. It isn't anything. It isn't even a fetus yet." Jill was crying suddenly, and I couldn't tell if it was with relief—because this was what she wanted to hear—or disgust, horror, anger, sadness, exhaustion. There were lots of possibilities. In case it was the former though, I kept talking. "If you're not ready, if Dan's not ready, you shouldn't do it. There are lots of good reasons to stop this right here."

"Like what?"

"Like if you're going to be resentful. Like if Dan's going to be resentful. Like if you don't want to set aside your whole life right now to take care of someone else's. This is not a part-time gig. You can't change your mind later. If you can't take care of it—"

"Why wouldn't I be able to take care of it?" Jill looked up at me and wondered with wet, hurt eyes.

"I'm saying if. I'm saying if that's true, you know, you *know*, it's not fair. To anyone."

"It would change my life," said Jill. An understatement.

"Having a baby would change your entire life," I agreed.

"No. I mean having an abortion would change my life."

"Why?"

"Because I would never forget."

"There are lots of things you never forget."

"Because what if this is my last chance?"

"To what?"

"To be pregnant."

"Why would it be your last chance to be pregnant? Clearly you're fertile."

"But what if I just don't ever get pregnant again for whatever reason?"

"If you want to, you will."

"What if I don't want to?"

"Then why would you now?"

"Because it's already here now. It's already decided." I remembered my flash of jealousy from yesterday afternoon, but I remained unconvinced. Indecisiveness is also not a good enough reason to have a baby.

"Indecisiveness is not a good enough reason to have a baby," I said.

We chewed Cheerios for a little bit and said nothing.

"How would it be? If you had the baby?" Katie ventured after a pause.

"You're changing the subject," I accused.

"This is hardly a different subject," she said.

"I guess I would drop out of school, get a job somewhere, get daycare all day. Work. Raise a baby." This sounded desperate and miserable, but it wasn't really. She wasn't just a child herself. She was not thinking about dropping out of high school. She was not even thinking of dropping out of college. This was a woman who already had a master's degree. We were talking about a Ph.D. in literature. We were not talking about her having to take a miserable minimum-wage job or two or three. We were talking about giving up the ten-thousand-dollars-a-year deal that is a graduate assistantship in exchange for a real job like normal people get. It had the ring of terrible, but that was someone else's version of this story.

"What about Dan?" I asked.

"I don't know. I don't know what he'll want to do." Katie and I exchanged glances and then let this go. I tried, but I honestly couldn't even put odds on what Dan would want.

"You could let someone else raise it, put it up for adoption," Katie offered. That's such weird phrasing, I thought. Put it up for adoption. Like put it up on an auction pedestal for bidding. Like it's a vase.

"That's stupid," said Jill.

"Why?"

"Because then I'd just have an abortion. Why would I give my child to somebody else to raise?"

"If someone else could do a better job of taking care of it—"

"Why do you guys think I can't raise a baby?"

"I don't think you can't raise a baby," I said. "But I don't know if you want to either. And if you don't want to, you'll do a bad job. This is important, Jill. You can't screw it up. You keep saying, 'I don't know. I don't know.' And you have to know, or you have to choose something else, and that something else might be the responsible thing to do in this case."

She thought about it. And Katie thought about it. And I thought about it. It was like we were in a fight, but we weren't really. Jill finished her Cheerios and slammed her spoon down. "I have to talk to Dan," she said. "I won't know anything until I do. I'm not even thinking about it until then." She picked up her things and left. She didn't even put her bowl in the sink.

"What do you think she's going to do?" asked Katie.

"I think she's going to have a baby. What do you think she's going to do?"

"I think she's going to have a baby."

Five

DANIEL DAVISON WAS one of those people for whom every-thing seems effortless. Walking across campus with him to get coffee took twice as long as it did with anyone else because everyone stopped to talk to him because everyone was his friend. The cool kids were his friends and the athletes, the Greeks and the poets, the theater kids, the marching band, the scientists. Deans and vice presidents and board members who knew only seven students by name knew Dan. They all stopped to say hi and to chat, and for each, Dan would know a little something. "How'd you do on that test you were stressing about?" he'd say, or, "I heard your party was awesome. I'm sorry I missed it," or, "How'd things go on that date you had last week?" Dan played intramural volleyball. He wrote for the student newspaper and the literary magazine. He was usually starring in a play or two each semester. He DJ'd for the campus radio station from one to two A.M. on Mondays. He was always in at least a couple bands.

We tend to think people like this can take anything in

stride. But for Dan, as for all people like this I suspect, it meant he couldn't accommodate anything unexpected—it was all balanced, all perfectly timed, all completely interdependent on everything else. Any addition throws everything off.

I knew all this because Dan was a student of mine my first semester in the classroom, his first semester at college. He was a smart kid and a good writer, warm, funny, the student who wins over the rest of the class for you because they figure if he likes you, you must be worth liking. He got As. On every assignment, every essay. Nonetheless, he came weekly to office hours. To go over my comments on his essays. To read me his rough drafts. To get explanations about semicolons, about passive voice. I couldn't figure this out. About midterm, I realized, amused, that he was already sitting in my office when I got there most days, that he wasn't talking to me or even listening to my responses to his questions nearly as much as he was flirting with my officemate. Jill ignored him all semester. "Stupid freshman. Like that's ever going to happen."

Three years later, Jill was bribed by the dean into being the faculty advisor for the Student Government Association. He didn't offer her very much money, but it was still more than she could refuse.

"It's not going to be worth it," I warned her.

"How much work can it be?" said Jill. "Besides, it's not my money being divvied up, so what do I care?"

I was right, and she was wrong of course. It was a lot of work. It was a lot of budget balancing and number crunching and spreadsheet making, none of which are the strong suits of English Ph.D. candidates. It was a lot of listening to presentations by an endless parade of student groups asking for more money. "It's weird," Jill marveled. "It's like they think I give a

crap." But mostly, it was a lot of refereeing between government geeks and fraternity reps. "The GGs think nothing on
earth is as important as SGA," Jill reported. "The FRs just
want to give all the money to each other for beer. This is the
stupidest thing I have ever done in my life." Meetings consisted
of yelling and nothing else.

Jill tried not caring, her usual approach to such things, until she started getting slightly threatening messages from the
Dean of Students. "It is vital that you succeed. Your graduate
career depends on it," one said. "We have entrusted you with a
sacred duty and responsibility."

"No one told me it was sacred!" Jill protested. Desperate,
she decided they needed new blood, people who were neither
self-important GGs nor FRs just in it for the cash. She fairly
begged for volunteers.

And so when Daniel Davison wandered calmly into the me-
lee of the last SGA meeting before midterm, she had to admit
she was pretty happy to see him. A senior now, he looked exactly
the same as he had sitting in our office three years before in every way that she could put her finger on, but in some ways that
she could not quite, he had changed. When she proposed they
all start fresh and do introductions and say why they were
there, most people offered some variation of either a testy, "Par-
ticipation in a democracy is an honor and a venerated duty," or,
"I'm here representing [three random Greek letters] because I
[drew the short straw; fell asleep at the meeting; lost at beer
pong; am being hazed]." Daniel said simply, "Hi, I'm Dan. I came
to help."

He was easy—easy smiles, easy ideas, easy friends. He was very
comfortable. He seemed to like everyone so much that they all
started liking each other too. And since he clearly adored the

advisor, there was a bipartisan movement towards cooperation. The advisor, for her part, wondered whether he "came to
help" SGA or her, but both clearly needed it, so she decided to
be grateful and not find out. Her question was whether he'd
stay or was there to make a show for one day only. But stay he
did. He came faithfully to meetings, helped mediate and plan
activities, and became wildly popular among student groups
who came to beg for money. Best of all, he could do the math
involved in the budget. Soon, SGA was running smoothly, and
there was peace in all the land. Everything was back to normal.
Except one thing.

"Shit," said Jill, "I think I'm in love with an undergraduate."

"Hurrah," said Katie, willing to overlook the swear word in
favor of the sentiment.

"He's twenty." Dan had skipped a grade somewhere along
the line.

"So?" Because everyone who's single is fair game at church,
many of the men Katie dated were about that age.

"I am twenty-seven," said Jill.

"And?"

"And I am twenty-seven. I am in graduate school. I do not
like to party all the time. I do not like to get drunk four nights
a week. I don't want to rock all day with my band and experi-
ment with drugs afterwards."

"Does Dan?" I asked.

"We couldn't even go out for a drink," she said, ignoring me.
"He can't even buy a beer."

"He could if he were with you," I offered. She shot me a very
nasty look. "You're just embarrassed," I said. "You're worried
about what people will say if you date an undergraduate. That's
not a good enough reason not to do it."

"When you're seventy-nine and he's seventy-two, it won't seem like that big an age difference," Katie giggled. "Your kids will think it's funny."

Jill rolled her eyes. "You're both idiots," she said.

She waited until after break and asked him out the first week of spring semester. She thought it only fair she do the asking and the taking since he had made his feelings clear from the start and had performed the miracle of saving SGA (and her ass). He was so glad, so purely, clearly glad she'd asked him, so happy to have the chance to prove himself worthy of her but also just to be with her. When you looked at him those first few weeks, he radiated simple, pure gladness. It suited him. And though there was some initial whispering around the department, it didn't last. Most people were just jealous anyway.

Most of a semester later, they were really happy. We all liked Dan. Jill was starting to think about next year, a thing you should never do when you are dating someone about to graduate from college. She knew this but couldn't help it. They were young and in love. It had ceased to be weird. But none of us could really guess how Daniel Davison would react to this late-April news. He was a good guy, yes, a nice kid and smart and in love for sure, but from there to graduate-from-college-and-raise-a-baby-with-a-woman-you've-been-dating-for-three-and-a-half-months was a long way indeed.

Six

THE LAST SATURDAY night in April no one was working. Jill was having Dan over—to make him dinner and tell him. Katie had a date. I was painting my bathroom purple. Between us, we had more or less a book to write and one to grade before next weekend, but we had, I guess, more pressing things to take care of. Jill was having a baby apparently. Katie was finding a husband. I had predicted that things were going to get more rather than less crazy at the end of this semester, and if I wanted the bathroom painted, I had to do it right away. It was that quiet right before a thunderstorm when you sit on the front porch watching it close in, soaking everything it crosses, unable to work up the energy or desire to move inside. It was coming, but there was nothing I could do about it.

Student Life folks are fond of saying that you do your best learning in college outside the classroom (I was an RA as an undergrad). What I had learned about personal narrative over those couple days was that as long as it's boring and mundane, it feels like it belongs to you, but the moment something happens, the moment it starts to look like a book or a movie, it stops feeling like your own. Suddenly, you have only the epic options of literature at your disposal instead of the boring but limitless ones you're used to. On most Saturday nights, Jill could go out, she could stay home and rent a movie, she could grade, she could read, she could go to the library, she could do countless boring random things, but that night, she had only a few, dramatic options—she could become a mother or have an abortion; she could make Daniel be a father or lose him to fear and bad timing.

For Katie, life was always like this. She thought the author of her personal narrative was God and considered her lows and highs part of the Grand Plan. So tonight's date, a setup, a friend of a friend, a guy she had not yet met, was already either *(a)* the love of her eternal life or *(b)* someone else sent to help her find the love of her eternal life. Which is a lot of pressure for a first, blind date. We were on the phone, finished with what she should wear—denim skirt, white T-shirt, cardigan (cute, casual but not too casual, layered for a range of temperatures)— and on to what she knew about him already.

"Dionne says he's cute, but Jenny thinks he's weird looking. She has strange taste though."

"What does he do?" I asked, hoping he was out of college. The undergrads hadn't been working out lately.

"Dental school, first year. He's twenty-four. Also," she added very reluctantly, "he's a Yankee fan." Not dating Yankee fans is my number two rule of dating. Katie knows this but doesn't care yet. Later, when he's no good, she will admit that dating a Yankee fan is stupid, careless even. Truly, this is foolproof relationship advice.

His name was Chris, her second Chris of the month, which

I knew would make him hard to track regardless of what happened on the date (good date or bad, he and the other Chris would remain a topic of conversation for at least six weeks). He went to church in a different ward. He had already been on dates with Annabelle, Alison, Kelly, and Dionne, the woman who set them up in the first place (the rule against dating one's friends' ex-boyfriends—my number one rule of dating—does not apply in Katie's world; a guy may not be in the plans for you because he may be in the plans for someone else).

"Anyway, we'll see. Annabelle really didn't like him, but she was still hung up on Josh, and they got back together the night after she went out with Chris, so he might be fine. Dionne said he's really nice." She was not very excited, not holding out high hopes for this one, I could tell. For Katie, like for most of us I suppose, dating is work rather than pleasure. She likes to shop for clothes for dates, likes to talk about dates good and bad, likes to talk to and about boys on the phone—it's just the actual dating she doesn't care for. Being friends with Katie is like being in eighth grade again.

"What are you doing tonight?" she asked.

"Painting the bathroom."

"Finally." I'd been musing out loud about a purple bathroom since January. "Should I come by when I get home?"

"Sure. I'll be up."

"When are you going to write?"

"I'll start tomorrow."

"Me too," she said. "After church. Ugh."

"Ugh," I agreed. For me though, it's all anticipation. I dread starting, but once I get writing, it will be fine I know. Katie is happy to do the research, but the actual *during* of the writing process drives her mad.

"I guess I better go," she said. "Good luck painting. Wish me luck with Chris."

"Good luck with Chris," I said. "I hope he's not really a Yankee fan."

"Thanks. I'll see you later."

"Bye."

"Bye." I'd gotten purple paint on the phone. And the rug. And was considering the relative advisability of using nail polish remover on either when the phone rang again. It was Jill. Of course.

"I'm sautéing fish," she said, preludeless. "How long?"

"What kind?"

"Halibut."

"In what?"

"That's the next question."

"I'd do about two minutes on one side then another five or ten or so, covered, on the other side. Until it looks done in the middle of the thick part."

"What am I sautéing it in?" she asked.

"Butter? Lemon? Some white wine maybe?" It was out of my mouth before I paused to consider that wine wasn't good for the maybe-baby and then that, really, the alcohol cooks off anyway. But enough? I had no idea. "Uh, let's say butter, lemon juice, and garlic."

"Sounds good. What about potatoes?"

"What kind?"

"Those little red ones."

"Nice. How about roasting?"

"How." More statement than question. She was down to shorthand.

"Chunk them. Salt, pepper, little bit of olive oil. 375ish. Stir often. Till they're done."

"Excellent. I am also having salad and bread. And I bought a cheesecake."

"Very fancy," I said. "You can knock me up anytime."

"Tell me everything will be okay," said Jill.

"Everything will be okay," I said. "He's a good guy. He'll be well fed. Everything's going to be fine."

Lull, lull. Quiet before storm. Unknowing before unknowing. The kind of calm you only have when you stop to realize that you are not panicked—something you never do unless you have just been or are about to be. Status quo on borrowed time. No one ever really knows what's going to happen next, but we're rarely so acutely aware of that fact because usually it doesn't matter yet. That night, the future had come strangely near. I sat on the lid of my toilet, getting used to purple paint on the walls, waiting patiently for everything in my life to change.

Katie came over at ten-thirty, bearing what she calls popcorn, but which is actually popcorn mixed with that gross glazed oriental snack mix you scoop out of plastic bins in the bulk section of the grocery store. Some holdover from growing up in Hawaii. She loves it. I just pick out the popcorn.

"So, how was it?"

"Mmm," she said, very noncommittal, by which she meant that it did not go well, but she wasn't ready to say so in case she was wrong and fell in love with him later. She gave me a highly typical play-by-play. Nice enough, cute enough, smart enough, but not overly impressive on any front. He talked a lot about mouths and teeth, to be expected I guess, but still a little alarming. He did his mission in Canada (a wussy mission, in my opinion, though it was evidently chosen for him by God, so who am I to say), his undergrad at Rutgers, his childhood in northern New Jersey.

"Doesn't that get him off the hook for being a Yankee fan? I mean he's from there. Everyone roots for the team where they're from."

"Root for the Mets," I said. "What else?"

"He taught high school chemistry for a year before dental school and hated it," she offered.

"Teaching's not for everyone," I said, though I am suspicious of people who don't like to teach. On the other hand, I'm not teaching high school chemistry and would rather die, so I really can't judge.

"His favorite author is *Sports Illustrated*." She tried and failed to offer this with a straight face. "He didn't know George Eliot. He didn't even know Charlotte Brontë had any sisters." Katie is obsessed with all three Brontës, but we are snotty about literature and know it.

"I can't think of the last textbook I read on dental care," I offered.

"Yeah, but then I told him that a friend of mine was unmarried and pregnant, and he wanted to know why I was friends with her, and I said I was already friends with her before she got pregnant, and he said why wasn't I doing something to stop her, and I said my friends' sex lives are really none of my business, and he said they were and got really annoyed."

I didn't say anything. It was a deal breaker, and we both knew it. Though in his defense, obviously, it was totally our business.

•   •   •

Meanwhile at Jill's, no one was eating anything. All of that beautiful dinner just being pushed around on plates. When Dan got there, she opened the door and told him right away. She couldn't wait. She'd been making herself sick about it. They talked for seeming days. Then she kicked him out, put everything in Tupperwares, and came over. No sense letting all that food go to waste. Not that we were much interested in eating either. It was late, and we were two hours into popcorn with nasty Asian snack mix.

"He said no," she said, which communicated nearly nothing.

"What do you mean, honey?" Katie prompted, arm around her overgently.

"He said no. He said . . . no." She looked dazed. She'd been crying. I couldn't think what she might have asked him to which Daniel could possibly have answered a straight yes or no.

"He doesn't want to be a father right now. He doesn't want a baby. He came over. I told him I was pregnant. He looked . . . surprised, but not mad, not unhappy. He said 'wow' a lot. He asked when I found out and when I would be due—he kept using this weird conditional tense right from the start. He did not ask if I were sure, which is good because that's a stupid, cliché thing to ask. He did not ask if I were sure it was his, which is good because that's even worse. He said 'wow' some more. He said, 'What are your thoughts?' He was being really nice, but he wasn't talking much, and so finally I just said, 'Daniel, I don't think I want an abortion. I think I want to have the baby,' and he said, 'Okay. I want to have an abortion.'" She stopped and looked up at us to make sure that our faces mirrored the incredulity in hers. They did.

"But he can't have an abortion." Katie started with the obvious. "He's not pregnant."

"Yeah, but he doesn't want to be a father," Jill explained. "He doesn't want us to have a baby. He wants us to have an abortion."

"So what did you say?"

"Well, I was really upset and really hurt and very sad that he didn't want to be part of this kid's life and very sad that he was willing to just let me go like that, but I was at least sort of prepared for this answer. I had a speech. I forgot most of it when the time came, but basically I was like, 'Okay, well, thanks, why don't you think about it for a while and get back to me about what role you would like to play, like none or just a little or what . . .' But he was shaking his head like I didn't get it, and he said, 'No, I don't want you to have our baby but I wouldn't be part of its life. I don't want you to have our baby. I want to get an abortion.'"

"That's not his decision," Katie whispered.

"That's what I said."

"What did he say?"

"He said, 'Why not? Just because it's not my body? It's my baby.'"

Seven

O N SUNDAY, WE retreated to our own apartments and our own computers and our own piles of books and wrote. It's funny that you can do that—just turn off the part of your brain that's in emotional crisis and turn on the part that thinks about the role of the reader in Dante's *Inferno* and let that one take over completely for a little while. It is nice to have days when you wake up and write, and seventeen hours later you go to bed, and in between you wander around the house a few times and eat leftovers for about five minutes standing over your computer and mainline water and otherwise write and write and write. By midweek though, I was ready for fresh air, ready for human contact, ready to find out what other people thought was important in the world (it probably wasn't the reader in Dante's *Inferno*). So on Wednesday, I went to grade and caffein-ate at Joe Bar. And it was there that I ran into Daniel.

Daniel looked worse than three days cooped up writing. Daniel looked like he hadn't eaten or slept since Saturday. He was sitting outside, wrapped in far too many clothes for newly

May warmth and sunshine, slunk down into a faded, once black, hooded sweatshirt, staring at an open—blank—notebook. He looked miserable. Even through the window, even in the glaring sunshine, he looked spent and very sad.

"Hey," I said gently, handing him a fresh cup of coffee and sitting down.

He looked up and smiled a "hey" that seemed full of relief, I suppose, that I was still talking to him but also maybe surprise that the world was still going round out there.

"What's up?" I asked.

He snorted. "I think you know."

"Yeah. How are you holding up?"

"Not well, actually. That talk did not go well."

"Have you talked to her since?"

"Why don't you know that?"

"We've been writing for a few days."

"I haven't," he said. "I don't know who should call."

"Uh, you?" I said. As in duh. As in obviously *obviously* you. How is that not clear?

"What? To apologize?"

"To talk more?"

"I said I'd think about it some more and call her when I figured something out. She said she'd do the same. I haven't figured anything out, so it seems stupid for me to call."

"Are you mad at her?" I was getting mad at him.

"No," he said, but he didn't sound sure. And then exasperated, plaintive, almost whining, "I don't want to have a baby, Janey."

"I gathered," I said. "But it seems like you might be having one anyway, so that's evidently not the decision anymore."

"Abortion is legal. It's safe. There's a Planned Parenthood

within walking distance for godsake. It's not killing a baby.
You don't think so. Jill doesn't think so. She's pro-choice—"

"Yeah, and I think she's choosing to have the baby," I interrupted.

"But why is that only her choice?" he demanded. He had
clearly been thinking this over and over for the last three days,
having this conversation in his head, concluded for sure that
he was right. And I just looked at him and couldn't say anything because I was sure he knew the answer. "I mean yes,
right, it's her body," he continued, taking in my face. "That's
why I can't force her to have the baby. That's why it's not fair
for the government to decide for her just because she gets pregnant. But that's not why she gets to choose to have it. That's a
different question. If I wanted to be a father and she wanted to
get an abortion, there'd be no question. Her body, her choice.
Now I'm saying I don't want to be a father right now. I'm graduating from college in a week, Janey. I don't have a job. I don't
know what I want to do with my life. I do know I want to take
the summer off and go to San Francisco with my band. I do
know that having a baby wouldn't feel magical or wondrous. It
would feel like I was being punished. It would feel like I was
giving up everything. It would destroy the future I have in my
mind where ten years from now I have a career I'm good at and
a wife I love and children I planned and chose. It would erase
that future. I would be resentful and angry and scared. I would
feel forced into it. This isn't what I want right now. I should be
able to choose something else. It's not my fault." He got shriller
and more animated, more sure, more upset as he talked. He
didn't want a baby. He was twenty. He'd been dating Jill only
since January. I understood. How could I not?

"Okay," I said softly. "You don't want a baby. They'll be

okay . . ." Even as I was saying this, I wasn't sure it was the right thing—I was feeling it out—but he was shaking his head.

"No, you don't get it," he said, impatient. "I don't want to desert my baby. I don't want to desert Jill. I don't even want to break up with her. And I don't want to go around my whole life knowing I abandoned my family and they're out there—this kid is out there—without me. I want it to not be this way. I want to undo it. I want it to go away."

"I don't think you can have that," I said.

"Yeah," he grunted sarcastically. "If only there were some safe and legal procedure to put a stop to this situation before it became an unwanted child."

"It's not an unwanted child," I pointed out carefully. "Jill wants it."

"But I don't," he said. "It's not like we would have tried to get pregnant. We wouldn't have. If we'd discussed it, we'd have said now is not a good time so let's wait. And what's killing me is we could go back there. We could wait. We could give this relationship a chance and have children when we decide to, when it's our decision, both of us. It wouldn't even be hard. But she won't. And I'm the bad guy for wanting to make her. It's a mistake. That's all."

"Mistakes happen though," I said. "Then you have to step up and take responsibility."

"I am." He was almost yelling. "I am taking responsibility. I will pay for the abortion. I will go with her and hold her hand. I will be with her while she recovers. I will be with her while she's sad. I'll be sad too. We'll be sad together. It's not like this is so easy for me. We'll get through this. We'll move on. That *is* taking responsibility, not doing what she wants just because she wants it."

"I think she wants this baby," I tried to explain gently.

"It's not a baby!" He looked at me, incredulous, a little wild-eyed. "You know how I know? Because I had you for Intro to Comp and her for a girlfriend. Plus several courses in biology."

"You choose no. She chooses yes. And it's her yes vote, so I guess that trumps your no." I shrugged helplessly and said nothing for a while, just sat with him quietly hoping that would help. "I'm really sorry," I added lamely. I was too. Sorry and torn. And not certain. Dan's arguments were compelling, the more so because he *was* being responsible. He was being honest. He sounded like he might be right. But I still didn't think he was.

"I'll talk to her," I offered. "I don't think she understands your position. Meantime though, you should think about what you want to do when she decides not to have an abortion. Because I think that's what she's going to decide. And I think it's going to be her decision." I laid my hand on the back of his hung head for a moment before I left. He didn't say anything or even look at me or move. Everything suspended for a moment, two. Finally he looked up at me and smiled. "Thanks Janey. I needed to talk. It was good. It'll be okay." But in his eyes, I saw that he didn't know how. And neither did I.

Eight

JASON WAS SITTING on the steps reading a clearly for-pleasure novel when I came outside having just handed in my final papers.

"Done?" He grinned, handing me one of the two iced coffees beside him. He was waiting for me evidently.

"Is it that obvious?"

"You're looking pretty postcoital," he said.

"You too?"

"Yup. That obvious?"

"You wouldn't smile unless you were done too." Finishing a school year rivals being in love for best feeling in the world. The jealousy of it knows no bounds, which is why I wouldn't talk to Jill or Katie for a couple days until they were done too. The sleeplessness and tedium of two straight weeks of reading, writing, grading, and, this semester, panicking, felt far behind. I had a whole summer stretched out before me. That I had slept four hours total in the previous forty-eight, that I started teaching summer session in just a couple weeks, that nothing had

been resolved, didn't matter at the moment. It was May at last.
It was warm and bright. I could do anything I wanted, guilt-
free, all day. Tomorrow and tomorrow and tomorrow barely
crept at all. I had survived another April. It was cause for jubi-
lation.

"I thought you were quitting the latte addiction after grades
were in," I said.

"April," he said as if that explained everything. "Besides, it's
not like I'm pregnant."

"Mmm," I said.

"Mmm? What does that mean?"

"Nothing. I'm supposed to be surprised you're not pregnant?"

"Oh come on, Janey. Tell me. My life is so boring. You have
to help me."

I scowled at him. Jason and his boyfriend Lucas had been
together for seven years. Good—and boring—as married. They
lived in Olympia, more than an hour south, which meant I had
Jason on my couch when he had to be at school late or early or
was too drunk or tired to drive home. Lucas was the head chef at
a restaurant in Olympia called Ever After. Very popular. He went
to work nearly every day. They paid him a real salary. He read
books only for fun. He was our hero. And pretty much as alien to
our lives as if he played professional baseball. "Your life *is* boring," I admitted finally. "How did you know?"

"Oh Janey, *everyone* knows." He rolled his eyes. I was stunned.
I couldn't imagine how anyone knew. "What's she going to do?
Is she keeping it?" It seemed remarkable to me that everyone
was going to be so willing to ask such a stunningly personal,
intimate question right out of the box. And the terminology
"keeping it" is weird. What's the opposite of keep?

"I think she's going to have a baby," I said and thrilled a little guiltily at the conspiratorial drama. He gasped, grinned, nattered on beside me. This news had shattered Daniel, the worst news of his life. But it thrilled Jason as it would most people who heard it. It was great gossip. It would prove endlessly, renewably interesting because it wouldn't end—she'd just get more and more pregnant and then there'd be a baby to discuss. It had the feel of scandal. We all graded half a dozen research papers each semester on the tragedy of unwed mothers. This was like that but without the heartbreak. It was the plot without the tragedy.

"What did Dan say?" asked Jason. Was telling a betrayal? I didn't want to gossip—not just because it didn't seem fair but also because, really, it felt like my life—but I also really wanted to gossip. Two weeks of literary criticism bred a craving to talk about things real. And nothing was more real than this.

"He's not so much wanting to be a father."

"Too bad?" asked Jason. It was a question. Is it too bad?

"I don't know," I said. "I guess she's going to do it without him?"

"He's leaving her?" Jason gasped.

I shrugged. "He isn't leaving her. He just doesn't want to do this. I don't know what they'll do."

"What an asshole. Too late to make that decision," he said.

"I don't know," I said. "You think he has to be a father if he isn't ready just because Jill is?"

"If he wasn't ready, he shouldn't have been having sex," said Jason.

"Oh that's bullshit. What are you—Focus on the Family? Besides, that's easy for you to say. You can have sex all you want, and no one gets pregnant."

"Ohmygod, speaking of which, Lucas's friend Ed called last night to tell us his ex-boyfriend Martin knocked up some girl and is getting married. Stupid fags. No clue how to use birth control . . ." And we were off. Jason moved seamlessly from one bit of gossip to the next, all equally titillating and ridiculous. He was a very close friend of ours. But Jill's crisis was as removed for him as his boyfriend's friend's ex-boyfriend's poor, knocked-up fiancée. Somehow I wasn't feeling that distance.

Nine

SECONDHAND SOURCES ARE never one hundred percent reliable. Firsthand ones, when they are pregnant and in love and borderline hysterical, aren't always much better. So I might be shaky on some of the details. I do know that Daniel was over at Jill's nearly every night after I ran into him at the coffee shop, that they talked and talked until neither wanted to talk about it ever again, until they didn't even want to see each other anymore. They talked and also spent a lot of time not talking and just holding each other and also spent a lot of time having a lot of sex because, at that point, why not? I know that Jill didn't just ignore his feelings on the matter, that she heard his point of view and deeply considered it, that Daniel didn't just up and leave, that he heard her viewpoint too, even tried to change his own, that they continued to love each other, that Daniel tried hard to grow up instantaneously those first few weeks after he graduated from college. I know that negotiations took place. I can promise that tears were shed on all sides. Hearts were broken, to be sure, but not recklessly or

thoughtlessly, and if I can't perfectly reproduce those conversations Jill and Daniel had, I can promise that they were had
with full hearts.

In the end, it didn't matter. One event changed everything.
If it hadn't happened, everything would have been different. I
think Jill and Daniel would have sat on her sofa and talked for
nine months, would have run their mouths until her water suddenly broke mid-sentence and there were no longer any options. And truly, I think Daniel would have fared just fine with
fatherhood thrust upon him. But there was a catalyst, an event,
a moment which changed everything and not just for us. This
is good for storytelling but bad for decision making, and it is
frightening to look back and realize, were it not for that moment,
all of our lives would have been so different. Maybe that's revisionist history. Maybe it's me making origin myths. But I
can't shake the conviction that Jason's boyfriend's friend's ex-
boyfriend's girlfriend changed the world.

We were sitting around the post-dinner table at my house,
all four of us, Katie, Jill, Daniel, and I, about three weeks after
graduation, not quite two months into Jill's pregnancy. We
were sated, had eaten and chatted our fill. We had talked very
little about babies and more about nothing at all. We had found
someplace comfortable in all this where things didn't seem
so urgent anymore. They had to decide, but they didn't have to
decide this minute. We had reached a place where we could
talk and think about other things, where we could joke with
each other, where it was almost old times (she wasn't showing;
she wasn't even throwing up). We could almost forget for whole
hours at a time. Things felt okay. Then Jason and Lucas
knocked on the door and came in bearing news and change
and, thankfully, cake.

The weird thing is it didn't seem that shattering to them, and later, when they tried to reconstruct the events they had set in motion, they couldn't, and couldn't believe that their little bit of gossip had changed everything. They didn't even lead off with it.

"We have cake," announced Jason, striding directly to the kitchen, taking out plates and forks, putting on water for tea.

"Left over from the restaurant last night. A whole untouched cake. Never happens," Lucas added. "I should make pasta more often. Everyone's too full for dessert."

"Not very good for sales," said Daniel.

"No," Lucas reflected. "But good for you guys. You get free dessert."

"I can't believe we're going to eat more," said Katie. I had made pizzas. I had also made salad, grilled vegetables, and garlic bread. We had started with hummus and crackers. But Lucas-cake was too good to refuse.

"Busy tonight?" I asked.

"So-so. That new place Grill Art opened last week, so some folks are going there." Lucas shrugged.

"We ate there for lunch yesterday," Jason said conspiratorially. "Terrible."

"It wasn't terrible," said Lucas generously. "The place just opened. Maybe it's better for dinner."

"Over-sauced. Nothing was hot enough. Too salty. Too bland. The man wishes he could cook like you."

"Oh sweetie," said Lucas, leaning over and kissing Jason on the mouth, "everyone wishes they could cook like me."

"What are you guys doing all weekend?" asked Jill.

"Not much," said Jason. "We have tickets to the ballgame tomorrow afternoon."

"We must do something with the lawn."

"I need to do some work for my summer course."

"And we really should go visit Elise," said Lucas.

"We don't even know Elise," Jason protested.

"Who's Elise?" I asked.

"I told you about her," said Jason. "She's Ed's ex-boyfriend's pregnant fiancée."

"Was," said Lucas.

"She died?" I gasped.

"No," said Jason. "Was pregnant."

"And was a fiancée," Lucas added dryly. Across the table from me, Jill and Daniel both hushed though neither had been saying anything.

"What happened?"

"She was in an accident on I-5. Someone two cars up blew a tire. She tried to swerve. Everyone tried to swerve. She got hit from the side and from behind," said Lucas.

"She's okay," Jason reassured us. "She broke an arm and banged her head badly enough that they'd like to keep her for a couple nights. And she lost the baby."

"And then Martin broke off the engagement. No reason to do it at that point. Said he did love her but not in that way, he'd been confused, he was really sorry, et cetera, et cetera. I feel bad for her," Lucas added, "but the guy is so obviously gay. You don't ungay."

"Plus, it's so much better to find this out now than later. Before marriage, before kids. This is a blessing really," mused Jason.

"Except she's so in love with him, poor thing. Gets in a huge accident, wrecks her car, wakes up in the hospital with a broken arm, a concussion, and no baby, and then Martin breaks up with her. Which is why we should try to visit her at some point this weekend. We cheer people up." The discussion had stopped being among all of us and was happening just between Jason and Lucas, who had slipped into private conversation, so comfortable that they didn't notice Daniel had turned greenish-white, and Jill's face was covered suddenly with a silver sheen of wet. She was shaking her head over and over, mouth open, nothing coming out.

"Uh-oh," said Lucas, looking up.

"She lost the baby?" Jill managed, barely a whisper, barely words.

"Oh honey." Jason was back with us now. "I'm so sorry. She did. She lost the baby. But it was okay. She was just barely pregnant. The doctor says she's fine in there. Told Martin they could start trying again right away," he added with a half smile because obviously Martin wasn't trying in the first place.

Small silence.

"You're fine." Katie cut to the chase. "It's not you. You're fine."

Jill was clutching her flat stomach, looking around a little wildly.

"She's fine too," I added. "She'll be fine in a couple days."

Jill wasn't responding, and we weren't, any of us, sure exactly what was upsetting her—the accident, the miscarriage, the broken engagement, the fact that it could all be lost so completely and so suddenly.

Daniel, his color starting to return, licked his lips and took his turn at trying to be comforting. "It's so much better for everyone this way," he said slowly into what felt like thirsty, gasping silence. "She'll find someone else, someone who really wants her and really wants to have a baby instead of trapping this poor guy into marriage and fatherhood with her."

I'm sure he didn't think about what he was going to say before he said it. And what he said was true. But also tragically
misguided coming, as it did, out of his mouth.

Jill got up from the table, walked directly to the purple bathroom, and loudly threw up. It was six weeks of repressed morning sickness, six weeks of denial and rejection, of fear and panic
and isolation, of endless deliberation despite the lack of any real
options. It was realization, finally, of what this all meant, how it
was going to change her life in ways which could not even be
construed as good or promising. It was realization, finally, that
she was probably going to have a baby, and she was probably
going to have it alone.

We sat in silence. You can't eat cake when someone is throwing up in a one-bedroom apartment. You can't eat cake when
your friends are collapsing. The vomiting and all it meant had
been six long, unnecessary weeks in coming. I exchanged
guilty glances with Katie. We had spent these first weeks evad-
ing decisions, responsibility, and reality, the truth, and we'd
helped Jill and Daniel do the same when it was the last thing
they should have done. We were complicit in this, and I felt just
as (well, maybe almost as) nauseated.

Daniel pushed back from the table, took an almost comi-
cally deep breath that went on and on—like the whole inside of
him was empty and he was trying to inflate—and walked to the
bathroom. He closed the door, probably in a vain attempt at
privacy, but really it was a very small apartment and cheap besides and poorly built. You try like hell not to hear when someone's puking in the bathroom, but of course this is disgustingly
impossible, and we tried not to hear Daniel and Jill's conversation, but of course that wasn't possible either. We should have

gotten up and left the house right away, but paralyzing gas seemed to be spewing invisibly from the cake.

"Sweetie, I'm sorry," said Daniel. "I didn't mean us. I meant them. I wasn't thinking."

Pause.

"Are you okay?"

"I have to have the baby," she said, shaky.

"Okay," he said.

"Daniel, what if I lost it?"

"I don't know," he said.

"I have to protect it," she said. "All my life."

"Okay," said Daniel.

I willed us to get up, to walk outside, but we couldn't move. We couldn't even look up from our plates. We were trapped in the unfolding drama and folded right in.

"I can't believe I almost lost this baby," Jill muttered. Daniel, quiet and resigned, taking it all in, seemed to be trying to decide how much of this was reactionary and irrational and how much was certain, and was coming just as surely to conclusions of his own.

"Jill, I can't." He was crying then. "I can't. I would be like Martin. I would resent it. I would want out."

"I don't want you that way. *We* don't." She was crying too.

"I can't make you. I wouldn't want to. But I can't do it." He was muffled. She was holding him against her. Or he had his face buried in her hair or stomach. Finally, they were both so hysterical and emotional and something else—intimate—that we were embarrassed enough to move.

"Perhaps a beer," suggested Lucas.

"Brilliant," said Katie, out of character, and as we left the apartment, it was like turning our backs on a fire, slowly catching, ready to rage.

By then it was late. We were all exhausted. We didn't want a beer or anything else. Jason and Lucas, heads hung and sorry, got in their car and went home. Katie and I went to her apartment, turned on the TV, and promptly fell asleep. Overload of everything. We woke up at six o'clock in the morning, went back to my place, and found Jill sound asleep in my bed. Alone. We crawled in with her.

"Hi," she said sleepily.

"Hi," I said.

"Hi," said Katie.

"He left," said Jill.

"Where?" I said.

"I'm not sure," said Jill, slightly puzzled, like it was a logic problem. "Before he said he wanted to spend the summer in California. Maybe he's headed there?"

"How did you leave things?" asked Katie.

"He did not want to parent. I did not want to abort. It wasn't what either of us wanted, his leaving, but, comparatively speaking, of the given options, it was what we both didn't want the least I guess, so at least we could agree on that."

"Are you okay?" asked Katie gently.

"No."

"Is there anything we can do?" I asked.

"Help me raise a baby?"

"Sure," I said.

"Sure," said Katie.

"Thanks," said Jill, and we all went back to sleep.

Ten

THE FIRST PROBLEM was that, left to her own devices, Jill still ate mostly saltines. She wasn't an overly picky eater. She ate well when we could afford to go out. She ate whatever I cooked for her. Occasionally, she supplemented the crackers with M&Ms and very occasionally the M&Ms with an apple or some orange juice. But mostly she just ate crackers and water. Great were she ever to be imprisoned in a nineteenth-century novel. Lousy for having a baby. The first problem we had to solve then, before the broken heart even, was getting Jill to eat.

The second, of course, was the broken heart. But as you know, mending those is tricky.

The third problem was financial. To the uninitiated, gradu-ate fellowships seem like a great deal. They pay your tuition. They pay you a stipend to cover living expenses. In return, you teach first-year composition thereby earning your keep while also gaining valuable career experience and building your ré-sumé. Unfortunately, the stipend is not really enough to live on. We were all getting by one way or another. Katie ran up crazy credit card debt (not, unlike school loans, with a low, fixed interest rate that would wait for payment until after she got a job). My parents gave me their old furniture. And paid my car insurance. My grandmother took me shopping when I needed new clothes. Jason had the good sense to fall in love with a man with a real job. And Jill ate saltines. Saltines worked for one maybe but wouldn't for two, especially when one of them also needed diapers, bottles, clothes, toys, car seats, blankets, a highchair, and regular medical attention.

The fourth problem was childcare. Graduate school is a full-time job. It is only about twelve to fifteen hours a week in the classroom, learning or teaching or both. But it's about a gazillion hours of grading. And about two gazillion hours of reading. So that's three gazillion hours plus twelve plus you still have to eat, sleep briefly, and do a little bit of something social to keep from going mad. You can try to grade faster. You can try to read faster, skim more, skip a few books altogether. But there's not a lot of time there for taking care of an infant.

We floated solutions sensible and ridiculous. We thought she could drop out of school and get a real job (solving problem 3 only). We thought she could become a professional food taster (solving problems 1 *and* 3). We proposed a reality TV show where teams of pregnant women go on scavenger hunts to restaurants across the country on a quest for meals which do not make them throw up (the footage of this would be dynamite, the feuds inevitable and profound, the public service rendered invaluable). But I kept coming back to the same thing. I tried but could find no way around it. When I was sure, I called her right away. Never mind it was three o'clock in the morning. I couldn't sleep for thinking about it. Why should she?

"We'll move in together," I said simply when she picked up the phone and grunted something close enough to hello.

Silence. Then, "Who is this?"

"Come on, Jilly. It's me. Wake up. We'll move in together. All three of us. We'll arrange our schedules so someone's always home with the baby." (Problem 4.) "We'll share expenses." (Problem 3.) "I'll cook." (Force-feeding Jill and Fetus. Problem 1 and maybe even 2 depending on how good the food is.) "I've thought about it. It's the best solution."

Silence. "*Who* is this?"

"JILL. Seriously. How is this not a good plan?"

"How does cooking help?"

"You have to feed this baby something besides crackers."

"I eat more than crackers."

"No you don't."

"Yes I do."

"No you don't."

"Any chance we could have this conversation tomorrow?" asked Jill, but I could tell she'd sat up, cleared her eyes and head a little. Finally she said, "Do you think you'd be a good father?"

I smiled. "I'd be a great father."

Eleven

WE WERE GLIB in the middle of that night, but we didn't stay that way. We debated. A lot. Jill didn't feel entirely comfortable asking what was really a rather large favor of us. Katie wasn't sure living with a ruined woman and helping her raise her illegitimate child was in line with church doctrine. We were all worried about our work. It was hard to imagine having even less time to get everything done and harder still to imagine reading and writing with a baby crying all the time. We also suffered, honestly, from some hesitation to live to-gether—me especially. I thought we were too old to have room-mates, that living together might well make us all hate each other. I couldn't believe that all the wait and headache of mak-ing my bathroom finally purple was for nothing.

But in theory, at least, it seemed very doable. We would schedule our classes at different times. We would try to overlap only on nights when Jason was sleeping over and could stay a few hours on either end. I would cook. It was just as easy, I told myself, to cook for three as for one even if it did yield fewer leftovers, and that way someone else could shop before and clean up after. We would split living expenses. It was going to be easy. There was no way it would go wrong.

Of course if that were true, there'd be no story. As everyone knows, saying there's no way things can go wrong precedes only by moments their actually doing so.

We got a dog from the pound, Uncle Claude, for practice parenting and extra love and silver lining—if I couldn't have my own small cute apartment all for me, if I had to have a great big house and share it with lots of people, at least that meant I could also have a dog. Uncle Claude was an angel dog, a Border collie mix, a genius (smarter than many of my students), a relentless, even compulsive, chaser of balls, a tremendous shedder (which we didn't realize until it was too late), and needer of a large backyard. So we found a house with a yard that was large indeed and huge inside as well. Four bedrooms so everyone—even the baby—got her own. Three baths so no sharing on that front either. A large kitchen, a nice porch, and lots of light. Even though I would have enjoyed another few months of freedom, we thought it best to do as much of the moving in and getting our lives settled as possible before Jill became too pregnant. Even in a city as liberal as Seattle, some people might be reluctant to rent to a family like ours. Three female roommates is nothing, but draw one a taut, rounded body over skinny legs, and suddenly we'd be a cult, a cause—at the very least, a lot of trouble.

Plus it was summer, so we had the time to do it. And it was fun. We culled our furniture, throwing out the worst pieces, each feeling like we'd gained a whole two-thirds of a house of new things. We shopped for bath mats and throw pillows. We bought candles and lamps and an afghan. It's amazing that even on so little money you can buy belonging, stability, commitment. Living alone, I realized after I wasn't doing it anymore, had felt like waiting, and so having a plastic grocery bag looped over a drawer handle felt reasonable. Now we were nesting. Together, we felt worth a real trash can. Together, we were making a home—for the baby but also for us. It wasn't that I felt undeserving when I lived alone. I had painted my bathroom after all. It's just that most things didn't seem worth it. What need had I for a real trash can? It had always annoyed me that people live in relative squalor for years, but the moment they become engaged, they need matching towels and sheets and expensive cookware (even when they do not cook). But moving in with Jill and Katie, I decided it isn't that newlyweds feel deserving because they are suddenly married; it is just the first time it seems worth the effort. I learned many things over the subsequent months, but the first and most lasting was the weight—of family, of being part of a unit—that one simply doesn't have on one's own. It was friendship too of course. And though I didn't recognize it at the time, it was motherhood.

It was also sick. Literally. When I was in second grade on a field trip to the zoo, I started a chain reaction on a bus that inspired the resignation of my first-year teacher, a woman who, by all accounts, was quite gifted in the classroom but simply chose, once I had revealed it to her, something other than the reality of seven-year-olds. Robbie Stafford, sitting across the bus from me and three rows up, leaned calmly into the center aisle about fifteen minutes into the trip and threw up his breakfast. "Ewwww," said Lizzie Donavan next to him. "Epic," said Mark Manther, whose boots were splashed but only a little and whose older brother supplied a steady stream of slang we were mostly too young to understand. "Gross," said Monica Sorrenson behind him. "Uuuuuurrrrrreeeeph," I said and leaned over into the aisle with my breakfast as well.

One vomiting kid seemed gross or cool, depending on your perspective. Two, though, boded ill in our collective seven-year-old brain. Perhaps we were being poisoned. Perhaps the bus was leaking dangerous fumes because it wasn't really a bus at all, and we weren't actually headed to the zoo but to a secret site for kidnapped kids. Maybe it was just the smell. But Eric Hynes behind me, Susan Jenson, Kelly Levine, and Harold Potter (I wonder where that kid is and what his life's like now, considering), all leaned over and threw up too. Maybe even other kids after that. By then I was pretty unwell and had lost count. Chain reaction second-grade vomiting, much of it unaimed, would drive anyone out of teaching. On my worst days in the classroom, I give thanks that at least I am not Miss Avramson.

The point of all of which is that other people throwing up makes me throw up. It's not so much the smell, though that doesn't help, as the sound—the retching, the violent cough just before it happens, the smack of all that digestive matter meeting porcelain/sidewalk/bus floor. Jill's latent morning sickness, awakened by Elise's miscarriage, never went back to sleep. Nor did it restrict itself to mornings. Jill yacked most days until about month seven. And therefore, so did I. I couldn't help it. Vomit is very unsettling. It would make anyone want to puke. I don't care how ridiculous that sounds.

So much throwing up, so much rumination, so much packing and unpacking, so many roommates again for the first time since I was a sophomore in college. I was drowning a little bit in everything. I was overwhelmed. And there was only one thing for it. The first thing all the responsibilities and machinations of motherhood made me realize was that I still needed mine. So the first Friday after we all moved in together, I got in the car and drove north over the border to see my folks.

I found my parents on the porch with my grandmother who was pretending to inspect the flower boxes but was really having a cigarette. They all smiled when they saw me, but their faces lit up when Uncle Claude trotted around the corner of the house at my feet.

"Hey baby," said my grandmother, and then bending down, "Who's this?"

"Meet Uncle Claude," I said, "your great-grandpuppy."

"You got a dog," squealed my grandmother, rubbing Uncle Claude's upturned belly with her non-cigarette hand.

"He's adorable," said my mom, elbowing to get some Uncle Claude space too.

"She," I corrected, pointing.

"Uncle Claude is a boy's name," my father said reasonably.

"Nonetheless."

"Oooo, who are you? Are you a girl? I'm so happy to meet you," my grandmother cooed to the dog.

"What possessed you?" my dad asked.

"Well, we have a house with a yard now so we could."

"If you can have a dog," my grandmother said, "you should. There's something wrong with people who can have dogs but don't." This was one of her rules of which there were many (such as not dating Yankee fans—her dating advice long before it was mine).

"Big yard," I said. "And I needed a silver lining."

"How *is* the new housing situation going?" my mother asked, still not looking up from the dog. "How's living together so far?"

"It's good," I said, but not very convincingly. "It's fine. A little hectic. A few more people around than I'm used to. They never go home after dinner anymore."

"You know I love Jill and Katie," said my grandmother, "but I'm not sure I'd want to live with them. Or raise their babies."

"Babies are a lot of work," my mom added, by which I didn't know if she meant "So it's a good thing you're helping out" or "So I can't imagine why you'd get yourself into this." She stood up from the dog and put her arms around me. I had been thinking mostly about Jill and the baby. My own family was much more interested in me. Which, of course, was why I'd come home. To be first to somebody.

"You're a wonderful kid," my mother said.

"We better go shopping," said my grandmother.

At the baby store, my grandmother threw teeny pastel towels and sheets and blankets and many hooded and footed things into a cart with reckless abandon. In contrast, my mother ignored the practical altogether in favor of the pedagogical and chose toys with mirrors, with bells, with balls, with crinkly stuff inside, toys to stimulate the eye, the ear, the first reach of tiny fingers, toys to cuddle and love. True to form, I tossed in books. *The Complete Tales and Poems of Winnie-the-Pooh, Where the Sidewalk Ends,* collections of bedtime stories to read aloud, soft books with only ten words total meant, evidently, to cuddle or maybe gnaw (I loved the idea that before you could really digest literature at least you could chew on it).

I was having nostalgia in the book section, surrounded by

my literary formatives, covers I hadn't seen in years whose interiors I still knew by heart. Before I even knew what they meant, their words had inspired a love for more words, for reading and storytelling, that had yet to abate, and I welcomed back into my life Ping and Max who makes mischief and Ferdinand and Mr. and Mrs. Mallard like old friends, for they were. In the book section, I was deluded and nostalgia-ed into imagining that hundreds of nights up at three A.M., hundreds of dirty diapers, hundreds of evenings we would rather go out to the movies, would all be worth it for the chance to read *Now We Are Six* to our own little one.

It was also all a little less scary now. If my parents and my grandmother had been horrified or even discouraging, I would have panicked about what I'd gotten myself into. I would have brought to the day what I only allowed myself to half consider in the dark—that we couldn't really make this work, that single motherhood was incompatible with being balanced and sane, that graduate school was a hopeless indulgence, that I was tying myself emotionally to a baby who would never be mine, a family which would never be a family. And if all of those fears eventually came true to greater and lesser extents, they still weren't good enough reasons not to do it.

I spent a few days at home then drove back to school with a carload of baby stuff. It was these supplies—not the vomiting, not the growing panic, not the ever expansion of Jill—that made it real. Katie and Jill were ecstatic at first—like I'd brought toys for them—and set it all up in a frenzy of Pooh curtains and mini bookshelves and heated debates about where to put the crib/changing table/swing in relation to the window/door/duck mobile. But soon we were all subdued, quiet, not sad, just thoughtful, setting up tiny furniture, arranging little plastic hangers with tiny outfits in order of months. (My father's point was that we weren't going to be any more eager or able to shop when the baby was three/six/nine months old than during week one though Katie doubted she would ever be unable or unwilling to shop.) It was still months before Jill was due, and once we had it set up, the room became sort of unofficially off limits. We didn't want to screw with its newness, its ecstatic energy, by studying in there, reading, grading papers. Still, sometimes I'd get up in the middle of the night to pee and find Jill curled up asleep in there on the floor or propped up against the wall looking up through the window at the stars.

A week after I got back with all the baby stuff, a huge box came in the mail. Inside were two new shirts for summer, a mug that said, "No. 1 Granddaughter," a package of my favorite licorice, two boxes of chocolate covered pretzels, and three rawhide bones. The card read, "For *my* baby (and her puppy)—Sorry we forgot about you in all the excitement. You're still my favorite baby of all. Love you. Guess who?" My grandmother signed everything "Guess who?" which made it pretty easy to guess.

People are always really gushy about nothing being more important than family and about real friends being like family. She's like a sister to me, we say of close friends, like family's not about blood or laws anymore but only love. Real family is much less sentimental than that though. Family is who you're stuck with. Jason's family disowned him when he told them he was gay. His father said he'd get AIDS and deserve it. His mother said he made her want to throw up. His sister said she'd pray for him but never wanted to see him again. Years of letters and tears and awkward conversations later, they achieved a sorry truce. Jason is welcome at holidays a few times a year as long as he never says anything that indicates he's gay. They've never met Lucas. They've never even seen a picture. But when I ask him why he even bothers, he scoffs, "Don't be naïve, Janey. They're family." Family, this technicality, mitigates all ills, no matter how diseased.

And mine, meanwhile, my grandmother and mother and father, I knew they would always love me first and best of all. Friends, even good ones, sometimes wouldn't, not just because friends sometimes get mad and leave your life, but also because friends are sometimes their own priority. Sometimes they put me first, for sure, when they can. But they also have their own families, their own needs. There's not the same non-negotiation with friends as with family. And it begged the question whether this baby would be family or friend and which, really, were Jill and Katie. Going in, I knew that no matter how hard this was, no matter what disasters happened as a result, if later I lost my best friends and a child who was like my own and all my money and all my sanity and everything that meant anything, whatever else happened, my grandmother would always love me best of all. I could only hope that would be enough.

Those nine months (six by the time we moved in together) felt electric. When school started up again, we all felt at the center of huge goings-on. Every time I left the house with Jill, I thought everyone was looking at us, noticing us. I was sure my students were whispering to each other about my living situation though I'd told them nothing of it. I felt like a minor celebrity around the department, at the center of everyone's gossip. And stranger still, I felt like I was getting closer and closer to birth with every passing week. I felt pregnant myself. I'd catch myself stroking my (more or less) flat belly while I read a book or sat in class or waited for water to boil or the grill to heat. I tried to talk about this once or twice with Katie, but she evidently wasn't feeling the same thing. It wasn't that I wanted to steal Jill's thunder, but I was so caught up in everything. It was the closest I'd ever come to scandal. It was the first time I'd made a major life change for someone else. It was my first baby and maybe my last.

In fact, of course, I wasn't pregnant. And in fact, no one really noticed us anyway. We didn't spend a lot of time out and about, and when we did, people just assumed I was Jill's friend, which, in fact, was true. We were gossiped about department-wide for about a week and a half before people moved on to other dramas. My students failed utterly to imagine that I had a life at all beyond the walls of the classroom. And though I was sleepless, breathless, about what we'd undertaken, about how it would transpire, this, truly, was the waiting part, the calm. The waiting I'd named before—waiting to find out if Jill was really pregnant, waiting to see what Daniel would say, waiting for a plan—was nothing like this. Every day, practically, she was bigger, rounder, less subtly pregnant. Every day, she would say feel how hard this part is here, or its feet are on my bladder, or my shoes won't go on anymore. We ticked off the seeming miles of those months in inches. We felt each morning one day closer to never sleeping again. We felt each morning the incremental loss of freedom and sanity. We felt almost moment by moment closer to a responsibility that would never go away and was so much bigger than we could handle. But only on some mornings was it oppressive. Others, I was full of joy at the prospect and promise of it all. I had that healthy pregnant glow about me.

They were a blur, those months. We took classes, taught

classes, wrote, and read. For practice, we watched *Sesame Street* and *Caillou* and *Reading Rainbow*. In fact, we started calling the baby Caillou as a working title, finding both the name and the cartoon character appropriately gender ambiguous. Jill would say, "Caillou will not settle down today," or "Caillou kept me up all night," or if she ate something gross she'd say, "Caillou did not like that salmon," or, "I like Caesar salad, but Caillou, evidently, does not." For real, we considered Anna Dana Megan Greta Rosalind Morgan Cora Hope Lanae. In case it was a boy, we threw around Will Pierre Oliver Dashiell Casper Nat Alexander. The Yankees won the World Series as they will. Katie dated two guys named Adam, plus David, Don, and Jeffrey. None were the ones. We got a car seat. I cooked enormous, balanced meals for all, determined to stuff Jill with protein, vitamins, and good eating habits. Daniel did not call. A week or so before Thanksgiving, we sequestered ourselves to study for orals, miserable exams where we picked one hundred authors from four different literary periods and read their complete oeuvres. We spent five weeks studying and doing nearly nothing else. We were only even showering every third day. For five weeks, all the time we weren't in class, we wandered around in sweatpants, reading while cooking, reading while walking the dog, taking turns reading aloud over breakfast so the other two could rest their eyes. The knowledge was useless and destined to be ephemeral. The process was worse. Jill mostly read lying on the sofa, feet propped on top of the armrest, so uncomfortable was she in any vertical position at all. Orals were ninety minutes in front of a four-person committee just after classes ended for the semester. On December 21, my exam was at nine A.M. Katie's was at noon. At three o'clock, Jill went in. At 4:30 she finished. At 4:31, she went into labor.

Twelve

I WAS HOME fixing dinner, and I mean really fixing it. I had
every window in the house open, never mind it was both
freezing and raining, to air the place out. I don't know if it was
really stuffy and smelly—though certainly it could have been
what with our showering only every third day, our laundry pil-
ing up on most of the chairs in the house, dishes left soaking
but undone, trash cans unemptied—or if it was just the stress
and anxiety and misery of studying for those exams that I
wanted to get rid of. I had both the stereo and the heat turned
all the way up, a full oven, and a stovetop simmering with relief,
boiling over with freedom from the printed word. We had
stopped delivery of the newspaper the previous weeks so as not
to be tempted to read something besides exam material, but now
I was loath to start it again, repulsed by the idea of reading anything at all (exactly what our graduate program in literature
hoped to inspire I'm sure).

I had called my parents to tell them I had passed. I had spoken
to my grandmother. I was on the phone with Nico, my college

boyfriend. Jill objected to my calling him that—"It's like you're still with him in an alternate universe"—but truly that's how we still thought of each other. He didn't feel like my ex-boyfriend, like someone over or finished or angry; he just felt like my not-at-the-moment boyfriend. "Maybe I *am* still with him in an alternate universe," I usually offered. I'd called him to tell him I'd passed but also because suddenly I missed him so much and longed to talk about something else—not books, not babies—with someone who knew that once—before the books, before the baby—there had been me with my own identity, interesting things to talk about, a life.

"How's your love life?" Nico asked. Well, okay, so not much of a life.

"Not even a hint of one." Nico, of course, was happily, stably, maddeningly partnered. Caroline. "It's okay though. It's not like I'm bored or anything."

"But it would be nice," said Nico.

"It would be nice," I admitted.

Nico and I met our first night of college at the requisite party for everyone who doesn't know anyone or have anything else to do. We were friends instantly. Nico came into school with a declared major in psychology, knowing that afterwards he wanted to go to graduate school for social work. He never changed his major or his goal, got into his top choice graduate school, finished a semester early, landed the job he'd fantasized about since he was four, bought a fabulous condo in downtown Vancouver overlooking the park, and was generally always leading a perfect life. Our first week of school, Nico felt a little stressed and overwhelmed, pressed for time, but he reasoned that there were 168 hours in a week, and there was no way he had more than 168 hours worth of things to do. So he sat down every Sunday night and made a chart. Twelve hours a week for class, eight hours a night for sleep, thirty hours for homework, five for intramural soccer, fourteen for eating, fifteen for socializing, two for psych club, four for choir, and so on. He figured in how many hours he wanted to sit on the bed shooting the shit with his roommate (four per week), how many he wanted to spend on the phone each week with his folks (one), how many he wanted for hanging out with me in the library not working (two at the beginning though that increased later when we started making out in the stacks). Every week, without fail, he had hours left over. That's the kind of person Nico is.

I tried to map out my 168 hours with him that first week, but I couldn't stick to it at all. I failed utterly to figure in time in the student union trying to decide if I wanted strawberry yogurt or strawberry-banana yogurt (about an hour a week), time to lie on my bed/sit at my desk/lounge at the library staring into space, reading glasses on my face, pencil in my hand, book on my lap, not reading anything (maybe five hours a week), time to feel guilty about how far off schedule I was (so many hours). I abandoned the project almost at once. We were not similar people, so we were perfect friends.

Which lasted for a whole semester and a half. We congratulated ourselves on how mature we were to have a "just friend" of the opposite sex. We sniffed pityingly at our friends' apparent lack of imagination, their insinuations and giggled suggestions that it was only a matter of time, that sex was inevitable, that one day we would get drunk and just take off all our clothes. Then one day we did. We were sitting against a log on the beach, watching the sun set over English Bay, hunkered down in the sand and huddled against each other for warmth—so cliché, I know—and one minute we weren't kissing and one minute we were. It was very sweet. We were blissed out enough not to mind the avalanche of I-knew-its and I-told-you-sos. We were blissed out enough not to mind anything at all. We were blissed out enough, in fact, to stay in that state for the rest of college. That's what I mean by college boyfriend; from beginning to end really, it was me and Nico.

But it was also a very present relationship. We never lived farther away from each other than a two-minute walk. We spent the night together most nights, ate most meals together, walked to class and home again, hung out in between and after. We shared the same friends and parties and activities. It wasn't as gross as it sounds; we hung out with lots of other people too, had loads of friends. But college is like that—we had few other responsibilities, a manageable workload, a small, tight community, dorm rooms in adjacent buildings, and the sleep needs of nineteen-year-olds. We saw a lot of each other. Which meant that graduate schools three thousand miles apart felt very far indeed. That much time on the phone, that many months without seeing each other, a relationship that had suddenly to rely entirely on words and memory with no touch at all, we had no basis for it. We'd never learned how. We tried, but we just couldn't do it. But we'd been together long enough to say gently to each other, "We'll always *always* be friends," and mean it. Sometimes though I wondered how it would be if we'd stuck it out. Sometimes I missed him so much it was like drawstrings between the organs in my chest and the ones in my stomach. In fairness though, I would have hated Caroline anyway.

"It's so hard to meet anyone," he sympathized. "Caro and I can't meet anyone either."

Were they swinging? This was new. "What do you mean?" I asked.

"We need some friends," said Nico, uncharacteristically plaintive. "It would be nice to have friends over for dinner or have someone have us over for dinner or have people to go to the movies with. Dating shouldn't feel this . . . isolating. But we don't know anyone."

"You have a billion friends, Nico." In addition to everything else, everyone loved him.

"Yeah, but they're not here. You're three hours away and always studying. My friends from grad school are all over. Everyone we work with is old."

"Maybe you should post a personal ad online," I suggested out of vengeance because that was what he always told me I should do, singularly because he had never even had to contemplate doing so himself.

"Yeah, sure, because 'Nice young couple seeks other couples or friends for fun, laughter, and good times' couldn't possibly attract weirdos or freaks. Besides, we don't want to try that hard. We want it just to happen."

"You and every single person on the planet," I said. "That's exactly what my students say about finding a boyfriend. That's exactly what I say about finding a boyfriend."

"Yeah, but you're lucky, Janey," he said. "You have so many good friends. You have people to do stuff with. You have more friends than time to hang out with them, and they're all near you. Finding love is easy—it's fate—you just sit back and let it happen, have faith that if it hasn't yet, it will soon, but then that's done, and you realize you're on your own for the rest of your life. It's up to you to make the rest of it happen because destiny is done with you, at least as far as your social life goes."

Did he mean Caroline? Did he mean she was his fate and destiny? Or could he mean me? I was considering this when the other line rang.

I clicked over.

I clicked back.

"OhmygodNico, we're having a baby. I gotta go. Shit. I have a stove and a half full of cooking food."

"Turn it all off and go," he said, excited too. "Call me as soon as something happens."

"Okay. Love you." I was about to hang up, but it occurred to me, "Nico? Having friends? Lots more responsibility than they're cracked up to be."

"Girlfriends as well," he reported. "Love you too. Bye."

You'd think that on the way to the hospital, I ruminated on the nature of love, relationships, and expectation, counted my blessings to have such wonderful people in my life, questioned mine and everyone's search for partnership and marriage, but you'd be wrong. I thought this: holy shit. I thought it over and over and over again. Every time I deep breathed long enough to clear my head and let my mind wander to the song on the radio or the exams or whether I'd turned everything off on the stove or the fact that I hadn't closed the windows before I left (perfect for newborns in December), I snapped immediately back to this: holy shit. Holy shit shit shit shit shit.

Thirteen

I HIT SOME traffic. I yelled and cursed. The hospital was only five miles away, and I freaked out for every one of them. What if I missed it? What if, after all of this, the baby was already there when I got there, already born, already a person? What if Jill thought I'd deserted her in her moment of greatest need? You would think people in Seattle would be good at driving in the rain. But you would be wrong. It is one of life's stupidest mysteries. When I finally got to the hospital and finally *finally* found Jill's room, nothing, and I mean nothing at all, was happening. Jill was lying on top of the covers in jeans and a sweatshirt. Katie was sitting in a chair next to the bed in the "genius outfit" she'd shopped for specially to take her orals in. They were talking about the exam. I couldn't believe it.

"Did they ask you about Elizabeth Barrett Browning?" Katie was saying. "They asked me about Elizabeth Barrett Browning. Who even reads her anymore?"

"No, but they asked me about Julia Kristeva," said Jill. "And

I *know* none of them has *ever* read a word of hers. They're delusional."

"They asked me about David Mamet, and all I could think of was that horrible movie we rented whenever that was with all the gold and the guns and everybody was trying to trick everybody else. Like I needed to go to graduate school for that."

"I cannot believe you guys are talking about orals," I said, coming in and wavering somewhere between relief that I hadn't missed anything and alarm that I was the only one who realized that the appropriate reaction to all this was: holy shit. "They're over. Who cares? You're in labor! Did you even pass by the way?" I asked Jill.

She nodded, opened her mouth to add something, then stopped mid-breath and held up a finger. "Hold on one sec." Then her face scrunched up, and her body got all rigid. I held my breath. Katie looked bored. Then Jill relaxed. "Anyway, yeah, I passed. But they asked some really stupid stuff. Did they ask you about Kristeva?"

"Was that it? Are you contracting?" I was almost yelling.

"I think contracting is when you're not a permanent employee," Jill said languidly, "but that's it. It's not bad so far."

"No one is alarmed," Katie reported. "They don't even want her to get undressed or anything yet. They said early labor could last hours, but they want us to stay here because her water already broke. Something about infection. They said we should both take a nap. They haven't even looked in on us in forty-five minutes."

"So we're bitching about the exams," said Jill.

Silence.

"What's new with you?" Katie asked brightly.

"I am freaking out," I shouted and paced the perimeter of

the room. "Why are you so calm? Does it hurt?" I asked Jill. "Does it hurt her?" I pressed Katie, not waiting for an answer from either. "Are you okay? Are you scared? Can I get you something? Did you call your mom? Are you hungry? Should you eat? What are we going to do? Shit," I finished. No one was even trying to answer me.

"We're just hanging out," said Jill calmly.

"Want to watch TV?" offered Katie.

I looked from one to the other as if they were insane. I checked the hallway in a vain effort to locate the team of nurses and doctors I was sure should be there. I searched my brain for information about what we should have been doing because I was pretty sure it wasn't watching TV. But there was nothing.

"I think we've earned TV," said Jill. It was true. Along with everything else, we'd put a moratorium on the television while we studied. So we sat and watched reruns of *Friends,* and every five minutes or so Jill scrunched up her face with a contraction, and we waited. We waited through four different *Friends* reruns, two *Simpsons,* and two incredibly bad reality shows Katie explained as we watched ("Okay, so that's Sophie. She's the mean one from New Jersey. She used to be blond, but Rob said he had a thing for redheads, so she dyed her hair. She's a hairdresser and aspiring model. He's not going to pick her." Et cetera.) We watched one *Law & Order* and one *CSI*-I-forget-where. We watched an old *West Wing* and another *Law & Order.* Jill's contractions got closer together but not a lot. The nurses came more often but mostly just offered not especially encouraging encouragement. "You're doing fine," and, "Keep hanging in there."

"Like I was going to quit and go home," Jill fumed. "I've decided to keep it inside actually. Thanks. Maybe I'll try again in a few weeks." She was getting cranky. Understandable. Katie and I, meanwhile, were getting bored and tired and cramped in the small hospital room. I was having fantasies about my very own bed, about going home and closing the windows, dumping the food, cleaning up a little, and getting a decent night's sleep. I hadn't had one in weeks because of the studying. I figured once this baby was born, I wouldn't sleep ever again. So this seemed like a good night for it. Jill was not at the moment in need of hand-holding anyway. She was dozing. The whole thing had gone from holy shit to feeling as mundane as waiting for your life to change forever possibly can. Katie and I flipped a coin to see who got to go home and who got to stay. I won.

I put my hand on Jill's forehead. She opened her eyes sleepily. "I'm thinking of going home and getting some sleep for a couple hours, get some things ready. I'm ten minutes away if things change."

"You're leaving?" Jill, panicked, propped herself up on her elbows. Looked desperate, positively desperate, to come home with me.

"Nothing's happening," I said. "I thought I'd go home, clean up, come back in a little bit."

"Don't leave me here," she whispered. "Please? I don't want to stay here waiting either, but you don't see me leaving." Katie rolled her eyes at me, but we both stayed. Katie climbed in bed beside Jill. I curled up across two folding chairs. None of us really slept. It was good practice I guess. By about four A.M., the contractions were three minutes apart, and Jill wasn't sleeping through or even around them anymore. She was eight centimeters dilated when the nurse came in to check at 4:45. By quarter to six, they had decided it was time to start pushing.

•   •   •

You have seen this part. Maybe you've given birth yourself or witnessed someone you love doing so. But even if not, you've seen this part like I had, on TV, in movies. Usually, real life is nothing like TV, but in this case, it was exactly like what they show there. Jill grunted and screamed and sweat and cried a lot, squeezed my hand and Katie's, complained of thirst, pain, and exhaustion. She was very brave. She was beautiful and also, you know, not. The baby crowned slowly, emerged sticky and red and covered in white, clumpy wet. It was just as you imagine.

The story they don't tell on TV is the one of the hand-holder, and it's because it's almost as scary but far less gallant. I was terrified. I was worried all that predawn morning and all the night before, but when they finally started, when we braced against her and pushed her knees back by her shoulders and the doctors and nurses came with all the lights and tools and just-in-case equipment, it was fear like I had never known. I was not excited. I was not in awe. I was simply terrified. My heart was beating so fast, so hard, it was difficult to think, hard to keep standing. I was afraid without words, and I am never without words. Jill squeezed my hand, and I squeezed back, just as hard. The baby came out and cried; Jill lay back and cried; I stood there still holding on to her and sobbed, not from mira- cle, not from relief, but because the fear still did not abate. I can't explain it, or maybe it's just that I won't. I won't look at what so terrified me or why. I have a family to take care of after all.

Far, far away, there were smiles all around.

"It's a boy," the doctor said.

"A little cliché," I sniffed with my racing heart.

"It's a boy, it's a boy," Katie was shouting and shouting, danc-ing almost, yelling at me as if I couldn't hear her. I nearly couldn't. Jill was steadying him against her chest with both hands, not so much holding him as pressing him there, face up, as if to keep him from sliding off.

"It's a boy, it's a boy," shouted Katie.

"It's a boy, it's a boy," whispered Jill, otherworldly, and as I swam up up up from someplace very far away and back into the room, my first coherent thought was: holy shit. Followed by: what are we going to do with a boy?

We had called Jill's mom, Diane, just before her daughter started pushing. Jill did not think it would be fun for her mom to be sitting and waiting through hours and hours and maybe days of early labor. Jill and her mother were very close but in that way where they sometimes wanted to kill each other. Jill's father left for good before Jill learned to walk; she has no memories of him whatsoever and only the dimmest of impres-sions. Diane had nothing nice to say to her baby girl about her father, so she said nothing at all. And so until she went away to college, for Jill, it was always just the two of them. She admired her mother when she thought about it, was glad her mom was home for dinner many nights. But also it was something she grew up with and so considered normal. As a kid, she thought her friends' families were strange, overly large and overly pres-ent, crammed into crowded houses with too many rooms and too many people. Then she went to college and took gender studies and learned with academic remove the struggles of single parents, the rigging of the system, and it was a familiar revelation. She recognized her mom and herself but as if in a clouded mirror or through something gauzy. Statistics never quite fit. Someone else's story is always worse. Still, Jill felt guilty about how hard her mom had worked and struggled, how much she'd given up, while Jill, her nascent-feminist only daughter, had failed to notice. When she called her mother from school in tears near the end of her first year to apologize, insofar as that was even possible, for taking all her mother's efforts so for granted, her mother, silent and incredulous, finally squeaked out, "You mean you didn't notice? All those years?"

"No," Jill whispered, mortified, sorry to the tips of her toes.

"Everything we did without? Everything we did alone? How much I had to work? How close we came to not making it? You weren't thinking about that all the time?" Diane asked.

"I wasn't, Mom. I'm sorry. I didn't know," Jill sobbed.

And there was silence on the other end until her mother finally burst out, "Oh thank God!" Jill was speechless. Later, when she'd recovered, Diane added, "I wasn't so sad about what I had to do without. Who needs new clothes when you come home to such a beautiful daughter? But I was so worried about you feeling hungry or alone or sad about what other girls had that you didn't. When you said you didn't notice? Shit, that was the best news I ever heard."

Jill knew that there was more to this story, that her mother must have given up her own dreams, that with the money Diane saved so her daughter could go to college, she could have gone to college herself. So Jill made sure to make it worth it—two majors, two minors, and no plans to be done with academia anytime soon. When she finished school, she decided she wasn't going to graduation. She thought the cap and gown ugly and extravagant, the ceremony beside the point. She told her mother she'd hang out with friends until the end of graduation weekend then pack up and come home. They could celebrate quietly, just the two of them. It took Diane a while to understand. "Do you mean to tell me you don't think you're going to your graduation?" she finally asked.

"Exactly," said Jill. "It's stupid. It's not important to me."

"Do not even for a moment think," her mother said quietly, "that this degree is yours alone. We are going to graduation. Both of us." Jill keeps the pictures from that day on her nightstand, requisite photos of a begowned graduate, Diane wearing the mortarboard and holding the scroll, arms around each other. Diane smiles for the camera, but also she looks like a soldier returning from war—shell-shocked, scarred by the horrors she's suffered, but proud beyond articulation of all she's done, of what she's saved.

Jill and Diane were both hyperaware of the statistics which say that children of single parents are much more likely to be single parents themselves than children raised by two. When Jill made it through high school without getting knocked up, when she made it through college too, Diane breathed easy for the first time since Jill started her period. She had raised a strong, proud, smart young woman who had escaped unscathed. She figured any babies born now would be wanted and planned. But when it didn't work out that way, when she heard our plan, she was also more sure than any of us that this arrangement could work. We weren't going to destroy all our lives; together we could do this. Three, after all, is even more than two.

I went outside to throw some water on my face and found Diane lost at the nurses' station. She turned and hugged me full-on and long as if she had nothing on her mind at all except how nice it was to see me.

"How are you, baby?" she asked me. "You look a little pale."

"I'm good," I replied, shaky, wondering if I should tell her or bring her to see for herself. She could tell though.

"I missed it, huh?" Diane looked at me closely, decided my paleness was due to an overly delicate constitution rather than something being wrong. Having assured herself of this, she asked nothing, preferring, I guess, to see for herself.

"You hardly missed anything," I assured her. "Nothing good anyway."

"A little squeamish?" she guessed, offhanded, but gripping my upper arm, guiding me to guide her to her daughter. "I remember. It wasn't pleasant," she said, laughing. "That's the one good thing about doing it alone. No one has to watch."

"Look who I found," I announced as we walked into the room. A miracle had occurred. The horde of doctors and nurses had been replaced by one clean, kind-looking woman in street clothes. The metal instruments and beeping monitors and just-in-case equipment had been swept away, replaced by a tiny bassinet. The blood, the white clumpy stuff, was gone. The sheets stained brown and yellow and red were now miraculously neat, clean, and white. The glaring lights were off, the shades thrown open, the windows cracked and leaking fresh air and what passes for sunshine in December in the Pacific Northwest. A screaming, sweating, hurting Jill had been replaced by a calm, dry one clad in a green nightgown (god knows where she got it; certainly it wasn't hers) and clutching to her chest a tiny, tiny baby, blue eyes wide open, also dry and clean and in new, soft clothes. Katie was madly taking pictures. Jill was oblivious, glowing, smiling blissfully at the new world outside. I stopped dead in the doorway. I thought of all those paintings of Madonna and Child. I thought of doves and larks, of church choirs and Benedictine monks, of puppies and spring and my breaking heart. I thought: what need we of baptism when we have whatever has happened here? I thought: the miracle of birth is nothing compared to the miracle that happened while I was in the lobby.

Diane was on the bed with her daughter instantly, both crying and crying. Into Jill's hair, she was whispering, "Oh my babies, my beautiful beautiful babies." Katie took like forty pictures of the three of them then exchanged glances with me, and we slid out into the hallway. It seemed the right thing to do. Plus, I suddenly realized, remarkably, I was starved.

"That was amazing," Katie enthused.

"That was disgusting," I tempered.

We went down down down to the cafeteria and sat under buzzing fluorescent lights drinking cocoa and eating rock-hard scones for breakfast (or dinner or lunch or whatever). All around us, everyone looked as tired and dazed as I felt except most of them were probably here with loved ones sick or dying, eating their eleventh meal of the week in the hospital, choking down oily, lukewarm soup with bad news and desperation. We ate quickly, said silent prayers of thanks, and went back upstairs to our bright day and our new baby.

When we got to Jill's room, Diane was sitting on a chair in the hallway. "They kicked me out to have a chat about breastfeeding. When I did this, nobody told me anything about anything let alone reached in, took out my breast, and helped me nurse." She gratefully accepted the coffee and muffin we'd brought her. "So how are you two doing?"

"Oh, we're so great," said Katie, clearly high on bliss or

adrenaline or something. "Janey's freaking out"—I hadn't realized she'd noticed—"but it's just so amazing."

"I have a grandson," said Diane, as if this clearly followed, starting to look a little freaked out herself. "What are we going to do with a boy?"

"That's exactly what I said." I nodded.

"Don't know nothin' about boys," mused Diane.

"Oh, they're just the same," said Katie, who had four brothers as well as three sisters and so should have been a good source of information on this point, but Diane and I were skeptical.

"What if he's one of those unenlightened ones who can't think of anything but breasts?" Diane wondered.

"What if he takes full advantage of the hegemony," I said, "and screws us."

"What if he thinks he's better just because he has a penis?" added Diane.

"What if he just thinks with his penis?" I countered.

"How do you even clean a penis?" wondered Diane to the amusement of everyone in the crowded hallway. "What if you all raise the girliest boy there ever was?" said Diane, and we were quiet, thinking about that one, wondering what sort of a boy we'd raise and how he'd get along in the world having grown up with three crazy academic moms.

"You all need a name," said Diane finally. And suddenly we had a surmountable task. We didn't have to raise him yet or nurture his maleness today or introduce him to the world this minute. We didn't have to start teaching him all he would need to know or immediately give ourselves over to his every need or protect him from the world or protect him from ourselves. All we needed to do was give him a name. For all the thinking we'd done already, we had all been pretty certain deep down that this baby would be a girl. We were all girls, weren't we?

The lactation consultant came out into the hallway and gave us a kind smile. "That boy is something, but he needs a name. You all had better get on it. By the way, we can order an extra cot tonight if you need it." No one seemed at all fazed about the four of us, totally manless, obviously not coupled up, all clearly parenting this child. No one asked about a father; no one looked at us strangely. I guess it's a new millennium and all that. Single parenting's not new and never was, and besides, it can't carry its persistent sense of shame into sterile hallways where it happens every day. But even beyond that, no one jumped to the obvious conclusion that we were all just friends, come to be supportive. It was more than that, and everyone seemed to sense and accept that. We all had to name this baby. We all might stay the night. We were family already, on sight, obvious to anyone who took any time to look at all.

"The lactation consultant says he's going to be a great breast-feeder," Jill reported happily when we came in.

"Who?" asked Diane.

Jill looked at her mother like she might be crazy and gestured at the baby with her head.

"I'm not sure who you mean," said Diane.

"My son," Jill laughed, but she got it. "We had a whole list of boys' names, but I never really liked any of them. I never thought we'd have to use one," she admitted.

"Jews name babies after dead loved ones," I offered.

"Bit morbid," Katie objected.

"I don't know any dead people," said Jill.

"We should name him something literary," said Katie. "An author? A character? A theorist maybe?" We mentally scanned our reading lists, wondering in silent horror about naming our kid Derrida.

"All the authors I work with are women," said Jill.

"All the books you read end badly," said Diane. "Wouldn't bode well. Probably why you don't meet lots of little boys named Hamlet."

"We cannot name him after tragedy," Jill said emphatically.

"Something with a happy ending?" Katie suggested.

"I don't want anything with an ending at all. No endings for him."

"Everything has endings," said Diane.

"Not Greek gods," said Katie. "How about Zeus?"

"Zeus is a whore," said Jill. "We need a name without tragedy, ending, *or* debauchery. Something big. Something titanic."

"Like Atlas?" said Diane, half joking, half not.

"Like Atlas," Jill echoed, under her breath.

"It's beautiful," said Katie.

"It's wide," said Diane.

"Other kids will make fun of him," I said.

"It's okay," said Jill. "With a name like Atlas, he'll be strong. He'll kick their asses. We'll give him a normal middle name. We can name him after his sister."

And so Atlas Claude Mattison came officially into—and into possession of—his namesake, the world.

Fourteen

THEY CAME AND swaddled Atlas up and put him in a bassinet that looked like a high clear plastic shoe box on wheels.
Diane slept in the "father bed" already in the room. Katie and
I shared the cot. I was certain none of us would sleep at all, but
once we turned off the light, I slept instantly and hard. I woke
up about sunrise, smashed against the metal rim of the cot,
and felt, remarkably, refreshed. I tiptoed into the hallway and
then wandered out into the morning. It was cold, drizzling,
looking on its way to raining for real, but still refreshing with
real air, not sterilized, not smelling of alcohol or death or even
birth, the whole world looking very much, unbelievably, exactly like it had yesterday. I called my parents and then my
grandmother and then Jason and Lucas and then Nico to report the news ("You're a mother now," he said a little wistfully.
"This is not how I always imagined this was going to happen.").

I went inside to buy coffee then came back outside to savor
it on a bench near the front door. It was freezing. But so good
to be outside. I watched patients pulling into the parking lot. I

watched elderly couples helping each other slowly in and out of cars. I watched people hustle into the building, heads bowed. People with flowers and balloons. People with white uniforms and stethoscopes. Many with briefcases and ties. Some negotiating obviously new wheelchairs and walkers, dragging oxygen tanks on wheels. A few people came in bearing baby presents, balloons, and stork signs announcing, "It's a . . ." I sat quietly next to the door, reveling in the heat that escaped every time it opened, clutching my coffee for warmth, and watching the come-and-go.

I was also waiting for Daniel. I didn't realize it at first, but I was. I was playing the movie scene in my head: I see a familiar figure I can't quite place walking across the parking lot, and as he gets closer, I realize it's him. He gives me a sheepish half wave and walks a little faster. "How did he know?" I think. Maybe Katie called him. Maybe Jill did. Maybe Diane had known his whereabouts all along (she'd always had a soft spot for Daniel) and called him after we called her, whispering, "Give her a day. Come tomorrow morning." Would I feel nothing but joy, no anger or resentment, just so glad to see him? Or would I pound his chest, demanding, "Where have you been?" Those are really the only options in movies.

"We named him Atlas," I'd say when I found my voice.

"Atlas," he would laugh. "That's perfect." Then he would start to go inside, but halfway through the door, he'd turn back towards me and say, "Thanks for taking care of everything for me, Janey. I'm back now."

But that wasn't what happened. Daniel didn't come. Would that have been a happier ending? Would it have been better than what really happened next and after that and after that? In some ways, almost certainly. In others, even knowing what I

know now, even after all that went down, I know I couldn't give
him up. I sat outside watching and waiting for an hour until it
was fully light then went back inside to confront the incredible
reality that in a few hours we would go home with an infant
child, a tiny new human, our very own Atlas.

Back inside, Katie was doing what Katie does best—ordering
people around. I fully expected a chore wheel by week's end, a
friendly note on the fridge in Katie's looping handwriting:

> *Breastfeeding: Jill.*
> *Bathing: Katie.*
> *Burping: Janey.*
> *We'll switch jobs at the end of the week.*
> *☺ K.*
> *(P.S. Electricity bill due Wed. Everyone owes $43.)*

When I walked in, she was actually saying to Jill, "Okay,
you wait here for the doctor," and Jill was laughing, rolling her
eyes at me. Like anyone else was going to do it. "Janey and I
will go home and get set up there. Diane, you stay with Jill and
get her home later, but call first please so we know you're coming."

"Aye, aye," said Diane.

We stopped at the grocery store on the way home. We already had a house full of tiny outfits, tiny diapers, bibs, cribs,
car seats, strollers, toys, books, bottles, rattles, and mobiles. I
couldn't imagine what else we could possibly need. Which is
why we had Katie. Katie always knows what you need at the
store, any store. She also knows which store has what you

need. She knows the fastest and best and cheapest places to shop. She knows what needs you have before you have them. When I suggested that we didn't need to stop at the grocery store because Atlas was too young to eat real food and we had a good supply of cloth diapers and a commitment to use them, Katie just looked at me pityingly. Inside, she loaded our cart with comfort food (for us, she explained, though by that point I was beginning to suspect as much), food in bags and boxes (even you are not going to have time to cook, she said), disposable diapers (just in case), disposable wipes (just in case), disposable towelettes (just in case, she said, and when I countered that we already had a package of three at home, she laughed hysterically. Have I mentioned that Katie is the oldest of eight?). She bought soothing shampoo and organic bubble bath, extra thick maxi pads (I blanched; I'd never seen them before, but I could imagine why they were on the list), the largest bottle of aspirin I'd ever seen (and when I raised my eyebrows, she just said, "Trust me," ominously, and I wondered for whom these were intended), and lots and lots of chocolate. Then we went home.

"Wow. What a lovely dinner you were making," said Katie, as if we might just be able to reheat it. It was freezing and damp in the house because I'd left all the windows open, but everything was nonetheless still reeking of the stalled feast. We stood in the front hallway and looked around. There was a full, leaking pot on every burner, onion peels and pepper seeds and green bean ends and stems of all varieties all over the countertops, empty cans and food packages, a full blender with spatter stains all around (I am not a neat cook). Besides dinner, there were clothes strewn on every horizontal surface, notebooks scattered on the floor, piles of books absolutely everywhere. Our

beds were not made. We had no clean clothes. Nearly nothing
in the house was put away. We remembered vaguely about
studying for exams, which at that point felt like several months
ago, but had forgotten how much everything—even the baby as
it turned out—had been on hold until after they were over.

"It's a good thing we aren't going home for Christmas," said
Katie, "because it's going to take us until next year to clean this
house." It is a sad irony that while I am a good cook, I am a
crappy housekeeper, and while Katie is a brilliant shopper and
organizer of humans, she's also a crappy housekeeper—she
says between us we make two-thirds of the woman we're each
supposed to be—and so the house pretty frequently looked, if
not quite this bad, not a whole lot better.

"We better get at it," I said, but neither of us moved.

"Maybe a quick nap first?" she suggested.

"We could just torch the place for the insurance money," I
offered.

"We don't have any insurance," Katie pointed out.

"Oh. My. God," said a voice behind us.

It was my grandmother. I actually wept with gratitude.

"What the hell happened here?" demanded my mom, coming up behind her.

"Man." My dad whistled. "I'm glad I brought the tools."

"I didn't know your family was coming," Katie squealed,
delighted.

"Me neither," I muffled from my mother's arms.

"Well we had to see this baby, didn't we," my grandmother
stated. "We left as soon as you called." My father nodded
bleary-eyed confirmation.

"Besides," said my grandmother, "somebody needs to clean
all this shit up."

We cleaned and cleaned, threw away dinner, made new food for brunch, scrubbed the counters and floors and corners all around the house, dusted, mopped, and disinfected, washed, dried, and folded, found homes (or at least out-of-the-way piles) for all the books. In far less time than I would have predicted, the whole house looked and smelled like a place babies might like to be.

"This place has *never* been this clean," said Katie.

"Enjoy it," said my mother. "It's not going to last the night."

Then as if we were back in that movie I'd been imagining, the front door opened, and there stood Diane, Jill, and an enormous bundle of blankets I could only assume contained Atlas.

There was a lot of jostling and cooing over and at the baby and passing him around. Our parents offered sage advice on the right ways to hold him and lay him down and stop him from crying. We all watched Jill feed him and tried not to stare at her breasts. My grandmother force-fed everyone (she gets this from me). There was actually a fight over who got to change his diaper. Jason and Lucas came bearing gifts. There were so many concerned and capable hands that later in the afternoon, Jill took a nap, Katie took a walk, and my dad and I went out to rent a movie. Atlas mostly slept. When he woke, he fussed only briefly and noncommittally, and Jill fed him, and he went right back to sleep. Everyone said what a good baby he was.

I started to suspect this might be easier than I thought. I started to think that clearly we'd lucked out with one of those easy babies, and we'd be able to do this no problem. I was so relieved. We were, all three of us, positively giddy. Our parents, meanwhile, were exchanging knowing glances that I only understood later on. Towards night, when my parents and my grandmother finally got in the car to go to the hotel, when Lucas and Jason left too, I did not feel panicked or lost. I knew we could do this. I knew they weren't far. When Diane hugged us all and walked out the door wishing us luck and promising to be back in the next day or so, I thought: don't hurry, we'll be fine. When it was just the four of us again—and the wonder of "just the" being followed by "four of us" stopped me but felt good and right—I turned off the light, put a blanket over Jill and Atlas napping on the sofa, sat with a small lamp in the kitchen, and started reading a book. For pleasure. It wasn't even like the movie anymore—not that dramatic or involved— more like a commercial for quiet dishwashers or soft light bulbs. It didn't look like what I thought my life would look like, but it felt like it, and that seemed realer and better to me. We had surmounted the hard parts, made a perfect baby, found another way to be a family. Happy ending! I wanted to turn off the lights, walk quietly into my bedroom, and roll the credits.

Of course, anyone with a brain realizes that birth is not an ending, it's a beginning. And also that even if your baby is pretty quiet his first day home from the hospital when lots of people are around and everyone wants to hold him and he's still a little stunned, that doesn't actually have anything to do with tomorrow.

PART II

Atlas(t)

(My love has come along)

Fifteen

I T WORKED, JUST barely, like this: Jill taught Mondays and Fridays from nine o'clock to noon, and she held office hours from noon to two after class on Mondays. She was taking Holocaust Narratives on Wednesday afternoons from noon to three and Advanced Gender Theory and Praxis on Tuesdays from three to six. Katie taught Tuesday/Thursday from twelve to three and was in Romantic Poets from nine to twelve Thursday and Lesser Known Victorian Novelists on Friday from nine to noon with office hours after Friday's class (Katie's point was that having office hours on Friday afternoons ensured that most students wouldn't come). I taught Monday/Wednesday/ Friday from three to five and was taking the Medieval Book Monday mornings and Shakespeare's Literary London Wednesday mornings with office hours Tuesday and Thursday afternoons. Plus we were all taking Early Modern Gender Studies together Tuesday mornings from nine to twelve. This meant someone could always be home, though handoffs were frequently tight, except for Tuesday mornings when Jason stayed with Atlas before he went and taught at one o'clock after Jill rushed home from her noon SGA meeting (alternate weeks only). For about the first week of classes, this seemed reasonable. We were tired—not getting a lot of sleep because Atlas was wanting to eat every two hours or so, and in those early days, when he was up, we were all up—but it mostly seemed like the usual beginning-of-the-semester chaos when everything is madness, but you know that it will settle down soon.

This didn't settle down though. It settled up; it upsettled. We had had to adopt Nico's approach of scheduling all our hours, but it soon became clear that all those unscheduled green blocks coded on the chart for free time were not nearly as free as they had seemed in planning. We had figured that we could read while we held the baby. I had had visions of me on sofa, book in one hand, baby in other, foot rubbing Uncle Claude, fabulously multitasking. In fact, it is harder than you'd think to read, take notes, cross-reference, write thoughtful marginalia, and tend to a rarely-asleep-for-more-than-fifteen-minutes baby. Or maybe it's exactly as hard as you'd think, but what you were imagining was closer to reality than what we were imagining. Like everything that must go exactly according to plan in order to work, this didn't.

The first thing that went wrong was Katie got sick. She is one of those people. Real or imagined, she is always down with headache, stomachache, cold, flu, sore throat. She has multitudinous, unspecified, shape-shifting allergies, premature arthritis, severe menstrual cramping, a heart murmur, an ulcer, and one leg which is an inch shorter than the other. She is selectively lactose intolerant (ice cream but not pizza, milk in a glass but not over cereal), fainted once due to lack of sleep, gets dizzy when she sits at a computer too long, and develops bumpy red rashes from ant bites no matter how small. My policy was usually to ignore all of it. But when she came down with a mysterious stomach ailment after church on Atlas's sixty-day birthday, one of whose manifestations included not just complaining but also lots of diarrhea, Jill tried to kick her out of the house.

"I am not leaving the house," said Katie.

"Atlas cannot get whatever you have," said Jill.

"Mmmmnnnnuuuhhhhhnnnn," moaned Katie pathetically, making her difficult to argue with.

"Fine," said Jill, "but you stay in your bedroom. With your door closed. And only use your bathroom. And don't come downstairs. Janey will bring you food and whatever else you need."

"Hey," I protested, "I don't want to be sick either."

"Better you than Atlas," Jill said without a trace of apology and hurried away from Katie herself.

I made Katie matzo ball soup and sat on her bed chatting about boys. Then I went downstairs to spell Jill. I went upstairs and downstairs all day, but it was Sunday, and it was fine.

The next day though, Katie wasn't better. I had to go to seminar, and Jill had to teach, and without Katie, there was no one to take Atlas.

"Probably whatever it is isn't contagious anymore," I suggested.

"You've got to be kidding me," said Jill.

I went up to check on Katie and make her an appointment at the health center. When I came downstairs, Jill had Atlas in fifteen layers and was toting a diaper bag too large to carry on an airplane.

"You're dropping him at the daycare center at school," I guessed, incredulous. It was staffed by early childhood ed majors. They were still learning.

"Don't be absurd," she scoffed. "I'm taking him to class with me."

"You can't."

"He's asleep."

"What if he wakes up and screams and cries?" I asked.

"Then he wakes up and screams and cries," Jill said.

"What if the only thing that will placate him is your right breast, and you have to nurse him in front of your whole class?"

"Then he wakes up and screams and cries," Jill said.

The good news was Atlas slept peacefully through class and offered the added bonus of inspiring hushed awe and rapt attention from Jill's students on that occasion and several others. The bad news was that Katie had amoebas. She walked into the house that night after spending all day at the health center and then at the clinic and then at the hospital where they'd sent her for more tests, collapsed dramatically across the living room floor, and announced the good news.

"The silver lining, if you want to see it, is that as long as I wash my hands real well, I'm not contagious."

"Hurrah," said Jill.

"We're waiting for test results, but they think I have amoebas."

"What?" said Jill.

"They think I have amoebas. That's why I'm always sick. That's why I have diarrhea. That's why my poop is weird. That's what it is. Amoebas." Having a baby, even for only a couple months, not to mention picking up dog shit in a baggy three times a day, makes you remarkably willing to have conversations featuring poop.

"You have amoebas in your shit?" said Jill, alarmed, trying to shove Atlas under her shirt.

"Yes, actually, and also in my intestine," said Katie. "From Guatemala, from my mission. The water wasn't very clean there. We boiled it for drinking and cooking, but you never know. One time I was drinking bottled water, and I was almost finished when one of the other missionaries suddenly clapped her hand over her mouth and screamed. There was this huge worm in the bottom of the bottle."

Jill looked pale. "That would do it I guess."

"No, that wasn't the amoebas. That's just an example of what can be in bottled Guatemalan water. The amoebas are too small to see."

"When will they go away?" I asked.

"No one's sure," said Katie, a little freaked, but also clearly enjoying how grossed out we were. "There are drugs, but sometimes they take years to work."

"You'd think you'd have shit them all out by now," said Jill.

"Evidently," Katie sniffed, "it does not work that way. The symptoms will come and go. There's nothing I can do. But the doctor said I should feel better from this bout soon. I already feel better. Did you make dinner?"

I started heating leftovers for her.

"When we were kids, we used to play a game called Amoeba Man," said Jill thoughtfully. "One person would hide under a blanket, like in the middle of the floor while everyone was watching TV or in the yard while we were just sitting around talking, and you'd forget about the person under the blanket and the amoeba man game, and then suddenly, when you least expected it, the amoeba man would jump up and try to tag people, and everyone would run away, but if the amoeba man tagged you, you got sucked under the blanket and became part of the amoeba. As more kids became part of the amoeba, the odds got worse for the kids who were left, but also it got harder to tag them because it was hard to maneuver with all those kids under the blanket. It was a fun game."

"That's really weird," I said.

"Then at some point the game morphed," Jill added. "And the older kids would capture each other and go under the blanket and make out and not try to capture anybody. They were more like two-celled organisms. Or one-celled ones that split. And the little kids would just giggle and hide and wait all out of breath, ready to run, like they would be tagged at any moment."

"Amoebas aren't one-celled organisms, are they?" asked Katie.

"No idea," said Jill. "You're the one who has them living in you."

"When I was in seventh grade, we had this really weird science teacher," I said. "He was kind of spacey. We were supposed to read chapters from the textbook for homework, but almost no one ever did, so class was never very productive."

"I've taught classes like that," said Jill.

"Me too," said Katie.

"Of course, I was a model student, so I always did the reading, but I never admitted it or answered any questions in class because it was seventh grade, and I was a total nerd and didn't want to make it worse by being an ass kisser or teacher's pet."

"I went to that seventh grade," said Jill.

"Me too," said Katie.

"So one day in class, he asked what an amoeba was, and no one answered him. He waited and waited, and no one said anything. So he called on this really popular guy all the way in the back and asked him if he was an amoeba, and the guy said, 'Um, yeah, I guess.' So Mr. Fields just stood there and looked real thoughtful and rubbed his chin, and then he asked the guy sitting next to the first guy if he was an amoeba, and that guy said yes, he was an amoeba. And so Mr. Fields went right around and asked everyone in the room if they were an amoeba or not, pausing and saying 'huh' and 'hmm' and 'I see' between each person and looking real thoughtful, and everyone said yes, they were amoebas. It was middle school. Everyone was stupid *and* totally terrified to be different from everyone else. Finally he got to me. 'Janey, are you an amoeba?' I was so frustrated and annoyed, having gotten the point half an hour before, that I blurted out, 'No, I am not an amoeba. An amoeba is a one-celled protozoan consisting of a mass of protoplasm. It moves by means of pseudopods. It is parasitic in humans.'"

"Tell me about it," said Katie.

"You *are* a nerd," said Jill.

"I said, 'Unlike me, an amoeba has no definite form but contains one or more nuclei surrounded by a flexible outer membrane.'"

"Actually, that kind of sounds like middle schoolers," said Jill.

"Why do you remember this?" said Katie.

"Everyone cracked up and was like, 'You're such an idiot. You don't even think you're an amoeba.' And Mr. Fields was like, 'No, you guys are idiots. People aren't amoebas. Amoebas are one-celled organisms without brains, which you guys would know if you ever used yours and read your homework.'

But it didn't matter. Everyone made fun of me anyway. All year long I was Amoeba Jane."

"Middle school sucked," said Katie.

"If it hadn't been Amoeba Jane, it would have been something else," said Jill. "Everyone I know and like now was a loser in middle school. You can either be happy for three years in middle school or be happy sometime after that, but not both."

"That's what my guidance counselor said. She cut out a *Far Side* cartoon from the paper and brought it in for me. It had an amoeba with a lasso and a cowboy hat, and it said, 'So, until next week, adios amoebas.' She pasted it on a card and wrote on the inside, 'For Janey, who says she is not one.' She said sometime it would all be worth it."

"I can't imagine a harder job than middle school guidance counselor," said Katie.

"Middle school science teacher," I said.

"I wish we could spare Atlas all that. Since we know it's coming," said Jill.

"Guys have it worse," said Katie. "They get made fun of *and* beat up."

"You aren't helping," said Jill.

"Can you imagine how frustrating it must have been for our parents?" I wondered.

"I'm starting to," said Jill.

"When I came home in tears every day? When I thought I was ugly and stupid and no one liked me? What if your little boy came home hurt all the time? You must want to pin the principal against a wall. You must want to barge in and start beating up little kids."

"Sounds like a plan," said Jill.

"Agreed," I said and went upstairs to call my folks.

Sixteen

WHEN SHE GOT well, Katie decided to try something different. On Friday night, she came downstairs skirted and perfumed, looking like a new person.

"I have a date," she announced.

"I guessed," said Jill.

"You always have a date," I said.

"This one is different," said Katie. "He's a graduate student. History. He got his M.A. at Oregon but came here for the Ph.D. I met him at the infirmary actually. He sprained his foot playing soccer. I love soccer players. I think he will be pleasantly surprised to see how cute I am since last time he saw me I was completely exhausted and dehydrated."

"You met him in the infirmary?" I was blown away. "He's been here all this time? A Mormon historian Ph.D candidate? How did you not meet him in church?"

"It's like a miracle," said Jill. "What's his name?"

"Ethan," said Katie, hesitant somehow, like she wasn't sure what his name was. "But here's the thing: he's not Mormon."

I almost dropped Atlas.

"You're dating someone who's not Mormon?" Jill asked slowly.

"I am not dating him. I am going on a date with him."

"Why?" I finally managed.

"What do you mean, why?"

"Is he religious? Is he a very devout and flexible Christian of some other kind?" I asked.

"I have no idea," she said, annoyed. "I think you're putting the cart before the carrot or the carrot before the horse or whatever. It's premature to worry about this. We haven't even been out yet."

We were all quiet for a minute. "Besides, if it gets serious, he can convert."

Jill and I were still considering this, stunned, when the doorbell rang. In hobbled Ethan with a cane and a grin and a soft cast on his right foot. He smiled at Katie, then at Jill, and then at me and Atlas. "You must be Jill," he said to me.

"Good guess, but actually I'm Janey," I said and put out the hand that wasn't under Atlas's ass.

"Sorry," said Ethan and then added to the baby, "Well, you *must* be Atlas."

"Better guess," said Jill and introduced herself as well.

Ethan took off his coat, sat right down on the sofa, and started talking shop. He wanted to know what classes we were taking and with what professors, what our specialties were, what we were teaching. He wanted to commiserate about having to teach required courses to unwilling students. He told a story about a kid in his History 101 class who'd shown up for the first time at the end of the second week of classes explaining that he hadn't been there because he'd gotten back late from winter break.

"That happened to me too," I said. "This kid came in at the end of week two and said he'd been working at a ski resort for January and wanted to stay for an extra couple weeks to earn some more money. He was really annoyed that this didn't seem reasonable to me."

"Parker Tamlin?" said Ethan.

"Yes!" I was totally amazed until I realized that it wasn't even that much of a coincidence. Most first-year students are taking both English and History 101. Ethan glanced at the TV. "Who's winning?" ESPN Classic was showing a Mariners/Yankees game from 2001. (By late February, I get so impatient for baseball I even watch reruns.)

"Mariners," I said. "One nothing. Top of the eighth."

"Enjoy it." He snorted. "Won't last."

I eyed him with disdain. "You're a Yankee fan?"

"God no," said Ethan. "Mets."

Katie smiled at me. Ethan smiled at Katie. She glowed back.

"You guys have fun," said Jill. "Remember I have library time in the morning, and Janey has yoga, so you're on Atlas duty."

"I remember," said Katie. "We won't be that late."

After they left, Jill and I deconstructed their relationship. They'd been dating for five minutes. It was time.

"He's going to want to have sex with her," said Jill.

"At the very least, he's going to want to take her out for a beer," I said.

"Maybe he won't be as creeped out as we are when he orders beer and she orders ginger ale." Katie has this way of making you feel like a degenerate for drinking anything that isn't pale soda.

"Maybe he won't mind not having sex. Maybe he'll like her that much."

"Maybe he will convert."

"Religious conversion *for* someone seems kind of wrong," said Jill.

"Maybe it can work," I said. "If you're convinced, if you believe."

"Maybe," said Jill, "but not because you fall in love with a girl and she's a Mormon and won't have sex with you unless you're a Mormon too."

"Love is transformative," I said.

"But he's fundamentally different from her. Religion's not just about what you believe. It's cultural. It's like saying race is just about skin color."

"They'll share other values," I said. "Education. Scholarship. Whatever."

"You just like him because he's a Mets fan, and he made you feel vindicated about Parker Tamlin."

"Stupid Parker Tamlin," I said. "Stupid Yankees."

"Plus he's a historian," said Jill.

"True." Jill and I share a distrust of history and people who study it. It wasn't like dating a Republican, but it was still good to be alert.

"It would be fun to have a wedding," she mused. "Put Atlas in a tiny tuxedo. Have a big shower for her. Sit around bridal stores while she tried on hundreds of huge white dresses."

"I think you're putting the cart before the carrot," I said.

We were still up when Katie got home. Ethan walked her to the door but did not come in. We couldn't tell if he kissed her or not. Katie came in, took off her coat and shoes, kissed an Atlas sleeping in Jill's arms, and asked how our evening was.

"Who cares about our evening," said Jill. "How was yours?"

"Mmm, nice."

"And?"

"And I don't know. He's nice. Did you guys think he was nice?"

"We liked him a lot," I offered.

"He seems great," said Jill.

Silence. Nothing.

"What did you do?"

"We went out to dinner. To the Hopvine. And then for dessert at Victrola."

Huge pause. Nothing forthcoming. This was highly irregular.

"And? Was it fun?"

"He had a beer," Katie said slowly, and Jill and I exchanged glances. "I didn't," she added as if she needed to. "But he didn't seem to care. He's doing interesting work. With Professor Carlson. He's nice and funny and cute."

"But . . ." Jill prompted.

"But not Mormon."

"Does it matter at this stage?" I asked.

"I don't know. I tried to feel out what he might think of conversion."

Jill shot straight up on the couch. "Are you mad?"

"I didn't come right out and ask him. I just hinted around. He didn't seem too open to the idea though. He said he believed in God but not religion. I don't even know what that means."

"It's a little early," I said gently.

"Yeah, we'll see."

"Will you?" asked Jill.

"We're going to have lunch Wednesday. If you can stay an extra hour or so with Atlas," she added in my direction.

"Yeah, of course," I said, bewildered. How can you tell someone who doesn't already know it that a first date is too early to ask someone to convert for you? On the other hand, for someone who knows already that this would be a deal breaker, maybe it isn't too early to ask; maybe it's the only possibility.

Seventeen

It wasn't experiments in dating that did it anyway. It wasn't amoebas or lack of sleep or our hanging-by-a-hangnail schedule. It was narrative. Narrative rose up and kicked our asses.

Jill's big project, her soon-to-be-proposed dissertation, was women's Holocaust narratives. At least it would have been if she were working on it. In fairness, I should emphasize that under normal circumstances, disserters taking months/semesters/ years off from writing their dissertations—while claiming instead to be reading, researching, teaching, traveling, exploring other angles, waiting for interlibrary loans, waiting for student loans, waiting for handwriting analyses, psychic readings, a sign from the heavens, and/or the (literal) death of their authors so that they can finally nail down a definitive oeuvre—is not only not unusual, it's pretty much expected. There are people in our department who started their master's degrees the year I started middle school. There are people in our department who took a year off from writing their dissertation so they could have a baby, and now that baby is graduating from high school. There are not people in our department—not even one or two—who have finished their dissertation in the purported year it is budgeted for. Writing a dissertation is not a linear process. No one minds. The unfinishable state of dissertations keeps introductory college courses staffed with practically unpaid labor and keeps the job market nearly impossible but not quite so completely impossible that riots ensue. I would go so far as to suggest that they must put something in the water to keep disserters distracted and ever nearer but never quite done, some Sisyphean chemical, except that would make me sound paranoid and insane.

Suffice it to say that Jill's not doing any work in and of itself wasn't cause for alarm, at least not to the department or the graduate program. But to we who lived with her, who watched her stop not only writing but also reading and researching to take up instead pursuits pretty much limited to activities that could be accomplished from the couch, including a remarkable amount of really bad TV, it was pretty alarming indeed. And there was lots and lots of crying. Maybe you are thinking that in a house full of women and babies there was bound to be lots of crying. But Jill is not a weepy person nor one easily put off from her goals, and we were worried.

Because it was Wednesday, I'd rushed home from my class to take over Atlasing so Jill could go to hers, but she was sitting in full lotus position on the floor, eyes closed, breathing deeply, listening to a yoga for mothers and babies CD with Atlas wide-eyed in her lap.

"Jill, you've got to go. Class starts in ten minutes. I hurried best I could but I ran into Dr. Brown after class and you know how that goes. He would not shut up. You're not even dressed!" I rushed in, breathless, in a very despite-practically-running-all-the-way-home-I'm-six-unmakeupable-minutes-behind-so-you-have-to-go-go-go place. Jill did not even open her eyes. She inhaled deeply into her navel center then her heart center then her third eye. She was wearing sweatpants. She exhaled slowly.

"I'm not going," she said as calmly and quietly as if this were normal. Grad seminars meet only once a week. You are expected—highly expected—to be there.

"You're not going?" Not that cutting class is some kind of tragedy. But I'd just rushed all the way home, and plus I had planned my day around not having my day. "So you're just going to sit there and do yoga?"

"Mmmhmmm," said Jill and breathed all the way in, all the way out.

"You've already missed this class," I added lamely. "You can't miss again."

In. Out. "I've dropped the class." Calmly. In. Out.

"What?" I shrieked. Uncoolly.

Jill's head turned towards me. She opened one eye. "We are chilling out," she said pointedly. Then added, "You are harshing on our mellow."

I said nothing. I went into the kitchen and made myself lunch. I tried to decide whether the anger I was feeling was virtuous concern or selfish jealousy or the stunning realization that dropping a class probably didn't portend the end of the world. Eight minutes later, I couldn't stand it anymore. She was stretched out on her back in savasana, hands upturned towards the ceiling, ready to receive whatever the universe had to offer. I was beginning to regret getting Jill into yoga. Either it worked too well on her or she didn't need it. She was already too calm.

"You're dropping this class or all of them?" I asked less shrilly.

"Just this one for the moment." So calmly.

"Can I ask why?"

"In a few minutes," she murmured from her yogic sleep.

I went back to the kitchen. Had I taken on this ridiculous schedule so that she could drop out of school? Had I consented to surrogate-parent her child so that Jill could sit around doing yoga while I rushed from place to place? Was Atlas not her son and thus her problem, and if so, why was I running madly home in the rain in my good shoes while she achieved enlightenment in the living room?

"Hey there," she said with a smile, sitting down and helping herself to half my sandwich without asking. I was too annoyed to eat and fed the other half to Uncle Claude.

"Where's Atlas?"

"Napping."

I could never—never—get Atlas to nap in the afternoons anyplace but my arms. When I put him down, he wailed and wailed. Jill set him in his crib, closed the door, and walked away.

"I can never get him to nap," I said, miffed.

"He was very zen from yoga," said Jill. I considered how killing her would be rude, bad for my karma, and impossible to schedule around.

"So you're just dropping classes?"

"No, I'm not just dropping classes. I have dropped this class." Calmly, gently.

"Why?" Annoyed, angry, irrational.

"Because I can't do it." Logical, simple, infuriating.

"How can you not do it?" I demanded. "This is your class. It's taught by your advisor. She's teaching it for you. It's the subject of your dissertation."

"All true, but it turns out I can't do it. I can't, I don't want to, I won't. That's it." Satisfied, smug, offering so little information. I believe the word is "maddening."

"Jill, how is it that you can't do it, but Katie and I can? We're taking on just as much as you are. We have just as many classes and students and pages to read and essays to grade. We aren't watching stupid TV all day every day. We haven't completely stopped doing any work at all. We are doing just as much child care as you are, and he isn't even our kid. How is that reasonable?"

"Because he isn't your kid," Jill hissed, suddenly icy. "And because you aren't studying Holocaust narrative."

"What the hell has that got to do with anything? I love him like he's mine. I take care of him like he's mine. I take time off from my own work like he's mine. And besides, Holocaust narrative is easier than Shakespeare. You've got fifty years of scholarship to go through. I've got four hundred and counting."

She slammed her water glass on the table, grabbed huge fistfuls of hair at her temples, and pulled hard. "There are no dead children in Shakespeare," she whispered through clenched teeth, too insane, apparently, to talk out loud, and while it is not strictly true that there are no dead children in Shakespeare, I kept my mouth shut as I suspected this was not her point. "I can't read about the dead babies." She started crying. "I can't do the kids starving to death, freezing to death, silent under floorboards waiting to die. I can't read about the children separated from their parents and marched off to gas chambers. I can't read about it, and I can't think about it, and I can't write about it. Even the survivors, even the happy endings, they're the kids who were all alone, who hid in latrines and haystacks and the homes of people who never loved them and were only trying to make money, and it's killing me. It's hurting my heart. I can't do it anymore. I don't even want to try to get over it. I don't ever want to read this stuff ever again."

I tried to think of something useful to say, but it's hard to argue to a going-insane new mother that she should read about mass graves full of dead children.

"Okay," I tried. "So you'll study something else."

"I can't start over. It's too late."

"It's not too late. You could start a whole new dissertation proposal, a new specialty, a new program altogether. You could switch to math if you wanted and still finish years before half the people here."

"People will ask why I switched topics. I can't say, 'Oh, dead babies,' because I mean probably if I didn't want to read about death, I shouldn't have picked Holocaust narratives."

"Things are different now," I said. "Pick something else. There are lots of uplifting literary periods."

"There are no uplifting literary periods," said Jill. And then, "I can't let words on a page ruin my life. So I have to stop reading them. Maybe all of them."

Part of dedicating your life to studying literature is realizing that storytelling is more than just make-believe and that make-believe is far more important than we all pretend—make believe—it is. One way or another, books tell the stories of their readers. But telling our lives is not the same as shaping them, whittling them away. Suddenly Jill had lost control. Her books had taken over and were in charge.

•   •   •

Later, Jill napped, and I sat with Atlas snug in my lap, reading him *Moby-Dick*. I don't especially like *Moby-Dick*. It is hopelessly long, and whaling is boring, and the allegory is painfully obvious though perhaps it wasn't before it became total canon fodder and probably not for a nine-week-old anyway. But *Moby-Dick* is beautiful—good for reading aloud—and it was one of Daniel's favorites. It seemed like what he'd have read to his son, and I am a firm believer in knowing people by knowing what they read, holding their favorite words in your mouth, running curious fingers along the spines of their books. Atlas watched me intently, eyes clear and bright and wide open, head pressed against my chest, warm and heavy in my arms. The consuming, epic, iconic hatred and passion of Ahab's quest for that whale seemed nonetheless dwarfed by the love I felt for this small, small person. I failed suddenly to believe in emotions as destructive as hate and obsession when such vast, all-consuming love could emanate from a tiny brand-new being and fill the room, the house, my heart. Atlas watched and listened, breathing in and out quietly, moving in and out as I breathed too, as Ahab paced the decks and watched the waters. Jill came downstairs rubbing her eyes and lay down on the sofa to listen quietly in the half-light. "You're skipping parts," she said after a while when I was sure she'd fallen back to sleep.

"*Moby-Dick* is long," I said. "And whaling is boring."

"But you're missing the point then," said Jill. "It's supposed to be long and boring and over-detailed so you feel what it feels like to be at sea for months on end, so you feel what it feels like to be totally lost with no power or control."

"It's just a bedtime story. It's not like he understands it anyway."

"Yeah, but why read it at all then?"

I didn't want to tell her I'd chosen it because of Daniel, but I suspected she knew. "It's pretty," I answered and added, "but I've stopped believing it."

"Which part?"

"All that hatred and vengeance and myopic anger. It doesn't seem believable to me. Real people aren't like that."

"They are when they don't have a choice."

"There's always a choice. You could chase a whale obsessively until it killed you and everyone else. Or you could chase it for a month or so and then give up. Or you could stay home with a book and care about something besides whales."

"You could but Ahab couldn't. You couldn't if you'd spent most of your life at sea, afloat, homeless, in danger, unloved. If you had no skills on land. If a whale had eaten your leg."

"Then I wouldn't be a real person. I'd be an allegorical figure."

"There's less difference than you think," she said.

"I'm just saying real people choose love or at least laziness, not hate, not anger, not fanatical whale chasing. The difference between real people and allegorical figures is we have choices."

"Not really," she said. "If you were in a book and your best friend got pregnant, you'd have to raise the baby. You couldn't leave even though you hadn't been stupid enough to get pregnant. You'd put your life on hold. You'd sit around all afternoon reading the baby's errant father's favorite book aloud even though you should be at the library doing your own work. You wouldn't have any choice. The frameworks of narrative leave no option for deserting your best friend and her out-of-wedlock baby."

"Sure they do. I could have left her and her baby, made my way in the world, and looked back with regret once right before my marriage, once when my first son died tragically of the plague, and once on my deathbed, having lived an otherwise rich and successful life."

"Only if you were a man."

"Only if I were fiction," I said gently. "I had a choice, Jill. We all did. We had choices all along the way. We still do. I have stayed not because I had to, not because of the bounds of literature, not even because of the bounds of friendship. This, given the circumstances and my infinite options, is what I choose."

"Or at least that's the story you tell," said Jill.

Eighteen

MEANWHILE, KATIE WAS suffering her own narrative constraints. Feminist narrative theory notes that for most of literary history there's been an imbalance between men's and women's stories. Male characters go out into a world of infinite possibilities. Female characters either get married or die. This makes enlightened female readers such as ourselves pissed off. But however much we deconstruct the narrative, however vigilantly we plow and apply the theory and read with our skeptical, over-educated eyes, still some lessons are hard to fully internalize, and the dream of happily-ever-after love, in real life and in literature, dies hardest of all. Which seems about right I guess. Because really, what's better than true love? We mock the concept. We bemoan what often must be done on the way to a love whose truth and timelessness turn out to be merely veneer. It's cheesy to talk about. But when it's good, there's nothing better.

Something you had been looking for that long, you'd think

you would recognize it when you saw it; you'd think it would be obvious. Katie's problem wasn't that she was in love with a non-Mormon, and it wasn't that she was dating someone she wasn't in love with. It was that she couldn't tell yet and had to keep trying to find out. Their second date, lunch in the food court at Uwajimaya, our Asian mega-grocery store, had gone very well. Ethan had been happy to share everything which is something Katie insists upon—she hates eating her own meal. They had tuna sashimi, miso soup, pad thai, and tofu summer rolls. They had seaweed salad, avocado curry, and a Vietnamese sandwich. For dessert, they had cream puffs and strawberry mochi that tasted like bubblegum. Katie also likes to have lots of options. They walked around and looked at the rows and rows of fish tanks, at the novelty snacks in pastel packaging with Japanese descriptions they could only guess about, at more receptacles for saki delivery than you ever imagined could exist. They held hands. She came home laden with leftovers and beaming. Only Katie could make a date of going to the grocery store.

"We're going miniature golfing on Friday night," she reported. "After he gets his cast off."

"You'll freeze," I said.

"Are you twelve?" Jill said.

"Are you going to the beach?" I said. "There's no miniature golf around here."

"There's one in Ballard."

"Is it indoors?" I asked.

"How did you talk him into that?" Jill asked, incredulous, nasty even.

Katie didn't even notice. "It was his idea," she said and danced out of the room.

• • •

Miniature golf also went very well—they dressed warmly—and, better still, loosened her tongue on all matters Ethan. I'm not sure what made her decide that she could talk about it without making it too real, without jinxing it, without confronting all the questions without answers, but something did. Miniature golf loosened her tongue in the other way too. They made out on a bench near the hole with the whale. They made out near the hole with the clown and the one with the castle. They went out for ice cream after miniature golf and made out in the car in the parking lot. Then they went to Joe Bar to get hot cocoa and warm up from the ice cream, and they made out there as well.

"He's very sweet," Katie reported, "and very . . . soft. And he smells nice."

"What are you doing?" said Jill.

"He's really smart. Some of the research he's doing overlaps with yours," she said to me.

"He's not going to convert for you," said Jill.

"You'll both really like him. He's funny and so sweet too. He sucks at miniature golf and wasn't even embarrassed about it. And we can talk about anything. I've never dated someone before who I could tell about my work and he understood let alone cared."

"And you're certainly not going to convert for him," said Jill.

"We like the same music. We like the same books. We like the same movies. We even like the same ice cream except I had to get sorbet because of the lactose, but back when I used to eat ice cream, I liked the same kind as he does."

"Well that's certainly more important than God," said Jill.

"You can't ruin this for me, Jill," Katie finally snapped and stormed out of the room.

"You know she has to work through this on her own," I said to Jill. "Why are you torturing her?"

"I'm not torturing her. She's torturing her," said Jill.

I took Atlas and Uncle Claude for a walk so I could call Nico to get a male opinion. And because I was missing him. Nico has this theory about dating that in order for it to work you have to be two things: soul compatible and actually compatible. You have to be attracted to each other and have chemistry and desire and desperation to be together and rip each other's clothes off and all that, but you also have to wake up on a Sunday morning and, having dispensed with the sex, want to spend the rest of the day doing the same things. A little bit of compromise will always be necessary, but it should be pretty minimal.

"Like us," Nico explained, as if this were the first time I'd heard this theory rather than the eightieth. "We were totally soul compatible and could spend hours at a time just gazing into each other's eyes, but after that, we wanted to spend a free day doing the same things—going to the park or having coffee or kayaking or hiking or going to shows or whatever. It wasn't like I wanted to go out rocking every night and take drugs, but you wanted to stay home and read and be in bed by nine-thirty. Or I wanted to hunt endangered wolves while you went to Greenpeace meetings."

"This is just like that," I said. "They have soul compatibility— they made out a lot during miniature golf—and they have a lot of actual compatibility. Much more than the guys she usually dates. They could talk about their work or go to the coffee shop and grade or attend, I don't know, a political rally or just go to the library together. Most of the guys she dates never go to a library. Remember how much fun we used to have in the stacks? Faced with your free-day theory, they want to do the same things."

"Not on Sunday."

"Who said Sunday is the only day that counts?"

"She did," said Nico.

Nineteen

SHE DECIDED TO ask before it got worse. She decided to ask before she fell in love and had to worry about hurting him or hurting her. She decided it was better to know than to wonder, to hope if there wasn't any. She decided Jill was obnoxious but possibly right.

"I'm not saying now," Katie told me in rehearsals, pretending I was him. "I'm not saying soon. I'm not saying you even have to decide now. I'm not saying I'll even ask you to in the future. I'm saying if. I'm saying *if* we fell in love and *if* we wanted to be together forever and *if* we wanted to make a life and a family together, would you be willing to convert? I'm saying if I loved you and you loved me, in a few years, would you be willing to become a Mormon?"

"Um . . . I don't know," I hedged, trying to channel Ethan. "It's a little soon. I can't know the answers to those questions right now. But I do like you a lot. I like where this is going. I know that I would like to do things to make you happy and that if you were that important to me and it were that important to you, I'd probably make it happen."

But that's because I was only practice Ethan. Real Ethan said no. Real Ethan said that though he more or less believed in God, he adamantly, vehemently, viscerally did not believe in religion. He said that converting so someone wouldn't dump you was disingenuous, offensive even to true believers with purer intentions. He said if she loved him, she wouldn't ask him to do something he didn't believe in. Converting was only suiting up for battle but was followed, he said, by the war—going to church every week and giving up things he loved and didn't think were wrong and building a life among people she liked so little she was willing to date a heathen like him. He said love me for who I am, or you don't love me at all.

"These are all reasonable points," said Jill.

"Why do you want to be so mean to me?" said Katie tearfully.

"I'm not being mean. I'm being truthful. This is how any normal person would respond. If he had said otherwise, then I would have been worried. What kind of reasonable person says, 'Yeah, sure, we've been on three dates. Let's talk conversion'? Ask Janey."

I looked hard at the floor.

"He said he would never ask me to give up my religion, just to practice it on my own. He said I should extend him the same courtesy. I said families don't operate on a 'live and let live' mentality. I said I couldn't be married to a non-Mormon."

"What did he say?"

"He said let's still be friends."

Jill laughed and Katie looked like she was considering strangulation.

"Actually I think it's sweet he even considered what you were saying," said Jill. "Most people would have freaked out that you even broached the subject after date three. It's better that you know."

Katie looked miserable.

"So he's not the one." I clapped, aiming for casual. I knew that being "not the one" was not a matter of failure on the part of either of them, just fate, and not a failure of fate, just a delay, and not really a delay as there is a time for every season under heaven. In any case, this situation—dates going nowhere—was not usually cause for alarm.

"I guess that's it. Not the one." She didn't sound sure.

"Let's make a list for him," Jill offered gamely.

Usually, there was a long, entirely quantifiable list of reasons why each guy was not the one. She actually wrote them down so that she could compare notes with the other women in her ward for whom he was also not the one (the vast majority) and to advise the one for whom he potentially was. They weren't bad qualities per se. They were just bad for her. They would be someone else's dream. So the list did not say things like "Chris: bad conversationalist, bad taste in music, not smart, not well read, boring." Rather they said, "Chris: talks *a lot* about football, obsessed with becoming a dentist, likes Led Zeppelin, favorite author—*Sports Illustrated*." Doom for Katie. Perfect, as it turned out a week and a half later, for Gracie, a high school senior in Katie's ward, cheerleader, Seahawks fan, Zeppelin diehard, and in possession of some regrettable teeth.

"Ethan: historian," I began.

"Taunts you with dairy-based ice cream," supplied Jill.

"Sucks at mini golf," I said helpfully.

"Not a Mormon," said Jill.

"Not the one," Katie sighed. "Except Ethan doesn't need a list. He's not going to be my problem to pass on. I don't know anyone who would date him. Problem is there's another list. Ethan: smart, funny, enlightened, feminist, liberal, academic. Hard to find all that at church."

"Ethan: you weren't that attached yet anyway," Jill pointed out.

"No," said Katie, "but I really wanted to be. I'm ready."

"It doesn't work that way," I said.

"No, that's exactly how it's supposed to work. It doesn't happen until you're ready, but when you get ready and you least expect it, that's when it happens."

"You are expecting it," said Jill.

"Oh my gosh I'm not," Katie said vehemently. "At this point, I'd be positively shocked." A lie. I knew what she meant, but dead scared something won't happen is not the same as actually believing that it isn't about to.

"Maybe you aren't really ready," said Jill.

"Of course I'm ready. I want this so much. My body is ready. Marriage and family is the divine plan. It's what everyone around me is doing. We're almost done with classes. I want it so badly."

"Which is not the same as being ready," Jill pointed out quietly, so quietly that Katie looked up suddenly, realizing it wasn't idle musing.

"What do you mean?"

"I mean maybe you aren't ready. You have to want it less. You have to be able to stand on your own. You have to know that you'll be okay without a husband. You have to want something else—something just for you, just about you—more."

"Thanks," said Katie. "I took Intro to Women's Studies. But that was really helpful."

Upstairs, Atlas started crying.

"You don't get things just because you want them. Just because you want them doesn't mean you're ready for them. Love and real relationships are a huge responsibility," said Jill.

"Really?" said Katie. "Like motherhood?"

"Whatever." Jill was tired of this conversation. She got up to leave the room, not mad, just bored of the petty direction Katie was about to take this. Or maybe going to get Atlas. I don't know.

"Oh, I'm sorry," said Katie. "We weren't talking about you, were we? Because you get what you want, ready or not. You don't even have to try for it. You just think about having a baby, and boom—you've got it. And you don't have to be ready for the responsibility because everyone around you ruins their lives to pick up the miles and miles and miles of your slack."

"Oh fuck you, Katie," snapped Jill. Atlas was screaming. I was glued in place. Katie looked like she'd been slapped so seldom did anyone curse in her presence. "I didn't mean to ruin your life. I made do with a less than perfect situation. I picked the least bad of a bunch of bad options . . ."

"Gee, I'm so sorry I couldn't be a better father for you."

". . . whereas you want to sit in this living room and plan out your whole perfect life without any sense at all of what the world is like out there. It's a pathetic fantasy. You're not ready for real life—you wouldn't even recognize it. You're that idiot walking across the heath in the rain hoping you'll faint and someone handsome will come rescue you when really you're just going to catch cold and die."

"Yeah, it's too bad I don't have your sense of the real world. I see how as a young, single mother you're working two jobs and spending a fortune on daycare and barely making ends meet. I see how you were so ready for the responsibility of the world that your baby's father wanted to stay with you."

"Daniel wanted to stay with me," Jill whispered, practically ice.

"Oh yes, I see him right here." Katie was yelling. So was Atlas.

"Daniel left Atlas, not me," Jill spat.

Katie shrugged. "If that's what you have to tell yourself. I don't see him around though. Haven't heard from him. Doesn't seem to be missing either one of you a whole lot."

"You are a bitch, Katie," Jill told her bitterly. "If it makes you feel better, you can knock me about Atlas. You can knock me about Daniel. But at least I've loved. And been loved. Maybe I haven't handled this perfectly, but I've handled it. Maybe I haven't done it by myself, but who ever said you were supposed to handle all the shit by yourself? Isn't that why you want a husband so badly? This is what you have friends for. I wouldn't even hesitate—I wouldn't even have thought twice had it been you asking me. I'm sorry if I've disappointed you. But I think it's you who's disappointed you." She stormed upstairs, but then we heard her cooing to Atlas, heard his sobs subside.

Katie paced around the room seething and muttering. "Where does *she* get off telling *me* about marriage and family and children? She is the last person qualified to give advice about love and relationships. I do everything for her, and she never does anything for me. Fantasy? She's the one living a fantasy." Et cetera. Finally, she turned to me. "What's your problem?" she snapped. "You think you just get to sit there and not say anything? You think you're so much better than we are?"

During all of it, I'd been pressing myself deeper and deeper into the corner of the sofa. Uncle Claude was curled into a tight ball in the corner too, head tucked under her tail. We do not do conflict, the dog and I. I don't yell. At anyone. Ever. It has literally driven people to drink so frustrated are they that, no matter what, I will not rise to yelling. And I don't like other people yelling either. When they do it on TV, I turn it off. When they do it in my presence, I leave the room. And when I can't leave the room, I try to disappear into the sofa. "I don't have anything to say," I stammered quietly.

"Fine," said Katie. "Me neither." And left the room too. So it was just me, sitting in the dark. Upstairs, Jill and Katie cooled off, felt better. Downstairs, I felt hot and much, much worse.

In the morning, Katie came downstairs early with a puffy-eyed Atlas and turned on the TV, plopping down onto the sofa and waking me up.

"You didn't sleep here?" she asked despite a good deal of evidence to the contrary.

"Apparently," I said, groggy and untrusting, wondering about her mood this morning, resentful that I had to live with such mean, spiteful people. She was puffy eyed too, so I supposed I had to cut her some slack.

"I've decided it's okay," she announced, not sorry for waking me up, not sorry for yelling all night. "I will stay friends with Ethan. I don't have to date him to be friends with him. He doesn't have to convert to be friends with me. That way I get all the benefits of hanging out with a guy I like who's smart and funny and interested in the things I'm interested in, and so if I have to date guys who lack some of those things, I still have a complete set. I just have to split it up between a few different people. Like Jill. She couldn't find all things daddy in one person. So she had Daniel for sex and sperm and you and me for childcare and support."

She sounded unconvinced. But not half as much as I was. "What makes you think Ethan's going to consent to being half a boyfriend?" I said.

"He was the one who said let's be friends."

"That's just something people say, Katie. They don't mean it."

"Who wouldn't want to be friends with me? With all of us?"

"Lot of work," I said.

"I already e-mailed him to invite him for dinner over here tomorrow night. Sort of a peace offering."

"Who's going to make dinner?" I asked as dryly as I could manage, not because I wondered—I knew—but because, you know, it's nice to be asked.

"You're the cook," she said because it was true and because she didn't get it. And, in fairness, because I discourage other people from cooking. Which, also in fairness, is because they aren't very good at it.

Twenty

I THOUGHT ETHAN might feel outnumbered by girls and English majors. I thought emotions and tensions were running a little high. So I invited Jason and Lucas too. Once you're doing it, it's just as easy to cook for four or five or seven. I made lentil soup, squash crepes, and couscous. I made three-pea salad for vitamins and corn bread for grounding. I made apple cake for sweetness and life and new beginnings where one didn't want to kill one's roommates. And I made sangria—a triple batch—for practicality. The only way to get through a dinner where Katie and Ethan were trying to be friends, and Katie and Jill and I were at least pretending to do the same, was going to involve alcohol. If Katie didn't like it, she should try to give me less stress.

Ultimately, squash crepes are a last-minute prep, which is both a blessing and an enormous pain in the ass. It is stressful at a dinner party to leave so much to the last minute and hard to get everything done and hot all at once. On the other hand, it is nice to have no choice but to leave someone else in charge of entertaining, conversation, and the baby. Ethan and Katie showed remarkable calm and grace though both seemed a little sad and defeated. And it seemed like forever since we'd seen Lucas or even Jason though obviously that wasn't true. Still, class together and studying together and library time together and showing up to babysit and crashing on our couch are none of them the same as dinner and alcohol and conversation about real and varied topics (not just books, not just babies). And peeking out of the kitchen at all of them, I felt something like forgiveness for the first time in two days. Jason and Lucas helped—if they could be a family in defiance of all society's proscriptions, surely so could we. Ethan helped too because if he didn't think we were total freaks, maybe we weren't. Mostly, a house full of people sounds like love. In the kitchen, Uncle Claude at my side awaiting what I dropped, I chopped and sliced, sipped sangria, listened to my friends laughing in my living room. For the first time in a while, I felt fine.

Jill and Katie didn't offer to help anymore because I always said no. They are inexact and careless in the kitchen. It takes longer to explain what I want than to do it myself, and help is only helpful if it's okay with you when you say chopped but get diced, and it's not okay with me. And it embarrasses me to cook in front of Lucas. It's not like what you make at home for dinner for friends is supposed to be like a restaurant anyway, and he always says nice things about my cooking, but it still makes me uncomfortable. Lucas says this is a problem he encounters with everyone he knows. Not even his mother will cook for him anymore. He never gets invited to friends' houses for dinner. If he wants a meal he didn't make himself, he has to go out. I'll cook for him occasionally, but not while he watches. Thus I had Jason and Ethan to sous for me. Since the former was already drunk, I put him to work setting the table. And since Ethan's skills were as yet untried, I put him on the task of dicing herbs and removing shallots from shallot peels. Do I sound like a control freak? Only when I cook.

Katie and Jill and Lucas watched Atlas roll over in the living room—new as of this morning—and I could hear them clapping and cheering every time he did it, Jill and Katie friends again as if nothing had happened at all. Ethan and I worked on dinner and talked about baseball. Sort of. I was cubing squash for the crepes.

"Those look exactly like those pillbox hats the Pirates wore in the seventies," said Ethan.

"Worst uniform ever," I said.

"Bad but not worst ever. There've been lots of uniforms worse than those."

"Name one," I challenged.

"All those powder blue road uniforms in the eighties. Those weird camo tops the Padres have been wearing lately. The all-one-color uniforms they were doing for a while—red hat, red jersey, red pants, red shoes, red laces. The Astros in the eighties."

"The Astros were having a coded coming-out party," I said. "Those uniforms weren't ugly. Those uniforms were gay. Rainbows? Stars? It's not even subtle."

"No gay man would wear a uniform that ugly," said Ethan. "What about those shorts the White Sox wore that one game?"

"They did not."

"Did so."

"No way. How could they slide?"

"No idea. I guess they got a lot of dirt in their underwear."

"I don't believe you," I said. He Googled it on his phone to show me. I was temporarily too stunned to cook.

"Are you guys talking about baseball?" yelled Katie from the other room. "Baseball is boring. Stop talking and make us some dinner. We're starved."

"You're missing all of this rolling over," added Jill, full of giggles. "Bring us food and a camera."

Tired of his belly that morning, Atlas had rolled over while I sat with him reading aloud about the plague years in late sixteenth-century London. He'd been able to push the top of him up for a couple of weeks, but that morning, he tucked one arm under, his left, and pushed himself right up and over onto his back. "Ohmygodyouguys," I screamed, forgetting that (1) I am not ten, (2) I was not really speaking to them, and (3) this would surely scare the crap out of them both. Jill, pale as death, was downstairs before I finished standing up, Katie not far behind her, completely breathless.

"He rolled over," I said, delighted, gesturing towards an on-his-back Atlas trying to put his toes in his mouth.

"You scared me to death," Katie scolded.

Jill burst into tears, making me feel terrible for hating her.

"I didn't mean to scare you," I apologized, putting an arm around her. "I was just so excited."

"It's not that," she sobbed. "I can't believe I missed it. I should have been here. I should never have been asleep. This is why new mothers are so sleep deprived. So they don't miss anything." And she sat down next to her son, put her face in her hands, and cried. Atlas reached his arm out towards her, tucked it underneath him, and rolled back over onto his stomach.

Over the next hour, we all sat together in our pajamas and watched him do this a dozen more times until he rolled all the way across the floor and under the sofa, and we dragged him back out, and he started again. Then I went running with the dog. Then I took a shower. Then Katie and I went grocery shopping. Then I called my parents and my grandmother to tell them Atlas had rolled over. Then I did some work. Then I started dinner. Jill just sat on the floor all day watching Atlas, determined not to miss anything else, exclaiming over each new roll as if it were the first (not his first, *the* first, the first time anyone anywhere had ever rolled over).

Dinner was good. We all got drunk, even Katie, though not on alcohol, just on proximity to us. We were silly and laughing, passing Atlas between us so everyone had a chance to eat, but not wanting to put him to bed either, not wanting him to miss this. At some point in the whirling, after cake, after coffee, still with the sangria, Jason leaned over to Katie and asked her to have his baby. We were all cracking up. We thought it was very funny. Except, evidently, he was serious.

"Kind of a large favor," said Katie.

"You're good at favors. You let me sleep on your sofa," said Jason. "And you owe me. I babysit. And I gave you all my notes from orals. That saved you so much work. Plus I'm very good in bed."

"It's true." Lucas nodded.

"We've been talking about this for a long time. We've been thinking about this forever. We're always thinking about this. We've always known we want to be parents together."

Lucas and Jason looked like love at each other. Katie started to look panicked. Jill and I exchanged glances, splitting the difference between amusement and coming down off our high. Ethan, still grinning, looked around for the hidden cameras.

"Why me?" asked Katie.

"You're perfect actually," Jason said eagerly. Clearly he *had* been thinking about this for a while. "Maybe uniquely among all the people I know, you understand sex just for procreation. You'd be bringing a new life into the world."

"A mitzvah," said Lucas.

"You'd be bringing a child to people who can't have one on their own. You'd be bringing so much joy to so many people."

"My mother would buy you many gifts," Lucas added.

"Are you crazy? Why would I do this?" said Katie, at which the guys brightened, thinking she was considering it, though really I knew there were actually and truly no circumstances in no universes past or to come that could make this happen.

"Well, we thought of that," said Jason. "The joy of helping others. The good and godly and spiritual act of making new life—"

"Why Jason?" I interrupted to ask Lucas. "How did you decide him and not you?"

"Actually, our first choice was for us both to have sex with Katie"—who was blushing so hard, with anger or embarrassment, I feared for her health—"so that we'd never know who the bio father was. But we don't look alike, so we'd probably know anyway, and we thought Katie would be more comfortable with someone she knew better. Also, sex with girls grosses me out. No offense. I'm not sure I even could."

"Oh my gosh, I'm not having sex with anyone," Katie blurted out. "I can't believe we're even talking about this."

Lucas kept talking as if he hadn't heard her. "Of course, we would buy you good health insurance, cute maternity clothes, anything else you needed. We'd also pay you thirty thousand dollars."

I choked on my sangria. Katie's face drained red to white.

Thirty thousand dollars was nearly three years' salary for us. Lucas might not get that, but Jason certainly did, and we all looked at him, waiting, stunned, for his explanation. When he'd said favor, I really thought that's how he'd imagined it.

"Actually, this saves us some expense as well as stress," he explained. "Surrogates, adoptions, having a doctor implant our sperm in you, these things are all really expensive. Plus the emotional trauma of all that. If we keep it among friends, we save the expense and the feeling that we're doing something really unnatural. We know who the mother is, so if we need a kidney or some medical info later—"

"God forbid," Lucas broke in.

"God forbid," Jason continued, "we'd know where to go. We know you won't change your mind at the last minute because you're a friend, and we know you'd never do that to us."

"And you're already surrogate parenting," Lucas added. "Atlas isn't your son, but you care for him as if he were. This would be like that, only with more work before and much less after . . ."

Lucas trailed off. No one said anything for a while. It would have been unbearably awkward if we weren't all so drunk. I knew Katie was never going to go for this. It was only, it seemed to me, some kind of pure love that had enabled Jason to convince himself otherwise. Katie had a lot of planned childbearing ahead of her. She wasn't about to start here.

"I love you guys. You know I do. But I can't . . . I wouldn't."

"Maybe think about it a little bit," Jason prompted.

"Don't rush it. Just consider it," said Lucas. "For us."

"The sex would be—I'm sorry to be blunt, but I know you must be worried about this part—gentle and easy and over fast. Not gross," said Jason.

"I'm not going to do this," said Katie quietly.

"We knew your initial reaction would be no," Lucas said. "But if you think about it a little more, it gets less weird."

"And you know we love each other," said Jason.

"You know we'd make great parents, provide a loving home."

Katie hesitated. Then she said, soft but steady, "Being gay is . . . not something I . . . condone—"

"Katie!" Jill gasped.

"What? They're allowed to ask me something like this at the dinner table, but I have to hold my tongue out of politeness?"

Lucas hung his head, but Jason looked ready for a fight.

"You know this about me," said Katie, hurt, like she was the offended party here. "Why did you even ask? What were you thinking?"

"That loving us means acknowledging we're not sinners?" said Jason. "That loving us meant you might think about helping us have a baby?"

"I don't . . . I can't condone raising a child in that environment."

"We would be great parents," said Lucas softly.

"Families need a mother and a father," said Katie.

"How can you say that?" Jason demanded. "What do you think this is?" He waved his hand vaguely around at us, the room, the house.

"What we're doing is great," she said. "But it's only temporary. We won't do this forever."

Not we can't. Not we might not. We won't. Like she already knew for sure. Like she already had an exit plan. "Why didn't you ask Janey?" she said.

"Janey would get too attached." Jason shrugged. "She wouldn't give the baby up to us."

"So, what, I'm just cold enough to do it?" Katie said crossly.

"You're just cold enough to do it," said Jason.

What can I tell about dinner parties like this one? They are shattering but also not so rare among friends that I really need to explain exactly what it felt like when eventually we hit lull and cramp, and anger bled into awkwardness, and everyone rose with excuses finally to go home, and those who lived there, those who stayed, felt very glad to have their house back and be alone again as if we'd been out too late and were coming home exhausted at dawn. Though always, too, dinners like this preclude return. You can't go back after you've asked a friend to make love and then carry a child for you even if deep down you always knew—and were relieved that—she would say no.

"I'm sorry, Katie. We didn't mean to upset you. But we had to ask. Do you still love me?" Jason said on his way out the door.

"Even though you totally embarrassed me? Even though you made me look like a horrible person?"

"Yes."

"Yes, I still love you. Do you still love me?"

"Even though you said no without even thinking about it? Even though you think I'm a sinner and are totally bigoted?"

"Yes."

"Yes, I still love you."

This is how it is with Katie. You have to hold two things in your brain at once. She really believes in what she believes in, even the offensive bits. This is her world. If you love her, and we do, you have to accept that part too. For her, these were the rules. Katie is very good about not trying to convert us even as she deep down believes we are all going to hell. Sometimes I am offended by this. I grant her it's a long shot, but doesn't she love me enough to at least try? And this, clearly, had been Jason's philosophy too. He knew she'd say no, but he loved Lucas enough to try.

"Thanks for everything," Ethan said, eyes a little dazed, hugging each of us in turn, walking out with Lucas and Jason as if they three had been friends since elementary school. "I had a great time. You guys throw a . . ."—he paused and finally settled on—"seismic dinner party. I'd love to come back." We closed the door, marveled for a moment at the bravery of Ethan's promise to return, left a million dirty dishes strewn throughout the house, and went to bed.

There, alone in the dark, I tried to decide if I was offended that they'd asked Katie and not me. I wouldn't have said yes either. They were right, I would get too attached. And though the sentiment "it's nice to be asked" rings true, you can't ask a question like that without truly meaning it. Committing it out loud is itself too intimate by half. Which is how I knew this wasn't off the top of their heads, wasn't a passing thought, wasn't a whim to finally ask her. They'd been thinking about it and planning for it, waited for her to break up with Ethan, jumped before she found somebody else. Must have considered every woman of childbearing age they knew, settled on the one person they thought had the foundation of God or of anything to separate sex from what it feels like and childbearing from motherhood. I have never been good at the former and clearly could not abide the latter. I would have said no. And besides that, saying no would have been hard and sad. But it would have been nice to be asked.

·   ·   ·

The next day, Katie had a plan.

"I have figured it out," she said happily over breakfast.

"What's that?"

"I will pray for husbands for all my friends at church. And they will pray for a husband for me. That way, it won't be me asking for something for me. It won't be me wanting a husband so much. What I will be wanting so much is happiness and husbands for my friends. Not selfish. Not obsessing. Outside myself. Very mature I think."

So this was how Katie circumvented her narrative. She realized from what Jill said that it couldn't be about her wanting so badly to fall in love and get married. She realized from what Jason and Lucas said that she was being selfish worrying only about herself and had to help her friends first. So she became a Jane Austen heroine, so genuinely committed to the love and happiness of those around her that she forgot all about herself while love ripened all on its own in the background as she unknowingly readied herself. All the outcome with none of the embarrassingly obvious effort. Or all the loopholes without any real change in attitude, depending on how you looked at it.

Twenty-one

ATLAS MUDDLED THROUGH that semester as we all did. It must have been hard for him, passed hand to hand, sometimes in tears, by one caretaker rushing out the door only half together to another breathlessly just home, still half in the library. I thought he would become overly attached to Jill, wail only for her, or worse, for another one of us, but he didn't. He was content equally with anyone, not just the three of us but also Jason and even Lucas and even Ethan, who still came now and again for dinner, and of course with his many grandparents—Diane and my family—who visited as often as they could but not often enough for Atlas to remember one visit to the next. He learned, I guess, I hope, that someone would always be there to love him though there was no telling who. He must have learned too though that that person would almost certainly be exhausted, often preoccupied, regularly in crisis.

Atlas was the most stable person in the house that semester. Jill was having a crisis of faith regarding her studies and research, Katie regarding the possibilities presented by love, men, and marriage, and me by, well, the two of them. The inability of my roommates to get their lives together drove me to exhaustion. Their undoing by the printed word and the failure of The One to show up on schedule, their inability to consistently get along with each other or make their own meals or maintain their own friendships wore me down. Taking care of Atlas was my joy. But it was also my burden—the fact of it crept slowly into my consciousness and moved in. Like everyone else, it would not leave. I resented Jill's every activity that was not the studying I had sacrificed my own for. I resented Katie's obsession with dating, saw through it to the exit strategy it implied. I resented that Jason spent one night a week with us then got to go home. Occasionally, I still resented Daniel though it seemed also that he had dropped out of our story almost entirely. Even his absence, so glaring after he left, so looming for the first weeks after we brought Atlas home, faded almost to airy nothing.

I knew that most of this anger was unfair. I knew that there was nothing I could do about it. I knew that it was interfering with the brief moments I had for uninterrupted, guilt-free work. But I couldn't make it go away. Jill strayed further and further from school and deeper and deeper into yoga and meditation. I am sure she needed it, and I am sure it helped, but it drove me near to madness to rush home for Atlas and find her sitting placidly in full lotus in the living room, garnering spiritual fulfillment from activities she used to mock me for doing. Katie stayed on top of her work but retreated too into manifest prayer. Church had always been there, of course, but now it was everywhere. She spoke constantly of God and prayer, of *His* control of all our lives and destinies. Again, I am sure it helped her, brought her peace, saw her through the same struggles I was dealing with, but I found it disingenuous, grating, and besides, I was jealous of the peace it brought her, rendering me none. I would love to think none of this impacted Atlas, but I know that can't be true. We all tell each other's stories.

For solace, for sanity, I started running again in earnest. I ran in college but stopped because it hurt my knees, and yoga seemed a much gentler, much more healing sport. Jill was ruining it for me though, and while I knew that yoga would preach all the ways in which Jill's doing it in the living room was a good thing for both of us, I couldn't bring myself to a studio to hear it. Whatever it does to your knees, running calms your spirit too. When all you can hear is your breath, your mind can go anywhere or nowhere as it likes. It's hard to be mad when you're gasping for air, when your legs are screaming to stop, but nonetheless everything in your body beats in time, pounds together, and carries on, forward and forward.

Running through winter also hastens spring and summer simply because running is the one thing it is enjoyable to do outside in February. Though it is dark and cold inside and out, winter allows you to exercise without being too hot. Which is a good silver lining. And which means that, though every other millimeter of your being is screaming for July, one small part of you (probably your thighs) is content with the slow creep of winter, and since, as everyone knows, nothing prolongs anything quite like your desperation to see it end, running brings an early spring.

Soon enough, there was an end in sight. It is one of the best things about academia—no matter how bad things seem, they end and begin anew every fifteen weeks or so. And you can do anything for fifteen weeks. Never mind that summer would not end Jill's depression or Katie's obsession or my anger or Atlas's muddled family, still it would be a new start, a chance to reevaluate, make a new plan. And whatever else, we wouldn't be taking classes, which would mean tons more free time comparatively speaking. We'd still have to teach and research and write, but it's not the same. When you've spent as long as we have in school, your body and brain automatically take the summer off.

Also, the coming of summer felt like completing something, like having survived the first round. It reminded me, of course, of last summer when all this started, and though I spent some time with nostalgia for last spring, my own apartment, my own uncomplicated days before all this, it felt so remote as to have been another life. All that chaos and uncertainty had been replaced in the intervening year with the sick feeling of an unsteady truce, a wobbly, barely holding on, desperate balance. But also in the interim year, chaos had become Atlas, and there was no denying the joy of that development. Things were, if not good, better than before. If not easy, making it. As I say, you can do anything at all for fifteen weeks, and so as weeks eight and nine became ten and eleven and twelve, my anger at the situation began to subside if only because soon this situation would be gone, and there'd be a new one in its stead.

One afternoon, I left to go running despite waning sunshine, an ominous sky, and foreboding weather forecasts. It was happening more and more that I simply lost track of everything when I was running—how far, how long, and where, and by the time it was really and truly raining, I was miles from home. It is not true that it always rains in Seattle, and when it does, it's rarely heavy, more like months and months of soupy drizzle. Torrential downpour is the purview of spring around here. I turned around, hot enough by then to be grateful for the rain, and ran home through what was, soon enough, late spring deluge. The streets and sidewalks became rivers of water, tributaries of which coursed down my hair, over my face, straight through my clothes, and into my skin until I was less jogging than jumping in giant, waterlogged sponges from puddle to puddle like a little kid out playing in the rain. Cars honked. Passengers inside them pointed and laughed at me or looked truly concerned for my sanity and safety, but I was breathless with laughter, hysterical to find myself so wet and still getting wetter, running through water, cleansed and cleansed and cleansed.

And better even still, rare as rainbows, I arrived home finally to a dark, completely empty house. I couldn't imagine where everyone was, and I couldn't have cared less. I stood breathing hard and dripping in the middle of my kitchen, listening to nothing, all the lights off, gathering dusk and entrenched rain clouds turning everything an undifferentiated, hidden blue, and considered my options. Taking a bath. Talking uninterrupted and un-overheard on the phone. Cooking dinner just for me. Simplicity matched only by luxury. It had been so long. I hadn't realized how, more than anything else, I missed this solitude. It's not selfish to think only of yourself when you're all alone. I stripped off sopping running clothes and left them in a spreading heap in the middle of the kitchen floor, donned dry sweatpants and sweatshirt, brought junk food to the sofa, and settled into it to watch anything or nothing at all on TV and listen to the rain in the dark all by myself. I closed my eyes and felt muscles I wasn't even aware of relax for the first time in months.

The glass door to the porch slid open revealing a grinning, dripping, naked Atlas on the hip of a grinning, dripping, naked Jill. She almost dropped him when she saw me.

"You scared me to death!" But she was whispering as if not to break the spell.

"Me too," I whispered back, shorthand.

"We were playing in the rain," she explained.

"I got caught running," I said.

She nodded. Inside, puddles formed around them, and their chill, drenched skin turned bright red. They glowed, slick and shiny, cold and hot. Even in near dark, they were so beautiful I couldn't take my eyes off them. Atlas laughed still—to be inside again I guess or at his slippery wet mother. Jill laughed too, left over from outside, from the quick scare of seeing me on the sofa, from a little embarrassment at being naked. And then suddenly, she was crying instead, not hard, not loud, not very different from the laughter and the rain except suddenly the water on her face came from inside instead of out.

"I'm so sorry, Janey." Barely a whisper. "I didn't know it would be this way. I didn't know it would be this hard."

"Me neither," I breathed back.

"I don't want to lose you guys." Into Atlas's hair as much as anywhere.

"You never could," I assured her, meaning it.

"I just want so much for him," she said. "It is worth sacrificing anything—even you, even me—for him to be loved."

"He always will be. You too. No one's been sacrificed."

"Do you think it'll be okay?" she asked.

I wondered what she meant. Our friendship, her career, my sanity, Atlas's childhood? "It will be okay," I promised, whatever it was. "It will. It will all be fine and better than fine," and added as evidence, "It's spring."

She smiled, then grinned, wiped her eyes and nose with one free hand, remembered again that she wasn't wearing anything, blushed even through her rain-drenched glow.

"Think this is what they mean by naked love?" she asked.

"Must be." I smiled, still entranced but coming back out of it. "You better get dry and warm before you both get sick," I said, channeling my grandmother. "I'll get him dressed while you take a bath. We can have potato pancakes for dinner." Her favorite. Not mine especially. But it is sometimes not true that the behavior has to shift so much as the attitude. I had to stop being angry more than she and Katie had to change. I had to remember about open, blind, knowing, unreserved, unambiguous, unconditional love—naked love—before any of it could make sense again. I had to find it the many places it hid, drag it out in the open and wrap it all around me, wear it around the house, feel its imprint on my skin, weave it into my hair, let it rain down wet and fresh from the sky before I could feel it, share it, be comfortable in its grasp, and understand, finally, what it all meant, at least this part of it, at least today.

PART III

Summer One

Twenty-two

S UMMER ONE. ALTAS'S first summer ever. The number one best season of the year. But mostly, in this case, first summer session. These short terms represent a flagrant disregard for natural laws, quantum mechanics, and the rules of physics that otherwise govern time. Cramming what normally takes fifteen weeks into five perhaps does not sound entirely outrageous, but it is, both in what it demands and in the compromises we all make to allow it to happen. I never teach Summer Two. I hate Summer Two. Summer One starts soon after spring semester ends, and it's easy enough to keep going, especially since the drop-off in workload is significant. Summer Two, by contrast, means you get five weeks off, but then you have to work straight through till Christmas. Christmas.

When they made me teach Summer Two one year and I complained to Nico about the straight-through-till-Christmas part, he focused exclusively on the five weeks off. People who work nine to five with only ten days off all year tend to fixate on that part. This is unfair. One reason is that people with real jobs get weekends off, and I do not. There's all that reading and writing and research to do. And then there's the grading. Two sections of comp, twenty-five students each, five papers per student, five pages per paper, five minutes per page—even I can do the math, but I needn't. Suffice it to say, it takes all weekend. Another reason only five weeks off till Christmas is unreasonable is that people with real jobs don't really work nine to five. They take coffee breaks and cigarette breaks and water breaks and go out to lunch and have parties for coworkers and do team building activities such as everyone takes the afternoon off and does a ropes course. We do all that too (not the ropes course), but it doesn't come out of work time; it comes out of sleep time because all the paper grading and lesson planning still has to get done. Nico's other point was that it was only five weeks off one way or the other, so what did it matter if it came first or second. Two words: until Christmas.

Fifteen weeks into five is also the kind of math even I can do. What it amounts to is meeting for two hours every day, no days off, no time for slacking. It means that missing even one day puts students pretty much hopelessly behind even though it also means that they feel they can cut class more often because, jeez, it meets every day. It's the same amount of class time as a real semester, but it's only one third the amount of time for homework—one third the time for reading, for research, for writing papers, for completing class projects. One third the time for grading. So it's a challenge. On the other hand, I love summer sessions. It's nice to be able to concentrate on one thing instead of fifty. You get really close with the students. You feel like you get a lot done. But mostly, you get out of your house and away from your roommates (both teaching Summer Two) and their baby for the entire morning. If you

hold an office hour, meet a friend for lunch, and then go running, you won't see anyone until late afternoon.

There is also little as exhausting as summer session. It's a
good thing it's so fast because you couldn't keep that pace up
for more than a few weeks. Sometimes, you have so much grading and planning and meeting with students to do that you
barely have time for anything else. But as I say, it's not just a
quick session. Time bends. Abstract theories of physics come
to apply. And so sometimes, summer sessions are strange and
eventful despite all the time spent working. And during this
one, simply, the whole world changed. Five weeks later, it was a
different place, the old one but a memory trace, a whisper of an
old life, so remote as to not even be my own.

I was teaching English 102—Intro to Lit. The first day is always
the easiest. It's when the students most resemble the ones you
were fantasizing when you planned the course, when all they
have to do is listen and smile, laugh in the appropriate places,
and that's enough. On the first day of class, since they'd not
read anything yet for homework, I decided—Atlas-inspired—to
read aloud to them. We did *The Lorax.* Good literature is good
literature after all. We moved the chairs into a circle, and I
showed them the pictures and everything. The students started
off a little dubious, wondering if I thought they were in kinder-
garten or what. But soon enough, they settled into being read
to, remembered how nice it is to be told a story, how when it's
one you're familiar with you slip out of the narrative and into
the cadence, the lull of the reader's voice, the waiting with joy-
ous anticipation to be told what you already know and understand more than is written. There's a reason we read to our

kids, and it's not just because they can't do it themselves. It's because there's a difference between reading yourself and being read to. I was tempted to give my new students a metaphor about sex versus masturbation but not on the first day of class. I sent them home with a dozen poems to read and explicate, beamed at the smiles of relief I saw leaving the room ("She seems nice" and "This won't be so bad"), and went outside to bask in sunshine.

On the steps, I found Ethan doing the same. "What are you doing on the steps of my building?" I said, sitting down next to him.

"I didn't realize it was yours," he said.

I turned and looked at the sign above the door.

"It says 'English Department,'" I pointed out.

"So it does," Ethan admitted and shrugged. "Summer session. They're redoing the history building for fall. Removing all the asbestos or something. Makes you feel really good about the last four years you've spent in there. In any case, they moved all our summer classes over here."

"What are you teaching?"

"History 102. You?"

"English 102," I answered happily, hugging my knees and grinning at him as if this were just an impossible coincidence. I love the first day of class.

"You're teaching *The Lorax*?" he asked, seeing it in my hands.

"Just for the first day."

"Sounds fun."

"What did you do?"

"Gave a mini-lecture summarizing History 101 in case they forgot or didn't take it."

"What's that take? About an hour?"

"Well, History 101 is roughly the dawn of recorded time to about 1499, but it's only Western civilization, so it's pretty doable."

"Do they seem nice?" I asked.

"So far," he said. "Yours?"

"Yeah, so far." We sat quietly and shared the mixed high/relief of the first class, coming down off the adrenaline of nerves and into the calm you get before the first homework assignment comes in when you don't yet know what you're in for and have nothing so far to grade.

"Want to have lunch?" he asked finally.

"I'm about to go running today, but I could do it tomorrow."

"Tomorrow it is," he said. Then, "Are you one of those people who likes to run alone? Because I'd love to run with you too. Not today of course"—he looked down at his khakis and tie—"but another day."

"What about your ankle?"

"It was only a sprain. It's healed. Maybe we can run slowly."

"Sounds great," I said. I don't in fact always like running with other people. But in the glow of day one, I could deny him—or anyone—nothing.

"I ran into Ethan," I reported when I got home. "We're having lunch tomorrow if you want to join us. And we're going running Wednesday."

"Oh yeah, I forgot to tell you he's teaching right upstairs from you," Katie apologized.

"How was day one?" said Jill.

"Good. They seem nice. Smiley. Participated some."

"How did they like *The Lorax*?" Jill asked but seemed distracted by Katie who herself seemed pretty distracted.

"They liked it. They got it. They had interesting ideas about . . ." I trailed off. "What's with you two?" Jill couldn't keep her eyes off Katie. Katie looked like she might explode.

"I met a boy," she shrieked.

I looked at Jill who suppressed, not quite, a smirk then swallowed it. "She thinks this one is different." She shrugged at me, bemused, eyebrows raised.

"His name is Peter. He just moved here from Utah for college. He's only twenty-one, but it's okay. He wants to major in zoology. He's very cute and nice. He paints. He's tall. He thinks I'm funny. He's in charge of food for the youth picnic we're hosting on Thursday, and since I'm in charge of games, we have to work together—"

"Why?" Jill interrupted.

"What do you mean?"

"Food and games have nothing to do with each other."

"Don't be ridiculous," said Katie. "These are five-year-olds. What do you think happens if you feed them ice cream and then do a sack race? What if he fed them macaroni salad and then I had them playing Marco Polo in the pool?"

"The horror," agreed Jill.

"So when are you going out?" I asked.

"Oh, he hasn't asked me out yet. But he will. I can tell. We're meeting tomorrow morning to discuss the picnic." And she danced upstairs to try on everything she owned followed by everything I owned and everything Jill owned.

•   •   •

On Tuesday, we tried to define the term "poem." It was hard. My students knew it needn't rhyme. They knew it didn't need to sound pretty. But they didn't know what it did need to do. At first they asserted that they knew one when they saw it, but I gave them some Robert Hass, and then they had no idea. It looks like prose. It sounds like prose. I assured them it was considered poetry and sent them home to write a response paper supporting that position or explaining why it was crap, whichever they liked.

Ethan and I carried lunch out of the sandwich place and sat under a tree on the quad and ate it. I told him about class, gave him a copy of Hass's "A Story About the Body."

"It's prose. It's totally prose," he said, laughing. "That's the wrong answer, isn't it?"

"Officially? There is no wrong answer."

"Actually?"

"Actually, it's a poem. Stark, visual, lyrical, opaque. Robert Hass is a poet. What did you do?"

"We started religion in Renaissance Europe. At this stage, it's mostly lecture, but it's really exciting. Telling them what happened and why and what it led to, this long chain of interconnected events . . . What?" I was smirking.

"It's make-believe," I said. "Storytelling. Fun with narrative."

"Oh, you're one of those." He rolled his eyes. "Why don't English majors believe in history?"

"Because it's all so much more complicated and suspect and full of half-truths and warped and incomplete than you're telling them . . ."

"Warped?"

"And they're just writing it down and memorizing it like it's what really happened . . ."

"You teach fiction, Janey."

"So do you," I insisted. "We don't have any kind of accurate picture of the history that was made, say, yesterday, so I know for sure that whoever spins it however many years from now is making it up."

"But you'll be dead then."

"So there won't be anyone to correct them."

"You don't teach history when you teach Shakespeare?" he asked. "You don't tell them about the printing press and the new settlements in the Americas and the plague and the influx of people in London?"

"I do, but only to show them what we don't know. Besides, that's not history; that's background information."

"You're drawing awfully fine distinctions there."

"Anyway, those are facts we know are true. We aren't making those things up."

"Can I just reiterate that you teach fiction?"

"Just because fiction is made up, doesn't mean it isn't true. What do we learn about life from Shakespeare's history? Maybe Shakespeare was Catholic, maybe he wasn't. Maybe he married willingly, maybe he didn't. Maybe he loved his family, maybe he deserted them at the first opportunity. Maybe both. We know nothing from history. We learn what's true from *King Lear.* Old age is frightening. It's hard to recover from the feeling of betrayal even when you know you're wrong. There are few things, even death, worse than madness, blindness, loss of power and respect and the love of your family. Storms in the world accompany storms of the soul. Both serve as powerful metaphors. Fiction is much more true than history. History is about other people. Fiction is about you."

"You're just using characters as models. So am I. It's just

what my characters did really happened. We learn from them the same way we learn from Lear. We try to honor what we admire and avoid what felled them. The particulars change but not the pattern, not the overriding—"

"Narrative?" I guessed.

"I admit nothing," he said.

We sat and thought awhile, enjoyed the weather. Then we threw out the remains of lunch and set a place and time to run. As we were walking away from each other, I turned around. "Ethan, speaking of inevitable narratives, Katie met someone."

"Oh, that's great," he said—because what else could he say?—but he may or may not have meant it. "Who is he?"

"His name is Peter. She met him at church."

"What's he like?"

"Haven't met him yet. They have their first date tonight." I'd had a text on my phone when I got out of class.

"Sounds pretty serious," Ethan said. "See you tomorrow." And I started home to find out just how serious it was.

Twenty-three

O N WEDNESDAY, I reported the whole thing to Ethan while we ran. For the first half mile or so, it felt like a betrayal, gossiping about Katie behind her back when Ethan wasn't so much a mutual friend as her ex (by contrast, I'd also relayed the whole thing to Jason that morning over coffee without a second thought). In my defense, several things: (1) being witness to Katie's love life was like being thirteen again, so why not act the part? (2) she was so high, I doubted she'd ever notice or care; (3) it is good to run and talk at the same time as it increases cardiovascular effort and ability; and (4) it was too much fun not to.

Peter had been on time, nearly to the second, and arrived in a tie with black and white patent leather shoes. Bearing flowers. He was cute, young, and obviously nervous, but he held his own against the three of us—Atlas screaming, Jill and I transfixed by those shoes. Katie had insisted on waiting upstairs so that she could make a grand entrance (sixty outfits later, she'd settled on a dress of Jill's with a wide skirt that flowed cinematically as she swept down the stairs). She was furious with us by the time she hit the living room because we could not stop giggling. ("You guys are not easy on a first date," Ethan broke in at this point. And I laughed, saying, "We were easy on you.") She glared at us then turned to Peter, all smiles and glittering eyes, took the flowers, cooing practically, and handed them to me without a word, without even turning her eyes from him (as if I were the maid), and fairly floated out the door on his arm. They'd been out to dinner and to a movie, and we'd ordered Indian and rented one and were paused in the middle of it, just getting Atlas down, when Katie and Peter got home.

We barely inquired after their evening and ran upstairs. "Are they always so giggly?" we heard Peter ask but didn't hear the answer. "They're like my teenage sisters," he said. The first thing she did—before she offered him something to drink, before she took off her shoes, before she dimmed the downstairs lights—was turn off the baby monitor we'd hidden in the corner. But lying on the floor in Atlas's room, staring up at his mobiles and listening to his baby sleep, we could at least catch the tone. There was a lot of laughing. Then a lot of soft singing quiet talk. Then nothing.

When she finally made it upstairs, alone, at quarter past four in the morning, she found me and Jill sound asleep under six or seven baby blankets on the floor of Atlas's room.

"Why are you guys sleeping on the floor?"

"Accident," said Jill. "We were trying to spy on you. This room is closest. How was it?"

"So great," said Katie, snuggling in with us, pulling over one of the blankets. "He is so great." She was already falling asleep which suggested to me that she'd just woken up. "We talked for a really long time. Then he kissed me. Then we kissed for a really long time. And then we fell asleep. Then we woke up and he went home. We're going out again tomorrow night."

"You mean tonight?" said Jill.

"Yeah, tonight." She smiled and turned over.

Jill and I went out into the hall. "Could just be NiCMO," she said.

"Maybe." I shrugged. "I'm going to bed." I had to teach in a few hours.

"It's true. It could just be NiCMO," said Ethan when I finished my story. "We had NiCMO."

"Yeah, I know," I said, panting. It is hard to tell long stories while you run.

"You do?" Horrified.

"Of course." NiCMO, for the uninitiated, is Non-Committal Make Out, Mormon-speak for hooking up. It differentiates itself from regular making out in that it holds no possibility of being The One. While this is in fact true for the vast majority of make-out sessions that occur on earth, most participants take that as a given or can at least usually make the distinction without naming it. Katie and Co. went ahead and specified. The Mormon church, which has strict rules against not only sex before marriage but also most kinds of touching (above or below the belt, above or below the clothes, even of oneself), doesn't mind making out and even recognizes that sometimes you might want to do so just because it's yummy, or at least many of its followers realize this. It's a weird religion.

Wednesday night I had to grade the is-it-or-is-it-not-a-poem papers. This time, Peter arrived in jeans and a T-shirt, less nervous, easier with us. Atlas had a cold and was on and off weepy, even in Jill's arms, but when Peter asked to hold him, he settled right down, nuzzled against him, and closed his eyes. Katie looked like she might cry. We chatted with Peter about school, about moving here, about home, his mission, his family, the youth picnic he and Katie were planning. He asked polite questions of us, gave polite answers back. Then they left, and Jill and I debriefed.

"He seems nice."

"He does."

"He's very cute."

"He is."

"He seems to like Katie."

"Which is a good thing because she really likes him."

"Think she's made her mind up?"

"Since before she met him," I said.

We were sitting on the floor in the living room, all three of us. Atlas had learned to sit up while I was at school in the morning and spent much of the evening, despite his cold, demonstrating for our squeals and applause. I was grading papers on my lap, clapping for Atlas, throwing the ball to Uncle Claude, and talking to Jill all at the same time.

"Think how good you'll be at multitasking when you have a baby," she said, and it stopped me because I had a moment, two, three, when I was confused by the word "when," when my brain flashed an unarticulated, confused "But I already have a baby" across the sky. I shrugged it off.

"You're getting worse at it," I said, not to be mean, just because she'd presented an opening.

"I was never very good at doing too many things," she said. "I like to put lots of energy into one thing—teach one class or take one class or write one paper or read one book."

"Graduate school isn't like that."

"Right, so I'm . . . cutting back. What's more important than being a good mother?"

I did not feel like just-a-friend with an undefined place in this family. I felt like a fifties father, like my parenting role was superfluous and unappreciated. Really, my job was to bring home the bacon. And shop for it and plan meals around it and cook it and clean up afterwards. Which hardly seemed fair.

"You've got lots of help parenting," I pointed out.

"I don't mean changing diapers and babysitting and putting him to bed or feeding him or whatever. I mean emotional energy, giving him my undivided attention, freeing myself up to notice his little progresses and setbacks, never saying, 'I have something more important to do.'"

"Isn't that a little . . . narrow? Wouldn't it kill you if someone's only thing in the world were you?"

"No, I think that would be lovely," said Jill. And then, "Why do you think he got all quiet when Peter held him?"

"Peter seems to have some experience with babies. Katie looked like she was going to cry. Didn't she say he has little sisters?"

"Yeah, but I mean we're good with babies, especially this one, and he was fussy all afternoon."

"He has a cold."

"Not when Peter held him."

"Change of scenery?"

"Change of sex."

Change of tone. I heard her voice catch and braced myself for what was coming.

"I think it's because he's a guy," she said.

"Atlas?"

"Peter. I think Atlas needs a man. Maybe a bunch of women isn't good for him. It must feel different being held by a man. Maybe there's some connection there we just can't provide."

"He has a cold, Jill. He has Jason. And that's not the issue here, and you know it."

Atlas, upright but precarious, looked nervously between us and smiled. He didn't seem to be suffering. He also didn't seem like he needed Jill's attention so much she couldn't pick up a book. He looked like he needed something nailed down to lean against. Otherwise, he seemed fine. I went to bed at midnight, and Katie wasn't home yet, so things must have been going well.

Thursday was the lull in it. In class, we did half a poetry unit, introduced the next paper. I went straight home afterwards to take care of Atlas while Jill and Diane had some much-needed alone time—sometimes a girl just needs her mother. It had suddenly occurred to Katie that she should play hard to get at least a little bit, so she decided, after the youth picnic, not to see Peter for the rest of the day. They spent three hours on the phone.

Peter turned out not to be much into baseball one way or the other, but he was a guy and mildly enjoyed games of all kinds. Having gotten out of the way the possibility of his being a Yankee fan, Katie invited him over for dinner Friday night under the no-pressure conditions of a family picnic on the floor in the living room while watching a baseball game so as not to have no conversation but not to have too much either. I

don't know if she was worried we'd say embarrassing and in-
criminating things or thought we'd be boring or feared we'd
grill the love right out of him with too many questions he didn't
want to provide—or she didn't want to know—answers to.

"Casual and laid back. No more than two courses," she warned
me, "including dessert. And make it baseball food—hot dogs or
popcorn or something. Maybe we should just order a pizza." As
if cooking a real meal would invite real conversation and spoil
the whole thing.

"Sooner or later he's going to find out that you're smart, you
read a lot, you vote for liberals, you're a feminist, you can't
cook, and your roommates are fairly overprotective and obnoxious," I pointed out.

"Fine, later," she said.

Friday then finally. "One down, four to go," I assured my students, already exhausted with only one week of summer session and one paper under their belts. Two days off. Two whole
days without seeing each other, without seeing me, without
having to think about poetry. I was jealous of their (probably
fictitious) carefree weekends at mindless jobs followed by lovely
summer parties since what loomed for me was a weekend of
grading and a picnic on the floor I was getting increasingly
nervous about. Anxiety, more than the flu, more than mono,
more than a rash, is very contagious. At home, I found Atlas
laughing hysterically in a bouncy seat at the edge of the kitchen
floor which Katie was cleaning with a toothbrush.

"What happened to casual and laid back?" I asked her.

"Because I am casually, laid backly, effortlessly neat and

clean," she explained, pushing hair out of her eyes with rubber-gloved hands.

"Where did those gloves come from?"

"I am a perfect housekeeper, so I obviously have tons of these stored under the sink."

"Where did they really come from?"

"I went to the grocery store and spent forty dollars on cleaning products."

"Very laid back," I said.

"Shut up," she said.

Jill and I spent almost as much time as Katie did getting dressed. Jill put Atlas in his tuxedo onesie as a joke only we got. I decided I couldn't just serve hot dogs and popcorn. It's not like I'm neurotic or never use a microwave or think I'm above ordering a pizza. I love pizza. But when you invite someone to your house for dinner for the first time, it is polite to actually cook. I fought with Katie for an hour before I convinced her that, though this was her date, it was my kitchen and therefore my decision. We compromised on real food that could nonetheless be eaten in front of the TV. Salmon burgers and salad and raspberry cheesecake bars. And indeed, except Atlas, we all looked appropriately casual in (carefully chosen) jeans and T-shirts and bare feet. Peter showed up similarly clad and, pointedly (which sort of defeats the gesture), ten minutes late. We sat on the floor and ate on our laps, cuddled with Atlas and Uncle Claude, chatted idly about the commercials, the color commentary, the occasional good play. The Mariners and Orioles played a completely ordinary baseball game, just one of 162, too early in the summer for standings to matter yet between two teams who weren't going anywhere anyway with a boring final score of 5–2. After the game, Jill and I walked the dog for a while. When we came in, Peter and Katie were in such deep conversation they didn't even look up. We went upstairs without even saying good night.

Six hours later, at five o'clock in the morning, Katie crawled in bed with me. "He said he had a dream," she whispered, less, I think, because it was five A.M. and more for something like reverence, "where he was in a bike race for tandems, and everyone else had two riders, but he was alone, and even though he was fast and strong and good, he couldn't catch up, but then he pulled over to have a snack, and I was there, and I said I'd ride with him, and then we caught up to everyone else and overtook them and won and rode all over the world together." She was crying.

"What do you think it means?" I said dryly.

She ignored me. "I told him I had a dream where I was asleep. You know when you fall asleep in your dreams? When you're just so tired and comfortable, you have to stop telling yourself stories and totally sleep? Except I was sleeping next to him with my head on his chest and my legs on his legs. It was the most comfortable feeling I've ever had."

"What did he say?"

"He said I was everything he ever dreamed of in a wife. He said he's been waiting his whole life to meet me. He said he wondered why God would send him to Washington of all places, and now he knows it was to meet me. He said he knows God wants him to get married. He says he sees me with Atlas and knows I will be a wonderful mother."

"What did you say?"

"Same thing. Different pronouns."

I hugged her, somewhere between delighted for her and

also thinking she might be insane. And also wishing she could wait and tell me these things at a more reasonable hour of the morning. But since I was up anyway, I waited until she fell asleep and then walked down the hall to wake up Jill.

"He all but asked her to marry him," I hissed.

"Who?" she asked sleepily.

"He had a dream about biking around the world with her. She had a dream about sleeping on his chest. He said she was everything he wanted in a wife and that God wanted them to be together and have children. She said she thought so too."

"They've been dating since Tuesday," said Jill.

"I know. It's insane."

"Where is she now? Singing in the front yard? Trying to find a wedding caterer open at six o'clock in the morning?"

"She's more calmly excited. Excited suffused with wisdom, purpose, godliness."

"Maybe she's just tired."

"Do you think it's too soon?"

Jill opened her eyes for the first time and looked at me. "Are you kidding?"

"Maybe after so much looking, she knows it when she sees it?"

"Since Tuesday."

"Should we talk to her?"

"I doubt we could put a stop to this even if we tried. It's like stopping the weather. Maybe he's less serious about this than she imagines." We heard Katie get up and go to the bathroom. Then she poked her head in the room. I did my best to look innocent. Jill did her best to will both of us to get the hell out of her room so she could go back to sleep. "Are you guys talking about me?" Katie said.

"No," I said.

"Yes," said Jill at the same time.

Katie looked thoughtful. "I think I'd like to have everyone over for dinner Sunday night," she said finally. "I think Peter should meet the family."

Twenty-four

Iᴛ ᴡᴀꜱ ᴀꜱ if we were hosting a coronation. In retrospect, it is easy to see how important the evening was, that the effort towards finery was warranted and worth it. At the time, we all thought we'd lost our minds, but none of us could stop. Jason and Lucas went without saying. They had a more or less standing Sunday-night dinner invitation. Ethan too these days. Peter's older brother Eli was in town, one night only, so he came. We invited Diane, who was seeming unhappy to Jill on the phone. Plus the four of us, even if one of us didn't get his own chair, made for too many around the table.

Katie borrowed a folding table and chairs from church, and we moved the plan outside, a good excuse besides for her to buy a few thousand candles, lanterns, and paper lamps. We invited everyone for late, even though Ethan and I had to teach the next day and even though Jason and Lucas and Diane and Eli had to drive home, so that we could have post-sunset glow and moonlit summertime to go with the soft light of candles and so that we had a better shot at Atlas falling—and staying—asleep. We

spent Saturday morning from nine to noon menu planning.
Nine to noon. Then I insisted on going running for an hour.
Then we shopped. One farmers' market, one co-op, two grocery
stores. This is a task I generally delegate, but the night seemed
too important to leave up to the mischievous gods of cooking or
my roommates, who tended to be less picky than one might
wish when it came to selecting good produce, the right chunk
of cheese, bread that was fresh, and so on, and did not take well
to instruction ("Fastidiousness," I said; "Annoying and control-
ling," they said).

A better question than why I was running all over the tourist-
mobbed city on a summer Saturday afternoon with one baby,
two roommates, a three-page list, and seemingly everyone else
in the Seattle metropolitan area is how I knew. Even though the
evening was important to Katie, even though I loved her and
wanted as much happiness for her as possible, I should also have
been able to relate to this from afar. Jill and I had lost somehow
the distance that allowed us to watch with wry amusement and
tinged alarm the pace and bubble of this relationship. We'd
been swept up. Like when you go to the movies and identify so
closely with the star that you go to the bathroom afterwards and
look in the mirror and feel vaguely surprised to see your face
and not hers looking back. Perhaps this was Atlas-effect too.
Jill's son was my son. Jill's problems were my problems. Katie's
love life, the possibilities so suddenly opening before her, were
my possibilities too? I wasn't as panicked, short-tempered, and
jittery as she was, but I was hell-bent on cooking for the queen.

We shopped for three and a half hours, rented a movie (*Big
Night* for perspective), ordered Thai food, and started cooking.
Sunday morning, Katie got up and went to church. Diane came
early and took Jill and Atlas to the zoo. Jill was sure Diane was

depressed. Diane was sure Jill was depressed. They were worried about each other and, both of them right, glad I think for the distraction from themselves. I put the iPod on both random and loud and danced while I cooked. I chopped and mixed and whipped. I made an epic, seismic, disastrous mess, covering every inch of counter with eggshells, corn husks, pea pods, food wrappers, cheese rinds, and tea bags. When I ran out of room, I cleaned up the mess in order to clear counter space. Then I made a mess again. Twice. I put the mini-quiches in about four, went into the living room to turn off the music and on the ballgame, and walked back into the kitchen to find Ethan standing in it, scaring the crap out of me.

"I was knocking, and someone was clearly home, but no one was answering, so I just came in. Thought you might need some help." Blissed out as I was on the loud, the dancing, the chopping, the house-to-myself, I wasn't entirely sure I wanted help. Plus, he was obviously stopping off at the tail end of a run and was grimy, smelly, and generally damp.

"You can help," I said, "but go shower first."

He grinned. He thought I was kidding. "But I'll miss the ballgame," he complained.

"Shower fast. You'll only miss the first inning."

"So this is serious," Ethan observed, coming downstairs pink and scrubbed, damp hair tousled, smelling for all the world like Atlas coming out of the bath (probably because Atlas's was the shampoo that was in the shower).

"Peter and Katie?"

"No, dinner," he said, laughing.

"Both evidently. I feel very nervous. I don't know why."

"Big night."

"Do you feel bad?"

"No. Why?"

"Because of Katie?"

"No, I'm happy for Katie. I'm a little worried about you though."

"Me? Why?"

"You seem to be suffering from the delusion you're cooking for eighty."

"It's hard to cook small," I said.

"I'll help," he offered, and started snacking on the tarts that were eventually going under the cream that was eventually going under the cherries. This was not helpful. What was helpful was that he stayed all afternoon, chopped what I told him to chop, and didn't get mad when I told him he was doing it wrong and made him start over.

Eventually, the sun went down, the house filled up with good smells and people I loved. Seattle in the summer is what makes Seattle the rest of the year worth it. The days are warm, sunny, cloudless, and very long. It's light until ten, and then the evenings are cool, clear, bugless, and beautiful. We glowed warmly from the candles and the wine and the talk, laughed loudly and even with our mouths full, ate and were sated. Dinner was good, my best effort, and the anxiety and weight of it all slipped away. Seattle in summer is so lovely that the end of the dessert course is really only the midpoint of the evening. No one showed any move towards going home. Presently, in the half-drunk, overfull, dreamlike aftermath, Peter stood up, stone-cold sober, and announced that he wanted to ask a question.

"Yes Peter," Jason called on him.

Peter cleared his throat. "I wanted to ask all of you for your permission and blessing to marry Miss Katherine Louise Cooke."

I couldn't look directly at him—it was too embarrassing—but sidelong sneaked peeks revealed he was not nearly as uncomfortable as he'd just made everyone else. We all sat in painful, awkward silence. He just stood there beaming. Katie slowly began to give off actual light and heat. Then she kicked me under the table.

"Say something," she yelled with her eyes.

"What?" I pled silently back.

Finally, blessings on his head forever, Jason spoke. If it wasn't the exact right thing to say, at least he said something.

"Why are you asking us?"

"It's tradition," said Peter.

"To ask her friends?"

"To ask her family." This is when Katie started crying. Just like that, he seemed worthy to me.

"You have my blessings and permission," I said, a little tearful too. Beams and smiles from Katie and Peter. Hard, scary glaring from Jill.

"Are you mad?" she demanded.

"No," I said.

"Drunk?"

"A little," I admitted.

"You've known her a week." Jill turned her wrath on Peter.

"Exactly."

"Exactly what?"

"Exactly a week. I met Katie a week ago tomorrow, but it's after midnight, so really it's today." He reached down and squeezed her hand.

"So you're asking her to marry you for your anniversary?" Lucas said wryly.

"Exactly," said Peter again.

"What kind of person thinks a week is long enough?" Jill muttered.

"I do," said Peter, practicing.

"How could you possibly?"

"I already know everything I need to. I know she is kind and smart. I know she is funny and fun. I know she wants church and family and children at the center of her life. She likes to share food and watch reality TV and eat sour candy. She does not like dairy-based ice cream. She prefers shopping to most other activities. She would do anything for her friends. She can't really cook or clean . . ." (Apparently some fessing up had occurred.)

". . . She wants to teach. She likes miniature golf and kite flying. She thinks sometimes that grad school is crap . . ." This was news to me. Also that "crap" didn't count as a curse word.

". . . She likes ducks. She speaks Spanish. She is the woman I am meant to spend eternity with." He stopped and thought about it. "That's it I think." It seemed like a fairly comprehensive list to me, especially for a week.

Jill remained unimpressed. "You honestly think that's enough?"

"The first few were enough," he said and recapped—kind, smart, funny, fun, church, family. "I knew right away actually. I could have proposed a week ago today."

"Katie?" Jason raised his eyebrows at her. "Is there anything you'd like to add?"

"Me too," she managed.

"So you've stopped talking now?" Jill scowled at her. Katie ignored this.

"Well, since no one here has ever been married, we might not be the best group to ask," said Diane. "But since I've got twenty years on you all, I suppose I'm as close as we've got to the wisdom of the elders. You've got my blessing."

"It's okay with me," said Lucas though his tone was less I-am-convinced than what-do-I-care-what-you-crazy-kids-do.

"Me too," said Jason.

"Me too," Ethan added uncomfortably. "I don't know why you'd want my permission, but it sounds okay to me."

"That's why I'm here of course," said Eli, which, come to think of it, made a lot more sense than that he happened to be in town just for the night.

Which left Jill. We all looked at her. "It's been a week!" she said defensively. I shrugged at her like sometimes you just have to trust that things will work out somehow, and maybe they really do know. Like they can always break off the engagement later when she really gets to know him. Like please say yes because the awkwardness here is killing me. But she just grumbled, "I'll get back to you."

That was good enough for Peter. He pulled Katie up by the hand he still had in his, got down on one knee, looked deeply at her for what felt like several hours, whispered finally (though, I mean, we were all sitting right there) that she was the most beautiful, brilliant, wonderful person he had ever known, and he was certain they would make a perfect life and family together, and would she be his for time and all eternity and, pending Jill's consent, agree to marry him. The rest of us looked hard at the ground, our plates, our shoes, the grass. I willed them to go away and have this conversation elsewhere. I prayed for Atlas to wake up wailing. I fantasized desperately a revisionist scenario in which, after Jill said she'd get back to them, I said we should do the dishes and was therefore inside while they had this discussion. But it didn't happen. "Yes" was all Katie managed. Then they both cried while they made out. I am sure it was a beautiful moment for them. I wanted to die. "Maybe we could clear the table," said Ethan after a while. We all jumped up simultaneously and started making stacks of serving dishes, wine and water glasses, plates—

"Actually, we have an announcement too," Jason began just as I thought we were about to escape. Everyone sat down again. He was holding Lucas's hand and smiling. "We're pregnant."

"Actually, my sous chef's sixteen-year-old daughter is pregnant," Lucas explained. "She doesn't want to end it, but she's not ready to be a mother either."

"They're Mormon too," Jason added helpfully. Katie cringed.

"Anyway, she liked the idea of two dads and of being able to keep in touch."

"And we liked the idea of knowing the mother and her family."

"She's due on Halloween."

They were beaming like proud parents-to-be.

"And the best part is," said Jason, drunk and giggly, "we aren't carrying the baby ourselves, so we can still drink lots of wine."

"Well, no, that's not the best part," said Lucas. "The best part is we're going to be daddies." They gazed into each other's eyes, thinking deep and profound parental thoughts, and for the second time in ten minutes, I positively longed to be doing dishes.

We asked a lot of questions. The usual. What's she like and who's the dad and do you know the sex and what about child-care and have you thought about names. Really, it was too soon for all of that yet, and I knew from experience that it takes nine months, not just to grow a baby, but also to get used to the idea of having one. This one, clearly, would be more complicated than most though I also knew from experience that even when the circumstances are more strange than a-married-man-and-woman-make-a-baby-together, at its heart, it's still a new family, sleepless, turned upside down, sometimes despairing, and often overjoyed. Suddenly, getting engaged to someone you'd known only for a week didn't seem nearly so weird—we all do family a little differently. And raising my best friend's baby, just like that, lost any sense at all for me of being anything apart from perfectly ordinary. I was just his mother. It was no more complicated than that and no more simple, of course, than families ever are.

I have this impression that at that point we were in wee hours of the morning, that it was practically light. We were starting to fade for sure, tired of eating and sitting, tired from the wine and the food, emotionally drained from the evening, and aware that we had, many of us, still to drive tonight, still to get up in the morning. Answers—to marriage proposals, to baby plans—could wait until tomorrow, until next Sunday's dinner. I thought tiredly, deliciously, of rehashing all this with Ethan tomorrow while we ran, with Jill after I got home, over leftovers for dinner tomorrow night just Jill and Katie and Atlas and me.

And then Diane, just barely audible, said, "Me too. I have something to tell you all too."

My first flash was she was dating someone. My second was

that she was pregnant herself. My third was full of hell and night, as I noticed that Diane looked pretty miserable, and remembered how depressed Jill thought she'd been. Cancer? Heart something? Diabetes? Probably cancer. And in just those few moments, while Diane steeled herself to tell us, I saw her shrivel and waste away, all bones and dark, faded eyes, and leave us before Atlas would even remember her. I saw it so clearly that therefore my response to what came next was at first something like relief.

"I've heard from Daniel," she said, a defiant quaver in her voice, like she was laying this fact out for our inspection and constructive feedback but was unwilling to accept complete rejection. I could almost see it, lying there among all the dishes, a big bubble of bad news, glowing and angry and quivering as if there were thousands of tiny creatures inside trying to chew their way out. We found ourselves silent again, listening in on another moment in which we did not belong. This was obviously a conversation Diane should have been having with Jill alone. And it was obvious too that she couldn't. Safety in numbers. Or is it strength? We were there, I guess, to protect Jill from the news and Diane from Jill.

"First, he was calling once a month or so, then every couple weeks, then we met for coffee, then he started coming to the house sometimes. He's not met Atlas—I won't let him come when I'm babysitting or anything—but he'd like to. He just doesn't know how."

Long, long pause during which we all sneaked sideways looks at Jill, who went hot and bright red and kept standing up and sitting back down again. "Since when?" she finally managed.

"Which part?"

"Since he started calling."

"He started calling a couple months before Atlas was born."

"A couple months—before— Are you kidding me?"

"He wanted to know how you were."

"Why didn't he call me?"

"It was complicated, Jill."

"Why didn't he call Janey at least?"

"Because you were living with her," said Diane patiently, maddeningly. "He wanted to make sure you were okay. And the baby."

"He wanted to make sure I was going through with it after all," said Jill darkly, eyes narrowed, "because if I changed my mind he could have his girlfriend back."

"Maybe. But he kept calling after. Wanted to know the sex, the name, how he was, how you were. He felt bad. He didn't have to keep in touch."

"He didn't," said Jill, bitterly. "And now you're dating."

"He asked if he could come by one day when Atlas was over. I said no. So he asked if we could meet and look at pictures. We had coffee."

"But not just once."

"Atlas kept growing. I kept getting new pictures. Dan kept wanting to see them."

My head was spinning. I put a hand on Jill's trembling arm. She seemed to be having trouble catching her breath.

"And now he comes over, and you guys just hang out?"

Diane shrugged. "I work, Jill. It was just easier than meeting him out someplace all the time."

"All the time?"

"He brings dinner sometimes. We sit and talk and look at pictures of Atlas."

"What do you talk about?" Jill was shouting.

"Atlas. What he's doing. You. Him."

"Me? Him?"

"He wonders if there's some way he can be part of your life. If it's too late. Why he couldn't stay at the time. What's different now. What's the same. We talk about why I hadn't told you. And how I might."

"And?"

"And I said I was afraid you'd be angry. You'd not understand. You'd think I'd betrayed you."

"And you haven't?"

"I've been doing this for you. He just needed a little help is all. I was trying to make him better for—worthy of—you and Atlas."

"Oh. My. God." Jill banged her plate loudly on the table, pushed her chair into the garden, threw her napkin to the ground then looked around for other stuff to bang, push, or throw. Finally, as if on belated, eventual cue, Atlas woke up and started screaming upstairs.

I was the first one up but only by a beat or two—everyone was on their feet right behind me. I went up to grab Atlas. Katie started an extensive good night with Peter and Eli. Jason, Lucas, and Ethan sneaked into Atlas's room with puffed out "holy crap" cheeks and rolled eyes to whisper thank-yous and apologies for leaving me alone with all this. But in the dark, I rocked Atlas back to sleep and realized that I never felt alone anyway when he was with me. Through the open window, outside in the garden, Jill had uprighted her chair and sat back in it but was still talking to her mother in harsh tones.

"What's he doing? Where the hell has he been?"

"He got a job. He's living in Renton, alone. He's playing in a band." I could hear Jill's snort from upstairs.

"Why didn't you tell me? And don't say you were afraid I'd be mad. You've never been afraid to talk to me before. And of course I'm mad."

"I was waiting to see. Waiting to see if he was serious, if he'd matured, if he was worthy or could be made worthy . . ."

"How are those your decisions?"

"Because they were offered to me."

"And?"

"And what?"

"And is he worthy?"

"He's getting closer. Honestly, there's probably no one in the world I'd consider good enough for my daughter, my grandson. But I'm working on it."

"So . . . what? He can come back?"

"That really wouldn't be my decision," said Diane.

"But that's what you want."

"Not quite. More like if it turns out that that's what he wants and that's what you want, what I want is for him to be a better guy, a better partner, a better father. Mothers never get that opportunity once the decision's been made. So I took it in prelude."

They sat quietly for a while. Atlas and I did too. For a minute, the only sounds were Atlas breathing and Katie and Peter whispering downstairs.

But then, "What if he wants custody?" Jill shouted. "What if I have to let Atlas spend weekends and holidays and every Wednesday and all of summer break with him? What if I can never move more than fifty miles from Daniel fucking Davison?"

"Maybe we can't have this conversation anymore tonight," Diane said gently.

I heard Jill slam the front door behind her mother and spend twenty then thirty then forty-five minutes violently banging dishes in the sink and leftovers into Tupperwares (though, upon further inspection later, the kitchen didn't look much cleaner than it had when she started). Then I heard her bang into the living room.

"You're still here?"

"Yeah."

"And you're talking about me?"

"Um. Yeah."

"Well, what do you think?"

"I really . . . don't know."

"WHAT DO YOU THINK?"

"I think your mother loves you. She just wants what's best for you and Atlas. She found herself in the middle of a hard, awkward situation and did the best she could. But I also totally get why you feel angry and betrayed. I mean, I would. She should have told you right away."

"Why would you want to be part of this totally fucked up family?"

"I feel like I already am."

"Fine. Then I give you my fucking blessing," said Jill.

"Thank you," said Peter.

Atlas sighed and smiled in his sleep as if all were right in the world, as if his weren't about to turn upside down.

Twenty-five

AND THAT WAS only week one. Week two: the short story. The challenge of the poetry unit is making any meaning at all; short stories are much harder. That's why they come second. They seem much clearer than poems, but that's only insidiously so. Poems are surmountable. They have rhymes and rhythms to help you make meaning. They're short enough (at least the ones you do during Summer One are) to read and reread until you've made some sense of them. Short stories are a different ballgame. You read them and understand the words completely. You know what happens in each sentence. You follow the dialogue and action. At the end, you know exactly what's happened. And also you have no idea. Or sometimes, you get to the end, and you think there must be more to it, but no, it's not that kind of short story. It really is just describing a walk through the woods or the memories associated with a quilt or old age. Short stories scare students because with poems they know there's more than they're getting at first, and they're game for finding it. It's like a scavenger hunt. With short stories, there may be more or there may not. And if there is, you have to find it like a reflection in one of those fun house mirrors—it's there but in pieces and odd angles, and reconstructing it involves as much seeing as looking, as much imagination as observation.

Talking about layers of meanings, digging them out, thinking about how stories can mean one thing and also their opposite, thinking about how details can mean everything or not much at all, it was hard to talk about these things in class all morning and think they applied only to short stories and not to my life. Once you start doing literary analysis, you see it everywhere. You can't turn it off.

I walked home after class wondering about the coincidence of incident and timing, what it meant that Peter had proposed, one week in, the same night as Daniel came back into our lives, one year absent, that the fulfillment of Katie's longest and strongest desire came with Jill's . . . what? Darkest nightmare? Deepest dread? Or was it her ultimate desire too? I realized I had no idea. We had simply stopped talking about Dan. His leaving his would-be baby had seemed so much more monumental than Jill and her boyfriend breaking up that we'd never addressed it, never mourned it, never really even thought about it after. The usual girl commiseration (ice cream followed by margaritas followed by till-dawn-dancing; photo-burning session optional) had never happened. It was too lighthearted I guess. You don't really hate all men. You don't really foresee a time when you'll need them only for sperm. You probably don't even really crave double fudge mocha swirl chocolate chunk brownies (with real chocolate chips), but it's a time-honored female bonding tradition, and it jump-starts the healing by performing, well, friendship. Even if you get dumped, even

when you're sad, it's okay because you have girlfriends. Girlfriends mean your life is not completely over.

In Jill's case, she'd been cheated. We'd all been so torn between understanding and anger when Dan left, between sympathy to his feelings and our own sense, deep down, that it was
not okay, that we'd dropped it entirely. Besides, needing Daniel, even wanting him, felt weak in our we-can-raise-a-baby-
just-the-three-of-us psych-up. And truly we'd needed to believe
that, but we'd missed something too, and I wondered how often Jill thought of him and how. With anger or longing, loath-
ing or love? Probably all of these.

Behind me there was pounding and panting, and I moved
absently to my right to let whoever it was run by. It was Ethan.

"Hey, I've been calling to you for a mile. Where are you?"

"Lost in my head," I apologized.

"Yeah. It's Monday? We were supposed to run?"

"Shit. Ethan, I'm sorry. I totally forgot."

"That's okay. Kind of a mind-blowing weekend. I think I'm
still full from last night anyway."

"Walk with me?"

"Sure. What are you lost in your head over? I mean specifi-
cally. I can guess the topic."

"We started short stories today in class. I'm trying to look at
this situation as if it were anthologized. We could read Daniel's
return the same night Katie gets engaged to mean he's ready to
settle down forever and be a family. Or we could read Peter's
proposal the same night as Dan's reappearance to suggest that
men in general are unstable and the institution of marriage is
rarely right for anyone."

"Those are opposites," Ethan observed.

"Yes."

"You poor lost children of Derrida," he mused sadly. "He has you guys all screwed up."

"Versus the discipline of history which would be really helpful to us here?"

"Not unless Atlas grows up to be an emperor or Peter and Katie are going to empower peasants or start an era of war or peace or industrialization or something. Otherwise, they're just statistics, patterns. History does teach you though that threads and connections are trickier than they seem."

"Meaning?"

"Meaning what seems relevant and meaningful now isn't a very good indicator of anything. Things that look like signs usually aren't. For instance, Jill and Katie could not be more different. What makes you think they're textual foils?"

"They're mirrors," I explained. "Opposite but the same."

"And you? Where do you fit in? No wayward boyfriend, no proposal or engagement, no baby of your own?"

"I'm the unreliable narrator," I said, sounding miserable even to myself.

We were quiet for a block.

"Do you feel sad because everything is in upheaval, and you're worried that one friend is rushing into marriage with a man she barely knows, and the other is about to be mired in a custody fight that's totally unfair because he had a chance to stay and instead was a coward and deserted? Or is it because no one proposed to you, and you don't have a baby?"

I couldn't think what to say. First because I didn't know the answer. Also because it was alarming how well Ethan was starting to see all of us. Also because none of these answers seemed good. He took my silence. At the end of our driveway, he said, "Cheer up. It's not so bad. You're forgetting about

Jason and Lucas. They're going to be parents. What does that signify?"

"Loss of babysitting?" I guessed.

"You're so literal," said Ethan.

"Do you want to come in?"

"Are you kidding? And get more involved in all this drama? I'll see you tomorrow."

Inside, Jill and Atlas were both looking pale. "He threw up," Jill reported, first thing. "I think it's a symbol, a sign." In a house full of English majors, no one is immune.

"Things that look like signs usually aren't," I said. "Babies throw up sometimes." I took Atlas from her and hoped we wouldn't both be puking all afternoon. He was a little clammy. It was unclear if this was because he was indeed ill or because Jill, herself looking pretty unwell, had had him clutched like death against her. Or maybe it was a sign. He was calm though, in which state, judging from Jill's wild eyes (not to mention hair), my spacey brain, and a kitchen still not cleaned up from the night before, he was alone.

I rocked him against me. Atlas was sometimes very calming. Better than yoga, better than meditation. When he was peaceful, you looked into his angel face, felt his perfect weight and perfect warmth, listened to his even baby breath and knew, *knew*, that as long as he was all right, nothing else could be all that wrong. It wasn't just because he was so lovely and all-consuming though he was both. He just put everything in perspective. He made me feel like I was stepping up to take my place in the great wide history of time. Everyone had a baby, and this was mine. Everyone felt this way about her baby, and indeed, this was how I felt about mine. However confused our situation became or seemed from outside of it, holding Atlas in my arms felt timeless. It didn't matter who he was or who I was or where or when we were. We took our place among mothers and sons, and nothing else mattered. This was not true when he was screaming for no discernible reason (or throwing up for that matter), but there were also these perfect moments in between, and already I was trying to hold on to them as if they were in limited supply.

Jill, in contrast, was not having a moment of any kind. She was freaking out. So I kept Atlas and put her on washing dishes. She looked at me wide-eyed when I suggested it like it had never occurred to her that dinner for nine needed to be cleaned up after, but it was the most wonderful idea she'd ever heard. She plunged in with something akin to delight. It took her two and a half hours to dig down to the bottom of the kitchen, but when she finished, it was well and truly clean. She talked through it, almost nonstop, which was clearly what she most needed to do, and Atlas cooled and dried and slept soundly in my arms, neither feverish nor vomity, and it seemed that a kitchen full of dishes was all anyone needed to surmount any problem the world could devise. And devise it did.

"I talked to my mom," she began. "I couldn't not talk to her. I was so mad, but I was a shit for like three years when I was a teenager and she forgave me, so I was just being a bitch sending her away all angry like that. I thought if she got in a car accident on the way home, and we ended like that, I'd just kill myself. So I called her. She said she was trying to teach him how to be a man. You know, like she thought he was essentially, ultimately worthy and better than that, really a great guy for me and for Atlas. She said she always thought so, but he wasn't ready yet. He was too immature. He was confused. She thought confusion shouldn't be a deal breaker, shouldn't be a fatal flaw. Confusion was to be corrected and forgiven as perfectly understandable, not punishable by Atlas doesn't get a father, I don't get the love of my life—these are her words you understand—he spends all eternity feeling guilty for youth and a brief lapse of judgment, for abandoning his family.

"She wanted to fix it. But she couldn't tell me that because she thought I would freak out, and I would have. I did. And she couldn't tell him that because you can never really hear something like that about yourself. So she tried to . . . tutor him I guess. Teach him to care about his son, to think about me while he thought about himself, to think of us as one unit rather than me and my needs versus him and his. That being a father wasn't that scary. He could still play volleyball. He could still be in a band. That everyday life wouldn't be that different, just better, fuller. He would sacrifice some freedom, sure, but what's he really doing with it anyway, and adulthood is different than purported, and what he'd get in return would be so worth it. She didn't lecture him or anything. She just showed him pictures, told him about us, told him lots of stories about when I was little, about being a parent and what she gave up and what she gained and what she maintained—her friends and social life and whatever. She said she gave him some stuff to read. I don't know—allegories or poems or letters I wrote when I was a kid or something? Literature about single mothers? I have no idea. Anyway, that was the upshot. Some sort of reeducation. To make him worthy. How can I be angry with her about that?"

"That's what happens to all the guys in Shakespeare," I said.

"Everyone dies in Shakespeare. They learn and then they die. How does that help me?"

"Only in the tragedies," I said. "In the comedies, they learn and then get married. There are these guys, and they're so flawed. They're untrusting and untrustworthy. They're mean and spiteful. They have these completely unrealistic ideas of love and relationships or totally screwed up priorities where they only care about beauty and money. Or they're so into their guy friends and messing around they can't be adult men. And these women, they're so amazing. They see through all that to the good men these guys can be. The women see the strong, kind, intelligent people these guys will mature into, and they know for a little investment of time and effort, a little patience, these men will be worthy for the rest of their lives. So they train them. They tease and tutor them and whip them into shape. They dress up like other boys to tell them because you're right—no one wants to hear this about themselves and least of all from someone they love. But eventually, these guys grow up and come into their own. They do learn, and it's a testament to how right and wise these women are that they can see what we don't at first. And they're all rewarded with love and marriage."

"But you feel like shit when you leave those plays," Jill objected. "Hero is stuck with this guy who's totally untrusting and mean. Helena marries her awful ex-boyfriend who only loves her again because of magic fairy dust. Viola ends up with this sappy, pouty dude who's probably gay anyway."

"Well, okay, but that's the point. Those guys didn't learn, so they get married at the end, but you don't feel good or happy about it. But think about Beatrice, think about Rosalind. These are marriages you do feel good about, not because the guys or even the heroines were perfect at the beginning but because they've learned. No one's perfect going in—no one's ever perfect—it's the ones who hear their detractions and can put them to mending who you're happy for."

"Yeah, but doesn't that mean my mom and Daniel are going to get married?" Jill giggled.

"It's just a metaphor, Jilly."

"What do you think I have to learn then?" she asked.

"What do you think you have to learn?"

"Isn't someone supposed to help me figure that out?"

"Sometimes. But usually the women have to come into it all on their own."

"Isn't there supposed to be a sidekick? Someone to tell the heroine the answers?"

"No one can tell her the answers. Figuring it out is her job. Fixing it isn't the hard part. It's learning what it is needs fixing in the first place. Beatrice learns that being harsh and afraid does her no good. She decides to love and let herself be loved—and she is. Rosalind realizes that time is short and love is precious. She finally gets that she doesn't have unlimited time to screw around pretending to be a boy and messing about in the woods. She's afraid Orlando won't love her anymore when she's not so young and pretty and the novelty wears off. She has to learn to trust that he'll always love her even when she's old and gray and they've been together for eighty years."

"But I wasn't afraid to let myself be loved. I was ready. He said no."

"Then that's not your thing," I said.

"What is?"

"Can't tell you." I shrugged. I didn't know. And it was her journey besides. The difference between Shakespeare and life is the absence of fairies, long lost twins, and really knowledge-able cross-dressers to solve all your unsolvable problems. On the other hand, the kitchen was clean, the dishes dried and put away, the counters scrubbed, and Atlas sound asleep and not even throwing up.

Twenty-six

I DID NOT know when the phone rang. I knew in the instant between saying hello and hearing the reply. Maybe I recognized the held breath on the other end. Maybe the pause was just longer enough than usual to herald a quick and unthought thought. I picked it up and said hello and felt my heart seize in the half moment before he said, "Hi, Janey," softly, sad, but also holding down something bigger. And I couldn't say a word.

"Are you there? It's me." Faced with silence on the other end of the line, Daniel stopped sounding small and afraid and turned back into Daniel again. He'd identified a problem he could tackle. "Okay, you don't have to say anything. Just listen. I'll keep talking unless I hear you hang up." I wasn't too angry to speak. I simply couldn't think of how to start talking. The everyday pleasantries that fill most conversations, particularly with people you haven't seen in a long time, didn't seem appropriate, but neither did skipping them and plunging right in. "I know you must be mad," he said, "but I also know you'll hear me out. Not that I have a big speech planned. Diane called to tell me she told Jill. I thought I'd better call."

He stopped and no one said anything, and I wondered if that was it. "I haven't been staying away because I don't care about her. I miss her. I still love her." The *her* felt conspicuous. "I just thought I should give you guys—her—some space, lots of space. Like I made my decision, so now I didn't get to half-ass it—call when I felt like it or ask after . . . you know, how things were, when I said I didn't want to. It was like all or nothing, and having chosen 'not all,' I had to take nothing."

"Okay," I finally managed, then added, "How are you?"

He let out a long, loud breath, and I heard him smile, whether from relief or absurdity I am not sure. "I'm okay. I got a job tech writing in Tacoma for a startup. I play sometimes in a band. I'm fine I guess. I miss you guys . . . I miss Jill."

He didn't elaborate, and he didn't ask me how I was, how we were, knowing, I guess, that I couldn't tell him without talking about Atlas, about Jill, about the joys and challenges of taking care of a child who wasn't quite mine and wasn't quite his. So we were out of things to chat about. "Would you like to talk to Jill?" I asked. And quietly again, cowed, he said he would. I put my hand over the mouthpiece and called her name. She walked downstairs holding Atlas, took one look at my face, and knew as well. The blood drained from her face so quickly I expected to see it puddle at her feet. I handed her the phone and got up to leave the room, to leave her the downstairs and the comfortable chair, a small, warm, private hole in which to curl up as tightly as possible and have this conversation. I was halfway up the stairs, and she still clutched the phone without saying anything into it when she called my name, and when I turned around, she handed Atlas out to me without a word.

•   •   •

Upstairs, Atlas and I sat on the floor of his room with the door closed and played with (chewed on) blocks. I did not want to eavesdrop, and I certainly didn't want Atlas to hear a word or even the tone of it, but I did want to tell someone (well, everyone) that Daniel had called. I called Katie. She was at Peter's. We had this conversation:

> Katie: Hello?
> Me: Dan called. They're on the phone now.
> Katie: I'll be right home.

Not even young love and a new engagement would keep her from this. She arrived less than ten minutes later. I thought she was so flushed and out of breath because she'd run home, but no, Peter had dropped her off. She was flushed and out of breath because she had dragged up the driveway and then up the stairs an enormous bag full of something odd shaped and cornerful.

"Where is she?" she wheezed, slumping exhausted to the floor and laying her head in Atlas's lap. He thought this was hysterical.

"She's down there. In the living room. You didn't hear her when you came in?"

Katie shrugged. "She wasn't talking, and she wasn't crying. Or if she was, she was doing it very quietly."

"What is that?" I nodded at her Santa bag.

"Oh, it's Peter's laundry bag. It was the only thing big enough to fit."

"To fit what?"

"All the wedding stuff," she said happily. Out of Peter's laundry bag came half a dozen bridal magazines, binders of sample wedding invitations, stacks of folders from florists, caterers, photographers, DJs, cake decorators, party planners, reception sites, tuxedo renters, and hairdressers. She had books about how to pick the perfect dress, plan the perfect reception, choose the perfect color scheme, make the perfect wedding favors. She had a sheaf of brochures with beaches and hand-holding couples on their covers bound with a pink ribbon and "Ideas for your perfect honeymoon from Suns and Lovers Travel Agency" written on a card in perfect script. When the bag was finally empty, she found her purse among all that mess and produced from it six pieces of cake in Ziploc baggies. "Samples," she announced excitedly, and unsure how long it might take Daniel and Jill to sort out what they had to sort out, I was delighted someone had thought to bring food.

Not ten minutes later, we had everything stacked in neat and organized piles. Atlas was passed out cold on the floor, covered in white and pink frosting, his hair and hands matted with crumbs. Katie and I, also a little frosted and becrumbed, paged through the bridal magazines, turning down the corners of pages with dresses we liked and, much more frequently, holding up the whole tome to show dresses so alarmingly hideous and inappropriate, it never stopped being funny when we said, mock serious, "How about this one?"

After a while, we couldn't look at bridal magazines anymore. We woke Atlas up, gave him a bath, and put him to bed. By then, wedding cake samples aside, we were well and truly starved. We did a mental survey of the fridge and pantry, considered what we could run downstairs and grab unnoticed that wouldn't have to be prepped, heated, or eaten with utensils, and made a dinner plan that included cheese cubes, cherries, pretzels, vegetarian bologna, and some leftover lasagna (not strictly finger food but desperate times and all that). We crept stealthily downstairs and by only the light of the fridge were just finishing our scavenging mission when Jill said, "I'm off the phone. I'm just sitting here. You guys can turn on a light."

I felt bad because frankly I was having a great time. It was fun playing blocks with Atlas and feeding him tiny pieces of cake. It was fun to look at bridal magazines and wedding stuff. It was even fun to sneak into your own kitchen with the task of procuring a dinner, silently and unseen, that needed no more preparation than slices of wedding cake in plastic baggies. Meanwhile, here was Jill, sitting in the dark all alone in some kind of paralyzed depression while I considered what kind of improvements might be made to a stealth dinner menu with the procurement of night-vision goggles and a jar of mustard.

Katie flipped on the kitchen light, and Jill blinked like a night creature, buried her head in her hands.

"Where's Atlas?"

"Sleeping."

"He . . . got into some cake samples."

"What are you guys doing up there?"

"Looking at wedding stuff."

"Thanks for giving me some space."

"Sure."

"Is there any cake left?"

Katie and I exchanged miserable glances. How could we have failed to save her at least a token piece of wedding cake? On the other hand, how were we to know she'd feel like eating? Optimistically, I took this as a good sign, reached under the counter for the big Pyrex, and started making carrot cake.

"So, what'd he say?"

She hadn't moved from the corner of the living room, hadn't removed her hands from her face, but, at this question, toppled over into fetal position on the floor, hugging her knees to her chin, and becoming a big ball of Jill.

"We just . . . talked I guess," she muffled from behind her knees. "He told me about his job, his apartment, his life. He said sorry for talking to my mom behind my back. He was worried about me—not really about Atlas though. He said sorry for not calling sooner. He said he wanted to call right when Atlas—he just calls him 'the baby' like he doesn't have a name—was born, but he didn't feel like he could, and then once he hadn't, it just got harder and harder, and he couldn't call then because it was too late and besides what would he say. He offered to send me money, which is ridiculous. He kept asking really deeply how I am, which is also ridiculous. He asked about Atlas but not like he really wanted to know. Besides, how do you answer that question? 'How's the baby?' What do I say? 'Well, he threw up earlier, but he seems better tonight, or at least he did until my roommates fed him cake.' He's never even met this person, so I don't know what he means by 'how is he?'"

"It's weird," Katie mused, "because that's not what your mom said."

"What?"

"That he wasn't interested in Atlas. She made it sound like he was all desperate for information and to see pictures and was thinking of moving in here or asking you to marry him or something."

"She wishes," said Jill dismissively, and I wondered what Diane did hope for, how someone whose fondest wish was only for Jill's and Atlas's well-being would want this situation to turn out. "He barely acknowledged 'the baby' at all."

"Maybe he didn't feel like he had the right to," I said. "Probably he was scared and nervous. Probably he felt awkward and guilty."

"So you're on his side."

"No." Absolutely completely totally not. No no no no no. "I'm just saying he probably wasn't trying to be a jerk. He probably wasn't a jerk. He just came off like a jerk because this is a difficult situation."

"You *are* on his side. It's a difficult situation because he made it difficult. He's the one who left. He's the one who deserted us. He's the one who hasn't called me but is secretly dating my mother."

"How did you leave things?" Katie changed the subject.

"He said he'd call me again in a few days. I didn't say anything. Then we hung up." A long pause then suddenly, "I'm out of here," pulling on shoes, grabbing keys and cell phone, heading out the front door. She was almost gone when she stuck her head back in and hissed, "Don't touch my baby."

We gave up on dinner. We followed up the wedding cake slices with at least half the batter of the cake I was making for Jill who wasn't here to eat it. Then we baked the other half and iced it with Jill's name and a smiley face, hoping it would make her smile too and not seem to be mocking her. It was weird she wanted to spin it now like he'd deserted her when at the time she'd insisted she was fine with his leaving and didn't want him around if he didn't want to be here. It was weird that she

was so angry that he didn't ask about Atlas when the night before she'd been so afraid he would want custody. And it was
weird that she thought I was on his side when I was so totally
on hers, on Atlas's, on mine. Because of course this was my life
we were talking about too. One way or the other, Jill and Atlas
weren't separable. One way or the other, Katie was leaving. If
Daniel came back or if he didn't, all I was guaranteed was
friendship, the opportunity to pick up the pieces. Daniel might
disappear again. He might get partial custody. He might marry
Jill and move in and be a family. But as far as Atlas went, I
wasn't guaranteed a thing.

I called Nico so he could be an impartial observer guaranteed
to be on my side.

"You are an amazing friend," he told me.

"Thank you."

"You are also an amazing mother," he added.

"Thank you."

"And you are going so above and beyond here. Jill shouldn't
be pissed at you. She should be on her knees before you, sup-
plicant with gratitude."

"She should."

"You are an amazing woman, Janey—the kindest person
I have ever known. Anyone lucky enough to have you in their
life—especially every day, especially right down the hall—
should be profoundly thankful," said Nico, which, of course,
was why I'd called him. Then he added quietly, "I understand
Dan. I know what it's like to realize you've made a mistake and
want to come back and not be able to."

"What do you mean?"

"You don't always get it right the first time. And not all mistakes can be undone. You're too young to see what you have when you have it. And then when you realize it, you get it in your head that it's just too late, and then it is. Dan's lucky. Atlas is his free pass. Since there's a baby, he has an excuse to come back."

"He wants to come back *for* the baby," I said.

"No he doesn't. He's willing to come back despite the baby. It's not the same. He wants to come back for Jill. Trust me."

"How do you know?" I asked. But he wouldn't say.

Later, I was in Atlas's room stuffing all the wedding brochures back into the laundry bag they had miraculously come out of. Usually, I am not scrupulous about my own mess, let alone someone else's, but I had this horrifying vision of someone rushing in to a crying Atlas in the middle of the night and fatally tripping over one of the four million pieces of bridal literature on the floor. Except for Atlas, I was alone in the house, and so I was comforting him aloud, even though he was asleep and couldn't understand. "It'll be okay," I promised him in whispers. "We'll all always love you and always be there for you. We're not going anywhere. We'd never let anything bad happen to you. Your mom's not really crazy. She's just having some stress. Your dad's not really evil. He's just . . . confused. Your mom's not really mad at Grandma or at me. She's confused too. You're a lucky kid. You are much loved. You live with a bunch of crazy people, but you are much loved." He just slept unperturbed, unconcerned. I felt actually, viscerally even, jealous of him. I envied him his rest and his ignorance and his powerlessness.

And the literalness with which he lived his life whereas I was mired again in metaphor. Maybe Ethan had been right—Jill and Katie, Daniel and Peter, weren't textual foils after all. Maybe Jill and I were the mirrors with wayward, prodigal, one-time lovers hinting about changing their minds. Being confusing. Being missed.

"Thanks for the cake," said Jill behind me. She was holding the plate in one hand and stuffing fistfuls of cake into her mouth with the other. "Mmfff gwaaaay," which I thought meant, "It's great," but could have been anything. "Look who I found making out on the porch," she swallowed, pulling an abashed Katie in by a sleeve. She had called Peter an hour ago to go for a walk. Apparently, they hadn't made it quite that far. "He came to pick me up, and we got distracted," she explained.

"That is a really big bag," Jill observed, red eyed but smiling, chastened, making up.

"Planning a wedding is a lot of work," said Katie gravely though neither Jill nor I were buying this. Katie loved planning parties. She thought it might have been her calling. If her two-doctorates-chaired-professor father wouldn't have thrown the biggest fit Salt Lake City had ever seen, she would have been a wedding planner for a living. "In all the excitement this evening, I forgot to tell you guys we picked a date. June twenty-ninth. We decided to do it right after Summer One ends, so no one would have a conflict."

"I don't think the Summer One schedule is the same next year," said Jill. "Did you ask someone in the Registrar's Office?"

"Not next year. This year."

We looked at her like she'd lost her mind.

"That's in a month," said Jill.

"Yeah I know," said Katie happily. "Isn't it great?"

"Why the rush?"

"We're not rushing. We just didn't see any reason to wait. Our bishop has the date open. We're going to do it in the backyard instead of in Utah at the Temple so you guys can all come. You can have a really nice wedding with hardly any notice if you're a good planner. And I am."

"You just want to have sex," Jill said. "You're both horny. That's why you're in such a hurry."

"Why the big party bag then?" I asked. It stood three feet high in the corner where I'd had to drag it (lifting it was out of the question).

"What do you mean? We have to plan the wedding."

"But you won't have time to order invitations or cakes or flowers. Caterers and wedding sites and photographers will all be booked. You have to do this stuff months in advance. When my cousin got married, she ordered her dress a year and a half before the wedding."

"You wait and see," said Katie. "Mormons are very industrious. We are excellent at pulling together beautiful, blow-your-mind, last-minute weddings."

"Yeah," said Jill, "because you're all so horny."

Twenty-seven

THE OTHER THING about short stories is, of course, they're short. Novels, movies, even plays pull you down and hold you under until you stop struggling. You get to know voices, characters, intricate motives, and complicated plots intimately. You live a book for weeks at a time, carrying it around in your bag, thinking about its characters like friends, worrying about their worries as your own. Not so short stories because as soon as you get to know the characters and voices and plots and complications, they're over. Resolved or unresolved, clear or still completely obfuscated, either way, there's nothing more . . . unless you're taking a class in which case you've probably been assigned five or so a night. The result is jarring. As soon as you get into one story, it's suddenly, cruelly over, and, worse still, you have to jump right into another one. It's like serial dating. The short story unit renders all of us sluts.

For the short story unit, my students write one mini-paper a day. These daily essays are short, but they still have a brain-scrambling effect, and by the end of the week, no one—not me, not my students—can keep track of anything. What we're reading, what we're writing, what we're learning, what we're doing next—it all jumbles together until we have class discussions that feature Alice Walker characters in Eudora Welty stories, star heros such as, "You know. That guy with the candy? His name starts with *J*?", and yield comments during workshopping sessions such as, "This is a really smart paper, but the event you reference in paragraph three isn't from this story but that other one we read on Tuesday." It's tempting to cut something, but the department is insistent that three credits is three credits, however jammed together, and we must accomplish in a week what usually takes three.

On the other hand, grading the short story papers tends to have the opposite effect on one's life. There isn't time for much else—no wedding planning, no Daniel-crising, no thinking about Nico, no fighting with roommates, no solo-Atlasing for more than an hour or so at a time. I was still running with Ethan, and I did make time for a midweek lunch with Jason to update him on developments and see sonograms (plus one photo of Jason and Lucas grinning on either side of a belly— "The before picture," Jason said as he handed it to me). But otherwise, grading. And while everyone will tell you (and be right) that the grading is the absolute worst part of the job, it was also a nice distraction from everything else.

By the end of week two, things seemed okay. Wedding plans progressed apace, and more important, Katie and Peter seemed still to like each other. Daniel called once more but only once more. The conversation seemed to be better. More quiet afterwards. No blowups. My students felt they'd come through the hard part, and it was all downhill from here. They were right. After the marathon of poems and short stories, they had in front of them drama, film, novel—easier to make meaning if more difficult to understand. We bid goodbye Friday like old friends, wishing each other not good weekends but long ones. I went running with Ethan. Then he walked me home. The whole time, running through my head as my feet pounded pavement and my breath struggled to keep pace, was one word over and over. O-kay. O-kay. OkayOkayokayokay. It was going to be fine.

And it was. At home, Katie and Jill were at the kitchen table going through the big binders of sample invitations, and Atlas was on the floor chewing on Tupperware. Ethan and I sat down and started looking through invitations too. Then we all switched to wedding dresses. Then it was towards dinnertime, and I didn't feel like cooking, and Jason called and offered to drive up with Lucas and lunch leftovers from the restaurant, and Peter knocked on the door with iced coffees all around plus Sprites for him and Katie, and Daniel did not call, and Atlas went to bed without a fuss, and everything was okay.

Then the phone rang, and it was my mom, and my grand-mother was in the hospital.

"Okay okay okay," I repeated again, over and over, all the way north, though this time it was less a tentative observation of the situation and more a fervent prayer. My mother, reflecting on my sleepless week grading, begged me to wait until morning to come up.

"There is no point in coming now," she said. "She's fine. She's sleeping. She won't even know you're here."

"But you will," I said.

"You haven't even showered since we ran," said Ethan. "You haven't even eaten. You should eat something."

"I am never going to be hungry again," I said.

All the way up—okay okay okay okay. Night drives have that quality to them anyway, lend themselves to bisyllabic mantras as miles tick past, as two axles follow each other over seams in the asphalt, over lane dividers and road reflectors, as evenly spaced streetlights illuminate one stretch of road after another and alternate bright with darkness as if half the time you're only guessing where you are, where you're going. Light dark hump bump okay okay okay. She had not collapsed, so that was good. She had not stopped breathing or suffered heart failure, been rushed in a wailing ambulance, been rescued from a crowded restaurant or resuscitated on the floor of some public place by a stranger. She would have hated any of that. She had been to the doctor Monday. He had called this afternoon and suggested she check into the hospital for some tests. She had calmly driven herself over, checked herself in, called my mother once she was roomed and begowned. This made my mother insane and was classically my grandmother, so that boded well for everything being okay okay okay. But it seemed to me, the more I drove, that when the doctor called with test results and instead of giving them asked you to check yourself into the hospital for more, things were rarely okay.

I got there. I found my parents. I cried. They cried. Then, almost immediately, the doctor came out. It was like that *Far Side* cartoon where the owner is yelling at the dog, telling her what she's done wrong and how frustrated he is and what will happen if she does it again, but all the dog hears is "blah blah Ginger blah blah blah blah." I was that dog. The doctor said a great many things, and he said them kindly and patiently, but the only one I heard was "cancer."

After the doctor, after my parents went downstairs to find some coffee, I went into my grandmother's room where indeed she was asleep. Under covers tucked tightly around hospital gown and bracelet, she looked . . . old. It was this setting finally which insisted I realize how different she was than the picture I carried of her in my mind, a picture no doubt formed in childhood, a twenty-plus-year-old composite much larger, more colorful, more robust than the woman whose sleeping hand I held, whose face was sunken and pale as her sheets, whose brow was wrinkled, whose tiny form barely moved the blankets around it. How long had she looked like this? How had no one noticed? She had always been old—grandmothers are old by definition—but I was certain that word didn't mean this. I stroked her hand and whispered—though without her hearing aids, she had long since stopped being able to hear anything that wasn't shouted at her—"okay okay okay okay okay."

I called home. Jill picked up on the first ring.

"Is everything okay?"

"Nothing is okay."

"What's going on?"

"She has cancer." A rustling as this information was relayed to Katie and whoever else was still there.

"Oh Janey, I'm so sorry. What else did they say?"

"About what?"

"You know, how she is."

"She has cancer," I repeated.

"I know, sweetie. That's terrible. Did they say what happens next?"

"Next?"

"Is it operable? Is it treatable? Will she have surgery or radiation or chemo or what?"

"I don't know." This must have been what else the doctor was saying. The good news, the hopeful part if there were any.

"Let me talk." Katie. Then more rustling with the phone.

"Oh Janey, I'm so sorry. Is she okay?" she said. "We'll do whatever we can. Is there anything you need? Peter and I could run some clothes up to you tomorrow. We could just come sit with you?"

"No, my folks are here. I'll borrow some clothes from my mom. It will be fine. I'll be home soon—I have to teach Monday morning."

"We can cover your class for you," Katie said, "or whatever you need. We'll pray for your grandma," she added, and this seemed, honestly, like the best idea I'd heard in days, maybe weeks.

Five minutes later, my phone rang. It was Ethan.

"Oh Janey, I'm so sorry." Everyone was sorry.

"That was fast."

"I asked them to call me when they heard from you. I didn't want to bug you, but I was worried. Are you okay?"

Was *I* okay? Was *I*? No one had asked this of me yet, not even me, and since the answer was so unambiguously, totally, screamingly NO, I immediately started crying again. Jill would have pestered me with questions. (Are you freaking out? What happened? What are you thinking? What changed?) Katie would have rambled until she turned blue just to distract us both. But Ethan just waited and was quiet with me. When I was done, he said very quietly, "My grandmother lived for years with cancer. Lots of them." And he told me many things about new treatments and really good drugs, how advanced medicine was treating this disease, how she didn't suffer, wasn't in pain. It was comforting that there were things to realistically hope for, things to be done. And it was more so just listening to him tell me about them softly over the phone.

"What will you do now?" he asked.

"Go back to my folks'. Try to sleep. Come back in the morning."

"Maybe you'll call me later? Chat a little more before bed? Might help you sleep."

"It'll be late."

"There's no one here to wake up."

"Except for you."

"Except for me," he admitted, "but that's okay. I don't mind."

Twenty-eight

THE NEXT MORNING when my parents and I got to the hospital ten minutes in advance of visiting hours bearing flowers, cream sodas, salt and vinegar potato chips, cheese sandwiches, and chocolate covered pretzels—my grandmother's favorites—Katie and Atlas were already in the waiting area, Atlas sound asleep against Katie, Katie sound asleep, head back against the wall behind her, mouth wide open. I laughed out loud, waking Atlas, whose face lit up when he saw me, who reached out his little arms to me to be picked up. But in the half beat I took to savor that moment, I lost the opportunity. Too slow. Already, my mom had scooped him up and was kissing his cheeks, his belly, the bottoms of his feet. He was laughing and squealing and reaching for her mouth, wriggly and pink and overjoyed. Katie roused more slowly.

"What are you guys doing here?" I was delighted to see them.

"We thought you might like some company," said Katie. "And we thought your grandma might need some Atlas-love."

"Where's Jill?"

Katie's eyebrows did a little dance. "Out with Dan," she whispered under her breath. "Went late last night right after we talked to you. Stayed out all night. Called at like five A.M. to ask if I could watch Atlas all day too. We were up, so we got in the car and came here."

"How did that happen?" I hiss-whispered back.

Katie shrugged. "Her phone rang around eleven, and she just left."

"Are you all going to bring me that baby or just stand out in the hall chatting amongst yourselves?" my grandmother's voice boomed out from her room.

She was a different woman from the one whose hand I'd held the night before. She sat up against fluffed pillows on a made bed, fully dressed with brushed hair, rouged cheeks, and street shoes on feet crossed casually at the ankles (the sin of shoes on the bed lost to the sin of looking weak in front of one's granddaughter I guess). In the shuffle of depositing flowers and food, fetching water for the former and ice for the drinks, much hugging and settling, I noticed that her eyes shone warmly, that her smile was real and easy, that she seemed herself again. She brushed off the hushed how-are-yous, looked me right in the eye. "Child, I'm fine." Certain, decided, nearly annoyed that anyone would suggest otherwise. "Now give me that baby." My mother relinquished Atlas to her mother's arms.

And there followed, finally, okay okay okay. My grandmother babbled at Atlas who babbled back. My mom and dad asked Katie questions about Peter, about Ethan, about what was up with Jill and Daniel and Diane, about Jason and Lucas's soon-to-be-baby, about wedding plans, about school. My grandmother chimed in too, never taking her eyes off Atlas.

She knew a great seamstress who could do a last-minute wedding dress. She was sure Diane was sorry and had only everyone's best interest at heart. ("It's hard work sometimes to be a grandmother," she said. "You wait. You'll see.") She thought it was just great that two nice young men could have a baby nowadays, and nobody could say boo about it. She was feeding Atlas tiny pieces of cheese sandwich—pushing them into his mouth and then scooping them off his chin for reinsertion, her own tongue miming the intake and rejection.

When the doctor walked in, we all jumped up in a fumble of lunch leftovers, scooping at the corners of our mouths with napkins, hurriedly tucking food boxes and trash out of sight, wiping the traces of laugh from our faces like we'd been caught sneaking food in class or laughing too loudly in the stacks at the library or passing notes during the (I sweartogod so mind-numbingly boring) lecture on "Verse and Vertigo" by a visiting Ivy League professor of Victorian poetry. Not that anything like that has ever happened to me.

"I'm glad to see you're feeling better." The doctor nodded at my grandmother though to me he leaked insincerity and seemed to be saying, "I'm glad you're feeling better because what I am about to say will ruin the rest of your life." Or, "How on earth can any of you be smiling when this is the worst news ever in the worst place ever, and none of you has any reason whatsoever to feel any joy ever again?" Or, "RWAAA, HAAAA, HAAAAA." What he was actually saying was, "We have to wait for the oncologist, who won't be in until Monday, and for the results of some tests which we should have by morning. We would like to keep you here for at least the rest of the weekend so you can get some rest, and we can keep an eye on you."

"If anyone in this hospital thinks I am staying here another night, they are going to be sorely disappointed since there is no way in hell," said my grandmother calmly. "As you can see, I am already packed and ready to go. My family is here to take me home. You can call me when you get the test results. In the meantime, I will rest very nicely at home thank you very much."

The doctor looked taken aback. He was probably not used to anyone, let alone a tiny old lady, talking to him like that. I wanted to take her determination to be home as sure sign that she was healthy, that the kind of cancer she had was the kind you could live with, symptom free, for years and years. But a nagging voice where my spine hit my brain pointed out two things: (1) her determination to be home might as well be a bad sign as a good one, a secret knowledge that there was nothing they could do for her here, that she'd rather spend her time at home, that there was much there she suddenly had to take care of, and (2) that it didn't matter how much pain she was in, my grandmother would grit her teeth and ignore it. She would have her way.

We brought her home. My parents spent the afternoon getting her settled and resettled. Katie and Atlas headed south. I called Nico and told him to meet me on the beach at Stanley Park. Our beach. "Come alone," I said. I waited for him against the log where we first kissed. (Was it actually the same log? It was close enough.) I looked out across English Bay, sunlight pirouetting on the water, over the kayakers and water taxis and tourists towards the mountains out beyond. It was beautiful. Did I feel the majesty of nature, the mystery of God, the tiny insignificance of life and humanity and the brief flash of time during which they overlap for us? I did not. I felt bitter and angry, closed off, small, and miserable.

"Do you want to cry?" said Nico, hugging me, holding me.

"No," I said.

"Do you want to drink?"

"No."

"She'll be okay," said Nico, bless him. "She's a very strong woman. She's got a lot of fight in her."

"Yes," I said.

"You'll be okay too," said Nico. "You're also very strong. You have lots of people who love you."

"Yes," I agreed.

"What can I do?" said Nico.

"Sit with me," I said. "We don't have to say anything. I don't want to say anything."

So we sat and didn't talk, sat and remembered, sat and thought about other things. Living with women and babies, you forget how nice it is sometimes just to sit and be, quietly. Finally, Nico said softly, squeezing my hand, "We need comfort food. Let's go get Indian."

"Okay," I said. It was too hot for Indian food, but misery made me very agreeable.

At my parents' house in the middle of the night, into dead silence, dead sleep, the phone rang (tore, screamed, threw things). Before I was even awake, my brain was screaming, "NOT YET." I held my breath and from my childhood bed listened to my mother's half of the conversation. It included sentiments such as, "Thank you so much," and, "I'll be right there," so I knew everything was at least sort of okay. My grandmother had gotten up to go to the bathroom, fallen, and then, unable to get back up, banged on the floor until the folks downstairs finally dragged themselves out of bed to find out what the hell was wrong with this woman and either help her or kill her depending on what they found. They called 911, and only eleven hours after she'd left it, my grandmother found herself back in the hospital.

We had her back home by eight A.M. Bruised hip, hand, wrist, shoulder, but otherwise okay. Warnings from more doctors. The medicines she was on now were making her weak and dizzy. No walking without a walker. No staying on her own. If she wouldn't stay in the hospital (she would not), she had to consent to round-the-clock nursing. If she wouldn't consent to round-the-clock nursing (she would not), she had to consent to one of us staying with her at all times.

It was in this way that I missed my favorite week of Summer One, my favorite unit of Intro to Lit. Drama is my mode of choice, not just because my life was full of it but because everybody's is. The drama unit is not just about plays but also play and playing, make-believe and making meaning, not just with words but more real, more solid than that—with sets and costumes, gesture and inflection. The drama unit is where we take back control. We become directors. We embrace the drama in our lives. We embrace the chance to tell our own stories, write our own endings, shape our own morals. Our trials, the hard parts, become opportunities to surmount them. The drama unit is always my favorite part of the term. Nevertheless . . .

"Go back to school," said my grandmother.

"Not on your life," I snorted.

"I'm fine, honey."

"Me too."

"You have school."

"There are literally hundreds of people who can cover for me this week."

"Do you mean figuratively?" she said.

"Whatever," I said.

My mother and I split up the week. At first, we planned each to take a shift in rotation, but it didn't turn out to be necessary during the day. My grandmother was a popular woman. It seemed like everyone in the building was her friend. During the day, there was a steady stream of visitors. Two sisters, easily ten years older than my grandmother, lived across the hall and brought over another friend and sat and played bridge with my grandmother for hours. A young couple who lived two floors down showed up one morning with breakfast for maybe fifty people—bagels, spreads, coffee, eggs—and stayed and chatted until afternoon when everyone was hungry again and then ordered pizza. "When we moved in, we didn't know anyone at all," the woman explained to me with her hand cupped over the receiver while on hold with the pizza place. "We expected to make friends with lots of people our age, but they just nodded in the elevator and went their own way. Your grandmother brought down a lasagna and salad one night, labeled a huge map for us with her favorite parks and restaurants and movie theaters, and offered to water our plants when we were out of town. She's an amazing woman." I nodded mutely. Did they not work or have a holiday or what? "Oh no." The woman waved me off. "When we heard she was sick, we took the day off."

The building's night security guard came up one morning after work with DVDs tucked under one arm and a bottle of wine under the other. A knock on the door early another morning revealed a haggard-looking woman in scrubs, obviously just off a very long shift, but with a puppy in tow. "I just thought it might cheer her up," she explained as the dog wriggled all over my grandmother. "She always cheers everyone else up. She's the friendliest face in this building." It was like this all day and all evening. Neighbors dropped by with food, flowers, gifts, and stories. She smiled for all of them, welcomed everyone into her home, did her best, ever the hostess, to make sure everyone had something to eat and drink. I mostly sat and watched everyone, sat and savored, but sometimes I left for lunch or went to the library or the coffee shop and worked for a few hours. Mostly I stayed though and alternated nights with my mom.

Those nights—and there were only three of them—were entirely sleepless though the nights I spent home with my dad I couldn't sleep either, so it hardly mattered. But painful though those nights were in yet another week without sleep, they were also, somehow, restful, peaceful, calm quiet full of breath. I kept vigil in the other room, out of her way but so that at her first move, I would be up and making sure. My grandmother, however she had consented to having me there nights, would never, never wake me up to say she had to go to the bathroom. She just wasn't that person. So I stayed up just in case. In truth, two of the nights she slept straight through. One, she wandered off into the bathroom and back again without incident. Still, I couldn't leave it to chance, and besides fears that she would fall, I kept finding myself in the bedroom, in moonlight, holding my breath to make sure I could still hear hers.

It wasn't the middles of the nights that were remarkable anyway. It was earlier than that, the time right before sleep.

The first night, she got ready for bed then called for me, and when I came into the room, she patted the bed beside her and said quietly, "Stay with me until I fall asleep?"

"Really?" I said, amazed at this show of something like vulnerability from my grandmother.

"No, not really," she scoffed. "That's what you used to say when I put you to bed when you were a little girl. 'Stay with me until I fall asleep.' You were very cute."

"Did it take long?" I asked, curling up beside her in bed anyway.

"It didn't usually even take until we had the lights off." Indeed, I have always been a quick sleeper.

"Listen," she said. "When the time comes—I'm not saying it's now but when it comes—you have to let me go."

"What are you talking about?"

"No heroic measures. No feeding tubes or breathing machines."

"Fine," I said. "Let's change the subject."

"No praying by my bedside either. No ridiculous promises to God that will give you stress and guilt for the rest of your life. No weeping and hand wringing and not eating. I don't want any of that."

"Okay," I said, as noncommittally as possible.

"I mean it." She sat up in bed and sounded like she did. "And don't let your mother do that crap either. Keep her in check. She gets two weeks of feeling sorry for herself after I die and that's it. You make sure."

"How am I supposed to do that?"

"Find a way," said my grandmother. "Once I'm gone, you'll have to be the toughy in this bunch. Your mother is too emotional. I'm counting on you. I don't want her miserable for years. I don't want her wallowing."

"I'll see what I can do," I promised.

"See that you do," said my grandmother, rolling over to go to sleep. "And don't think I'm kidding either."

I didn't. Not at all.

The second night I stayed, just after I kissed her good night and turned the light off, my grandmother called out to me to turn it back on.

"Look in the top drawer of my bureau," she said. "I have something for Atlas."

I caught on right away. "Save it," I said. "You can give it to him when you get better."

"I want to give it to him now."

"What is it?" I asked.

"Look and see," she said. I did. It was a black, velvet box (the box alone would send him into shrieking fits of joy) which opened to reveal pearl cufflinks inlaid with onyx and gold. They were beautiful.

"They were your grandfather's," she said. "I want Atlas to have them."

"That's very sweet," I said. "When he's older, you'll give them to him. He'll be delighted."

"Jane Eleanor Duncan, why are you hell-bent on making me spell this out?"

"It's not like you're dying," I said. "Maybe you'll be fine. Maybe you'll live with cancer for twenty years. Ethan's grandmother did. Ethan says there are amazing drugs now. Why would we tell ourselves you're dying when you might be fine?"

"Because I might be dying," she said, "and if I am, there won't be any later when I get a chance to give Atlas these cufflinks. He's my only great-grandchild—I'm sure that won't always be true, but he's probably the only one I'm going to meet—and I want him to have his great-grandfather's cufflinks, and I can't give them to him from a coma, and I can't give them to him from the grave, so I am giving them to you now to give to him later."

"Can we change the subject?"

"You can," she said. "But I can't. When you're dying, it's hard to think about anything else. When you're dying, you have a lot of other things to take care of first. It's very stressful."

"You think this is funny?"

"A little bit. Don't you?"

"I don't. Not at all."

"Oh honey, it's fine. This isn't a tragedy. If I were thirty, this would be a tragedy. If I were two days from retirement or my pregnant wife were about to give birth to our first child, if I hadn't lived long enough to know you . . . that would have been tragic. But baby, I'm eighty-seven. I've seen my child grown. I've seen her child grown. I lived long enough to meet Atlas even. I haven't been in pain. I haven't been sick. It's not looking like I'll spend a decade and a half in a vegetative state not knowing my name. This isn't a tragedy, baby; this is just sad. Sometimes things are sad, but that's nothing we can't handle. Sometimes, it's even nice to be sad. It means things have been happy. And that they will be again."

"I'm not ready to resign myself to this yet," I said tearfully.

"I know you're not, honey," said my grandmother, "but that's too goddamn bad, isn't it?"

It didn't seem entirely appropriate that she (old and sick) should be comforting me (young and well). It seemed like she was the one with the awful thing to come to terms with, like she was the one who needed me to be strong now. But even old and sick, maybe especially old and sick, she remained the adult and I the child. She was the grandmother, and I was curled up next to her, letting her rub my back. She remained the strong, stoic, in-control woman I had always let myself be a little girl with. And I guess, I hope, it was comforting to both of us.

The last night I stayed over, the night before I went back home, began like this: "Don't tell yourself this is the last night ever or anything. I'm not going to die tomorrow just because you're going back to school. Let's not get mushy." So we sat and watched the ballgame and drank Cokes and pretended that the reason my grandmother, who always wanted me to cook for her, did not want me to cook for her was because she had had a big lunch (when, in fact, I don't think she'd eaten solid food in days). And in the middle of the fifth inning, my grandmother looked thoughtful for a moment and, not taking her eyes off the TV, asked, seemingly out of the blue, "Is Ethan a baseball fan?"

"Yeah," I said, surprised.

She narrowed her eyes. "Yankees?"

"Mets."

"Good." Most people get their love of sports from their fathers. Neither my father nor I particularly like sports at all. But baseball isn't so much sport as narrative, storytelling, and I get my love of it not from my father but from my grandmother. She and my grandfather were living in Baltimore before they moved to Vancouver when my mom was born, and they were losing too much money at the track betting on horse racing. At some point, they made a conscious decision to become baseball fans instead—first Orioles fans, then Expos fans when they moved to Canada. Into the Expos tradition, I was born. Their poor attendance, their poor play never bothered us. My grandmother and I used to spend one week alone together in Montreal every summer, practicing my French and sitting in the stands at Olympic Stadium with five thousand other fans. My grandmother loved the Expos and the Orioles and the Mariners who she got on the Seattle channel on TV, but most of all, she hated the Yankees. Turns out these things are hereditary.

She seemed pleased to hear that Ethan wasn't a Yankee fan, but she dropped it. Then during the seventh-inning stretch, she said, "I have something for Ethan too, but he's not ready for it yet. When he is, you give it to him. But not yet."

Hard to know where to start. "What is it?" I settled for.

She nodded toward her bureau. "In my top drawer. Grandpa's watch."

"You gave that to Dad years ago."

"That was his good watch. This is something else."

I went over and retrieved it. We opened the box together. Its face was a silver baseball. Its hands were silver bats. The straps were made of leather and had the curved red lace stitching of a baseball. It was the coolest thing I'd maybe ever seen. On the back was engraved, "With love from your number one fan." I wanted it.

"It's not for you remember," said my grandmother, reading my mind apparently.

"How have I never seen this before?"

"It wasn't for me either. It's too big for us," she said, laying her arm next to mine, comparing our long fingers and nails, our tiny wrists. "I open that box though to look at it almost every day. It brings him back. I see his arm in that watch, his hand, his fingers. That was his everyday watch, not his good one. I see him coming home from work in that watch, eating dinner, playing with your mom. I see him touching me in that watch."

"Why do you want Ethan to have it?"

"Same reason."

"Because you see him touching you in it?"

"Because I might not be around later when it's time."

"Time for what?"

"I think you know," she said.

"Why don't you give it to him yourself? He's much older than Atlas. He won't put it in his mouth or anything."

"I can't do that."

"Why not?"

"Same reason."

"What's that?"

"I think you know."

That night while my grandmother slept, I thought about what she thought I knew. She thought Ethan was in love with me, and we would get married and spend the rest of our lives together and be happy forever, that she would be at the wedding only in spirit and so had to offer this family heirloom now, that he and I would have children together, her great-grandchildren, who would be pseudosiblings to Atlas, the one great-grandchild she would ever meet. At least that's what she wanted to think. She hadn't even met Ethan but had only heard about him. I did not think that. I did not think Ethan wanted to marry me.

I did not feel sure that I would always have Atlas in my life. I worried that I would never have any children of my own. And at the same time, I thought if I did someday get married, of course my grandmother would be there because what was the point of a wedding without her. I thought if I did someday have children, my grandmother would meet them because almost definitely absolutely certainly she wasn't dying and would be fine. It was a strange collusion of cloudy, wallowing pessimism and blind, ignorant hope: no one loves me or ever will, but as long as I don't acknowledge that she's sick, my grandmother will live forever and ever. Everything will be okay okay okay.

Sometime after midnight, my phone rang, jarring me out of—I couldn't believe it—sleep. It was Ethan.

"Oh Janey, I'm so sorry for waking you. You said you'd be up all night. I just wanted to check in."

"I wasn't sleeping," I slurred.

"You're still sleeping," he laughed. "How are things there?"

"Good. Nice." Mmmmm, sleep.

"How's your grandmother?"

"Very good. Getting stronger. Gonna be fine."

He seemed to think this odd and changed the subject. "Listen, I took your class today. Katie had an appointment at the dress shop."

"But you teach when I teach."

"We did a double class. We talked about literacy in Renaissance England versus the Industrial Revolution in the same place two hundred years later. Very literary and very historical. It was fun actually. Nice and interdisciplinary. We sat out under a tree and talked for a while. Then I paired everyone off with someone from the other class, and they shared ideas about the impact of the printing press on history versus literature and how that correlates with other, later technologies. It was really interesting. Maybe we should do it again when you're back next week."

"My grandmother thinks we're getting married," I said sleepily.

"Who?"

"You and me."

There was a pause during which he said nothing and I think I napped.

"Okay," he whispered finally.

"Okay," I mumbled and hung up and went back to sleep.

Twenty-nine

IT WAS A long, exhausted, miserable ride home. It was rainy, and there was traffic, and I had so much work to do, and Katie (and Ethan) had covered my classes but had not, I was sure, done the grading, but I couldn't concentrate on lesson plans or anything else. Instead, I was worried about my grandmother. I was worried about me without my grandmother, about how me-without-my-grandmother was even possible. I was worried about falling asleep while I was driving and how much this would piss off my parents who had begged me to wait and go home in the morning. I was worried about how I wasn't helping Katie enough with her wedding—what kind of a best friend was I? I was worried that Atlas would have forgotten me in the week since I'd seen him. I was worried that Daniel would come and take him away or take him and Jill away, and which would be worse? I was worried about deciding. I was worried about when I would grade and what the hell I might teach next week and when I would figure it out. I was worried about what I was going to find to wear to Katie's wedding. Did I need a formal dress? Would a sundress do? What about a skirt and a fancy top? How would I decide things like this without a consult from my grandmother who knew all about etiquette and other crap like etiquette? I was worried about how Jason and Lucas were having a baby and Jill had a baby and Katie would probably have like fifteen babies any minute now and even Daniel Davison had a baby, but I might never ever have a baby. I was very, very worried about how, in the middle of the night, from the depths of my first sleep in two weeks, I'd told Ethan that my grandmother thought we were going to get married. You should never talk to people in the middle of the night. And there should always be at least a fifteen-minute window between waking up and getting on the telephone.

I pulled into the driveway and my phone rang, and my heart stopped at my parents' number on the caller ID, but my mom, not counting on traffic and thinking she should have heard from me that I'd gotten home safe more than an hour ago, was panicked only over my whereabouts. My grandmother was fine. I was fine. Everything (nothing) was fine.

"Go to bed," she said.

"I'm still in the driveway," I said.

"Go inside and go to bed," she said.

"I have so much work to do."

"Do it tomorrow," she said. "They'll wait an extra day to get their papers back. It will be fine."

"I can't sleep anyway," I said.

"Lie in your bed and see what happens," she advised.

Inside, it was the end of Sunday-night dinner. I had forgotten. It is amazing how the world—even your immediate world— goes on while your own seems stopped. It is amazing too how people manage to eat even when you don't cook for them. (In fairness, they seemed to have ordered sushi.) Even Atlas was still awake. Everyone jumped up when I came in. Everyone crowded around and asked how I was and how my mother was and how my grandmother was. Atlas reached out from Peter's arms to me. Uncle Claude humped my leg. Three people tried to give me food. I was really glad to see them. I was. It felt as much like coming home as going to my parents' house, and I'd lived there for eighteen years. But I couldn't do it. I was just too tired. I made apologies and explanations, ate one piece of spicy tuna, and went to bed. Ten minutes later, Ethan knocked on the door.

"Hi," he said.

"Hi."

"I just wanted to say hi before you fell asleep this time."

"Hi," I said.

He sat on the bed next to me and brushed my hair lightly with his hand for a while.

"Are you okay?" he asked.

"I'm fine. Just tired."

"Okay," he said. "Good night. I'll see you in the morning."

I closed my eyes. There was a knock on the door. It was Jill.

"Are you okay?" she said.

"I'm fine. Just tired." My mantra.

"Poor Janey." She sat down on the bed. "Can I help you?"

"Not really. I just need to sleep."

"So what's going on with you and Ethan?"

"What? Nothing. Why?"

"Among other things, because he came up here right after you went to bed."

"He probably came up to use the bathroom," I said.

"Yeah right," she said.

"How's everything here?" I asked.

"Fine. Quiet. No news."

"Daniel?"

"I'll tell you tomorrow."

"Good." I smiled and hugged her waist. She kissed me on the head and whispered good night. I went to sleep. There was a knock on the door. It was Jason.

"I have a meeting early tomorrow. I decided to stay over," he said, climbing into bed with me.

"There's a sofa downstairs."

"Katie and Peter are making out on it," he said. "What time did you set the alarm for?"

"Eight."

"That works for me. See you in the morning."

I was too tired to fight with him. "Good night, Jason."

"Good night. Hey Janey? Are you really okay?"

I started crying. I don't know why then. I don't know why then and not when I'd said goodbye to my grandmother that morning and not on the long ride home and not in the driveway when I heard my mother's voice and not when I walked into my house and this family and not when Atlas reached his little arms out to me and not when Ethan came up to say . . . whatever he'd come up to say and not when I'd hugged Jill good night. Jason made soothing noises, held my head on his shoulder, fed me Kleenex. Jason said it would be better tomorrow, and I just needed sleep, and it would be okay okay okay. Jason said my grandmother was one of the most amazing people he had ever met. He said he wished his grandmother—to whom he hadn't spoken since she'd banished him to hell when he came out to her—could be like mine. He said she was one of the strongest people he had ever known, and he'd never seen her not get what she wanted. He said if she were here, she'd tell me to get some sleep. I snotted and sniffed and said thanks. I wiped my nose and eyes and tried to sleep again. Jason said, "Janey, what's going on with you and Ethan?"

Thirty

WHEN I PULLED into the driveway last night and my phone rang, did you think my grandmother had died? Did you think just at the exact moment I completed a dark and rainy drive full of dark and rainy ruminations, arriving at last at my well-lit, love-filled home, my mother had called to report the horrific and inevitable (never mind I obviously wouldn't have left if my grandmother hadn't been much better and that timing would have been quite a coincidence)? If so, as I explained to my students Monday morning, it's from watching movies.

The film unit always comes second to last. If you do it too early in the semester, students think the class is a joke. And besides, they can't analyze movies at the beginning. They can analyze poems on the first day because poems are obscure. You read them and don't know what they mean. So you have to figure it out. Movies seem easy to understand. Everyone knows what they mean. They don't mean anything. They just are. This is what students think when they come in. You have to wait most of the semester for them to see that in the same way that poems are meaningless until figured out, so are texts that seem straightforward, texts that seem to mean very obviously and nothing deeply right from the start. Also, if you don't take a break at some point, they're too tired for the homestretch. You get crappy final exams. Hence: film unit, second to last.

All of which is to say that already it was second to last. Granted, it was only three completed weeks into term. On the other hand, we only had two to go. We were almost done. Students get pretty close in summer session because classes are small, and they spend a lot of time together. By the time we got to film, a couple of students made popcorn for the entire class. Two students, having met three weeks ago, were now madly in love, holding hands in the back, considering, I worried, making out during the movie. Several others had already cliqued up, laughing at each other all through class, whispering, passing notes. It was all a bit like teaching ninth-graders but, I have to admit, pretty fun.

We watched *Memento*, which is a mystery told backwards so that the final resolution scene is the first thing you see in the movie. The point of the plotting, then, turns out not to be *what* happens but *why*; that's the mystery; that's what's important and what we want desperately to know. My students argued that this is because of the way this film is told—chronologically backwards—so that knowing what happened is pointless without the setup. Their moral: knowing what happens is meaningless— literally without meaning—until you understand why. My argument was that all literature is this way because all life is this way—the mystery isn't what but why. My students disagreed. They said in life you understand the why all along because you live it every day, and you're in your head; you're just desperate to know how it will turn out.

"Some examples?" I said.

"Will your current relationship end badly or in marriage?" volunteered the female half of the couple in back (the male half blushed so hard I could see it from the front of the room).

"Will a certain drunken and unprotected hookup result in someone we know getting dumped?" offered one of the cliquees, and I was relieved that the whole group of them broke into hysterics, which suggested it had happened to someone they knew but not to any of them.

"Right, but in that case, isn't the why the most important part?" I asked.

"Not of the mystery. We know why. He's a whore. She's a whore. They both drink way too much. She's been in this long-distance relationship since, like, high school. That's not a mystery. What happens is the mystery."

They had a point. It was this: they were nineteen years old. When you are nineteen, life is full of the what-will-happen-next kind of mystery, and the why seems perfectly clear and beside the point. Not that I'm middle-aged or anything, but it seems to me that the difference of just a few years is enough for a massive shift from what to why. It wasn't because I knew what was going to happen next in my life, and it wasn't because my life at the moment wasn't full of its share of intrigue, loose ends, unanswered questions, and seemingly insoluble problems. Somehow, though, none of that seemed the important point to me. It was the reasons we did what we did, held and chose and loved what we did, the motivations behind the actions—which, anyway, seemed just to happen, whether we would or no, and so were utterly beside the point. Why evaluate what you do not control instead of what you do? Any of which would have been very instructive given what happened next if I could have remembered this wisdom, or any other, at the time. When push comes to shove, maybe we're all nineteen.

And maybe it's why we watch movies too, to recapture the simplicity of a time in our life when all the whys are clear and make sense and the only mystery is what's next. We go to the movies when we're too tired to go out for dinner and conversation. We rent DVDs when we need a break because our brains hurt from reading/writing/teaching/thinking/working all day. Movies are about action, but they take the place of it in our lives. And whereas we expect most texts to follow logically from one point to the next, whereas we want our written endings foreshadowed in their beginnings and symbolized in their landscapes, at the movies we want distraction and surprise.

At home, I found the former if not really the latter. Katie and Jill were fighting. I could hear them from fifty feet away.

"You can't ask Janey—she needs rest."

"I'm not asking Janey. I'm asking you."

"I can't. I have a dress fitting this afternoon."

"How many times do you need to have your fucking dress resized?"

"It's not being resized. They're just making sure. It's my wedding dress. It's kind of important that it fits."

"It's not important, Katie. It's a dress. This is my life we're talking about. The love of my life maybe. The father of my child."

"Dan changes his mind on a weekly basis. I am getting married once for all of eternity."

"Dan only changed his mind once. And maybe not even that. But I can't know if we don't go out."

"Bring Atlas with you."

"He's not ready yet."

"Atlas or you?"

"Daniel."

"Well he needs to get ready, don't you think? He's a bit late."

"I'm trying but not all at once. Atlas has been really cranky the last couple days. I don't want to freak him out."

"Why are you posturing all of a sudden?"

"I'm not posturing."

"You're pretending it's okay if he doesn't want to see Atlas. It's like you're dating him and pretending you don't have a son. If he wants back in, why doesn't he want to see his baby?"

"Isn't this what you want, Katie? Nice nuclear family all back together again? That's not going to happen overnight. I have to work at it."

"It doesn't look much like work. It looks like going to parties and shows and getting drunk and having sex."

"You don't know what we do," spat Jill. "And I don't care whether you agree with it or not."

"As long as I scrap my plans to take care of your kid."

"Oh, so he's my kid all of a sudden."

"Not all of a sudden," said Katie.

"I'll take him," I said, coming in, realizing that waiting out in the driveway for them to stop yelling at each other was going to take too long.

Katie shot Jill a nasty look.

"It's fine. I'm fine," I said. "I'd be glad to take him. I missed him."

"Are you sure you don't mind?" Jill cooed, and Katie rolled her eyes, and Jill was out the door almost immediately.

I looked at Katie. "I was only gone a week."

She shook her head. "The first night they went out was the night you left—I told you about that. He called late and she left and called in the middle of the night and asked if I could hang on to Atlas the next day, but when I went to bed that night, she still wasn't back yet. And it's been pretty much like that all week. She checks in; she comes back briefly, but then she leaves again. She never takes Atlas with her. She hasn't really even seen him all week. She barely asks if it's okay with me, and then she stays out well beyond the hours I agree to anyway. She just expects me to pick up all your hours too. I had to call Jason twice this week to come up when I had to go teach your class. And I'm getting married in less than two weeks."

"What's going on with them?"

"I don't know. She won't talk about it. I ask and she blows me off. Sunday-night dinner was the first time I'd seen her for more than five minutes all week. And she'd only come home a little bit before you did. And she left after you went to bed."

As always, I spent less time considering my actual reaction than what I thought it should be. Or maybe I was just too tired to feel anything as exhausting as righteous indignation. It was unfair to expect Katie to do everything, unfair to discount the import of her wedding just because Jill thought it was too fast, unfair to foist Atlas on me when I had so much work to do, unfair to sideline Atlas's needs for Daniel's, and unfair to be so rude and selfish about the whole thing. On the other hand, this was momentous too. If Daniel wanted to see about being in our lives again, I guess she had to find out. She had to hear his story and tell him hers. They had a lot of catching up to do. So we'd just have to try and not kill her.

•   •   •

Jill didn't come home that night, and she didn't call. Katie and Atlas and I all went to bed early and without eating anything, all totally wiped out and cranky and feeling borderline coming down with something. In the morning, we had a text message from Jill that she would be home by noon, but I had to go teach, and Katie and Peter were driving to Portland to meet with caterers. Jill wasn't answering her phone. We called Jason, profusely apologetic, and he canceled a meeting with his advisor to come over and stay with Atlas for a few hours until Jill came home. I taught more about movies then spent the afternoon in the library catching up on grading and prep.

It is sometimes true that trauma at home, stress in one's personal life, sick relatives, annoying roommates, weddings to plan, and sunshine to sit out in prevent academic productivity of all kinds. And it is sometimes the only thing for it. Buried in the stacks, typing by backlight, I read about film theory, took notes, wrote outlines, and generally forgot about anything else. There is something too to this feeling of control. Some people clean the house (I wish); some plan parties or fund-raisers or church events; some people stop eating. It's the same motivation. I may not be able to control anything else, but if I want to know more about something, I can find out. It's very empowering. It is also like after exercise. I walked home feeling absolved and slightly high. I had learned something new, made productive use of my afternoon, prepped the rest of my film unit, caught up a bit. It's a different kind of endorphin rush, but it's there all the same.

On my way up the driveway, my phone rang. And that's when my life became truly filmic.

Thirty-one

IT WAS JASON, sobbing. Choking sobbing so he couldn't talk. I answered the phone to silence. If it hadn't displayed his name, I wouldn't have known who I was listening to on the other end. My heart sank and then my knees did, and kneeling in the grass outside my house what I thought was this: isn't it sweet for Jason to be so sad that my grandmother died? And already, *already* living without her, I started to comfort him. It's okay, it's okay, or something like that; she liked you so much; she lived a good life; thank you for loving her. Mindless, pointless, and not really listening because he had said no no no no many times before I finally heard him. And then, suddenly, in a rush of, I'm ashamed to say, relief, I realized it wasn't my grandmother he was weeping for at all. These weren't friend-sobs; they were parent-sobs. "Your baby?" I gasped, sorry immediately not to have put it more gently. "No," he finally managed. "Yours."

•   •   •

I don't remember driving to the hospital, but I must have. And when I got there, I couldn't remember ever having left. It felt exactly like that night sitting with my grandmother all tucked in, holding her hand. It felt like waiting in the ER after she fell. It felt like waiting with Jill in labor, waiting to take Atlas home, waiting for Daniel to return. But it felt like nothing so much as my own cancer, my own heart attack, my own heartbreaking labor, my own heartbreaking homecoming. I felt like I had always been in that hospital. I felt like a lifetime happened in those searing moments of searching the emergency room for faces I knew. And fleetingly, only fleetingly, came into my mind the cold comfort that this was the best place in the world to feel so entirely like I couldn't draw breath.

I found Jason, wet faced and wild eyed and shaking so violently I could see his shimmer from across the room, wedged into a corner as if for the protection afforded by the walls.

"He was still asleep when I got there at ten, and I was working all morning. I checked on him around noon, but I just thought he was sleeping, and then Lucas called, and then I got caught up in Kant, and I just didn't think to check on him again—"

"Why were you still there all afternoon?" Like that was the significant detail here. "Where was Jill?"

"She called and asked if I could stay longer. She said she and Dan had to talk some more."

"She's still with Dan?"

"I can't get her. I think her phone's off. I finally checked on him at like two, and there was vomit all over the crib. He looked all sweaty but he was still sleeping, so I rattled him just a little bit, and when I touched him, he was burning up and totally drenched. And then he started shaking all over. I think he had a seizure."

More crying. And seeing it in person, I realized what I couldn't on the phone. It wasn't friend-weeping or parent-weeping—it was blind-fear-weeping, total, all-encompassing, every toe, every hair, every day and tomorrow fear and horror. I could feel it coming on like a storm, and I struggled to keep it together long enough to get all the information I could out of Jason before it took me over too.

"I called 911. I didn't know what to do. I couldn't even put him in the car because I don't have a car seat. Was I just supposed to lay him on the floor in the back like groceries and hope he didn't roll around too much?"

We exchanged horrified half laughs, reminiscent of levity though it actually bore no resemblance at all.

"Where is he now?"

"I don't know." Jason shrugged, helpless. "Back there. They rushed him out of the ambulance and now he's back there. They said to wait here. Since I'm not the father I think."

A savior in scrubs came out from behind huge swinging doors. I caught a glimpse of the chaos back there—beds, stretchers, people with IVs, people running with clipboards, bandages, monitors—but no Atlas. In the—what?—maybe six strides between the woman in scrubs and us, I heard these words: I'm so sorry. There was nothing we could do. And these: False alarm. Ha ha ha. Common mistake. He's totally fine. And these, an echo: Cancer. It's cancer. It's always cancer. But instead, she asked a question: "Are you the mother?" And without a thought, without a beat to consider ramifications, without, even deep in the bone, any sense it wasn't entirely true, my answer: "Yes."

•   •   •

Back in the chaos, Atlas looked eggshell white and eggshell fragile with an IV in his tiny arm, a tube under his tiny nose, monitors on his heaving tiny chest. Again, I only caught the horrifying highlights of the explanation: flu maybe, probably had it for days with symptoms that had been ignored, dangerously high fever, dehydrated, decreased consciousness, waiting for test results.

How long had he been running a fever? When was the last time he ate? How much? Solid food or breast milk or formula? When was his last bowel movement? When was his last wet diaper? Any vomiting or diarrhea? Had he been fussy or quiet? Real tears or just wailing? How long had he been asleep? These were what the doctor needed to know.

Except I didn't know. I had been in Vancouver. I had been tending to my own family when this one fell apart, when everything fell apart, when the world came crashing down. Without me, no one could take care of themselves. No one could take care of anything. Jill was so wrapped up in her drama, she didn't notice her dehydrated baby, burning with fever. Katie was so obsessed with her wedding, she had no time for a child she didn't even think of as her own. Atlas had been passed off, one hand to another—I don't have time; I have better things to do; here, you take him. Warning signs like church bells pealing across silent nights, like alarms sounding in sleeping barracks, like howling dogs and angry babies and wailing widows and roaring angels, and no one, no one, to heed this cacophony. And all alone with a sick child, I could only admit that I did not know; I did not know how long he'd slept, how much he'd eaten, how often he'd cried. "I was out of town," I stammered.

"Who was with Atlas?"

"Um . . . a sitter?"

"The gentleman who brought him in? I'll send someone to bring him back."

"No, no. Another sitter. Someone else."

"Well, you better call them."

"Um, I can't. I can't reach them . . . her . . . right now."

"Well, symptoms would have been apparent for days now. How long have you been away? No one called you?"

"No. I don't think so. I don't know."

The doctor eyed me suspiciously. "We've taken blood and done a tox screen. Are you still nursing? If you're on something and he's ingested it, you should tell me now. Time is paramount in these cases. Is the father involved? Is there anything you *can* tell me?"

She was guessing. I was acting weird but why? I was on drugs and had passed them on to the baby? I was on drugs and forgot to feed him or notice whether he had a fever? I was on drugs and had left him home alone for maybe even days on end? I was on drugs and running from the law/an abusive father/a shady past?

I was not on drugs, of course, though I realized with a start that I wasn't one hundred percent sure that Jill wasn't. I had been out of town with my sick grandmother, a perfectly reasonable, guiltless excuse, but one I couldn't make because they wouldn't let me stay if I weren't Atlas's mother, and since I couldn't let him stay there alone and since I couldn't tell her that I really was Atlas's mother but not in an easy-to-explain way, I did the only thing I could think to do. I pretended that my strangeness was due to fear not ignorance, and then I lied.

"Sorry, sorry," I said, shaking my head as if of internal cobwebs. "He's been sleeping since early last night. He's had a little

bit of diarrhea, but the baby book says sometimes that happens. And some vomiting. He hasn't eaten since yesterday
afternoon—no—morning. He's not been crying real tears. I
first noticed his fever . . . this morning . . . but I thought he'd
just sleep it off. I'm not on anything. I don't think he's ingested
anything." Worst-case scenarios mostly. I figured best to paint
extremes and let the doctor take them into account than guess
it was less serious than it turned out to be and have more warning signs ignored. His being so tired and cranky last night
seemed normal to me because I was so tired and cranky. Since
I didn't want to eat, I wasn't surprised that no one did. He
hadn't seemed hot. He hadn't seemed sick. I had been in such a
rush that morning. All I could do was guess.

The doctor eyed me steadily for a long, undecided moment,
finally chalked me up as a distraught parent, and told me I could
stay with him while we awaited test results and that it might be
a while. I squatted beside his bed, somewhere between wanting to be level with his hot little body and actual prayer. Please
let this fever break; please let it be nothing; please let him wake
up, see me, smile, laugh; please make it okay, make him okay,
make him be okay okay okay. I prayed to no one. I could not
summon God. I remembered my grandmother's proscription.
But bargains with that No One floated through my brain.
Would I give him up if it would save him? If Jill married Daniel
and took him far away and I could never see him again, but he
would be okay, would I make that deal? Would I give up my
grandmother for him? If it were his life or hers, whose would I
choose? He's not even blood, and no guarantees because that
would be too easy. If I had to let my grandmother die, but that
gave him a 70 percent chance of making it, versus I let her live,
though she still has cancer, and his odds fall to 30 percent,

what then? These were the questions my brain demanded of itself, the self who had no power to grant wishes of any kind versus the self who had no power to offer anything of significance to relinquish. I tried to put my arms around him, under IV, under tubes, tried to spoon his little body into mine, and I closed my eyes against this world—fitful dreams, fitful nightmares, a hundred hundred nagging thoughts, and no energy left to fight the gathering demons.

I woke up because a large man with a large stick was roughly shaking my shoulder with a large and unkind hand. "Ma'am, you need to come with me." My heart seized, but Atlas looked . . . exactly the same as he had. Still overwarm, still too asleep, but right there next to me and nothing changed. No, I tried to protest, explain, but the large man was dragging me up, pushing me out, and already I was across the room, far away, reaching back out to an Atlas already gone. The large man, gripping my upper arm and pushing me from behind, steered me hard down one hall, through some double doors, down another hall, and into an otherwise empty room with one hard chair in it. We both stood.

"What is your name?" He sounded already angry, already not believing my lies.

"Janey Duncan."

"Are you this boy's mother?" Gesturing towards the door, the hallway, in, one presumed, the general direction of Atlas.

"Yes." I kept my voice level, made sure it didn't rise at the end, but I still sounded defiant rather than matter-of-fact, the way I imagined one would sound if one were the boy's mother.

"Why does he have a different last name than you?" Who

had given them Atlas's last name? Jason must have when he brought him in.

"Mattison is my husband's name," I said evenly, angry though that they'd concluded that this couldn't be my son simply because our last names didn't match.

"Then why are there two people in the lobby who claim to be Atlas Mattison's parents?"

I had no idea. "Two people?"

"Ma'am, I need you to be straight with me, and tell me what's really going on here."

But how could I do that? So I had to keep lying. I had no choice. There was no way to explain what was really going on here. I was Atlas's mother in all the ways that counted, and right now, Atlas needed his mother.

"I'm his mother." I shrugged. "I don't know what to tell you. I don't know who those people are."

He looked me up and down and studied my face for a while, his eyes going squinty. Then he sighed and said quietly, "One of the people out there is pretty upset. She's done a lot of yelling. Her name is Mattison too. And she's just left the building claiming to be on her way home to get a birth certificate. If she's lying, we're very sorry for this inconvenience, but, you understand, we have to be careful. There's a lot of crazies out there. If she comes back with a birth certificate though . . ." He trailed off, so I didn't know what would happen. I'd go to jail on kidnapping charges? I'd be denied access to Atlas? I'd be yelled at by the large man and possibly beaten with his large stick? I had no idea. But also, I didn't care that much. It was a gnawing detail way in the back because the first thirty rows or so were taken up entirely with Atlas who was hot and sick and seizing and I didn't know why. And next to that, nothing mattered. "We'll keep you posted," the guard said on his way out, neither kindly nor unkindly. "Please don't leave." I sat down in the chair and waited. What else could I do?

What I always did. Analyze. Why would I lie? Especially since, clearly, they were about to find out? Admitting it when you first get caught, laughing it off as a silly accident, a harmless misunderstanding, a perfectly-understandable-if-I-see-now-totally-unacceptable error in judgment, even a halfhearted, half-muttered apology, is always, *always* preferable and more sensible than lying more and worse. How do I know? Because I teach film. Because I have seen this movie before. Only twelve-year-old boys and everyone in the movies think that more lying will get you out of an initial lie. Every audience member (at least every non-twelve-year-old boy) shouts at the screen, if only in their own heads, "You idiot. You are making it worse. GO BACK." It makes audiences feel all squirmy and uncomfortable, knowing if these characters would only tell the truth, things might turn out, but since they won't tell the truth, they are almost certain to wind up dead within the hour, never mind that it is also only in movies that lying is an offense where the narrative justice is death. I had panicked I guess. And I felt my loyalty to and love for Atlas was being questioned. And I was his mother in many ways. And I was angry at Jill. But mostly, I think, I plead Narrative Syndrome. I had film on the brain, and in film, the only way forward is deeper.

Generally, I hate hospitals. Everyone hates hospitals I know. But of course, it's different when it's you. So I feel that, unlike everybody else, I *really* hate hospitals. They seem dirty and infectious places to me, cold and unfeeling and dangerous as hell because at any moment someone could come rushing in with a gunshot wound or drop down clutching his chest or cough until blood comes out in red chunks of—I don't know—lung? And I don't want to see that. And I don't want to catch whatever's causing it. But right then, the hospital was the most comforting place to be. They were taking care of Atlas, making him better. And they were keeping me from Jill. From Jill, from Daniel, from Katie, from everyone. And kept away was the only way I wanted to be.

I called my grandmother, just to check in, or really, just so she could comfort me, but as soon as I had her on the phone, I realized that I couldn't very well tell her that Atlas was sick with some as-yet-unidentified disease or that I was being held hostage in a hospital where at any moment someone could throw lung up on me. I couldn't tell her that I might soon be carted off to jail for claiming to have mothered a boy whose mother I was technically not. Come to think of it, the large man with the large stick had not asked me if I had borne Atlas. If he were my adopted son, the right answer to the question "Are you this boy's mother?" would clearly be yes. If he were my foster son, the answer would be yes. If he were my sister's son but she left him on my doorstep when he was an infant on her way to checking herself into a mental institution, even if she never informed the authorities, then clearly the answer would still be yes. So we were splitting hairs here. I hoped. In any case, obviously, I could not have this conversation with my grandmother. At the sound of her voice, I started crying and couldn't stop. But she is my grandmother, who understands without understanding, and said oh my poor baby very softly and promised it would be okay, and still, somehow, I believed her.

I had relocated from the chair to the tile floor, back against the wall, so at least I could stretch my legs and rest my head when the door flew open. The door was opened by large man, but large man immediately stepped out of the way, and two people instantly identifiable as real police officers rushed in behind him.

"Janey Duncan?"

"Yes?"

"We need you to come down to the station and answer some questions for us."

"Am I under arrest?" They stopped mid-motion, looked half surprised.

"Is there a reason you should be?"

"No." I tried to sound sure, indignant even.

"Come with us please." Not a request by any stretch. A command.

In the police car, there was no talking. I sat in the back, locked in and behind wire but not handcuffed. Not yet. Inside, I followed police officer one while police officer two stayed carefully behind me. In a room just as bleak as the one in the hospital but with loads more furniture (a table and two chairs), they turned on a light bright as day, slammed the door shut, and struck up movie cop poses—one straddling the chair with its back turned forward, one with arms crossed, leaning against the wall in the corner and looking angry and skeptical.

"Are you Atlas Mattison's mother?" asked the sitting-backwards cop in front of me quite calmly as if she'd asked, "Do you like chocolate ice cream?"

"No," I said, equally reasonably, as if answering the ice cream question.

She did not look surprised at all. She already knew this evidently. "Why did you say you were?"

"They wouldn't let me see him otherwise. I had to be with him." Still calm, reasonable, confident even.

"What is your relationship to the boy?"

A tough question that, and I really didn't know how to answer. "I'm his . . ." What? Mother clearly wasn't an option anymore. Babysitter did not convey the half of it. Aunt, cousin, in-law—these rung closer to truth but were really, of course, farther away. Friend seemed a small, cold, distant answer. And one I wasn't sure Jill would vouch for any more than the one I'd started with. "We share custody," I finally tried. "I live with him and take care of him." And then, "I love him," I added, though no one had asked that. The one cop exchanged a glance with the other and looked at me steadily, coolly.

"Why is he sick?" she said.

I can only imagine my face went to surprise, displaying the confusion with which my brain processed this question, because the officer softened visibly before I even answered.

"I have no idea," I managed.

"Did you give the child anything?" asked the corner officer.

"No!" Again aghast, confused, appalled as I caught on to what they were thinking.

"When was the last time you saw the child?"

"I've been in Vancouver all week, but I was with him all afternoon yesterday and last night. If anyone had known something was wrong this week, they'd have called me at my parents' house. When I got home, he seemed fine, and no one said anything, so they must have thought he was fine too."

"You didn't see him this morning?" said corner cop.

"No. I got up early to teach then spent the afternoon in the library."

"Where do you teach?" asked backwards cop.

"Rainier University." They looked impressed. Important note: when being arrested, it is useful to have an impressive-sounding job.

"Who is the boy's mother?" asked corner cop.

"Jill. Jill Mattison."

"And his father?"

I rolled my eyes. I may have gnashed my teeth. I sighed and shook my head and finally admitted, "Daniel Davison," with as much equivocation as I could shove into those two words.

"And you and Jill are . . . lovers?" asked backwards cop.

"No," I laughed, and both looked confused again. Suddenly I understood that they'd worked this all out in their heads—Jill and I were lovers raising her and Daniel's baby. Jill was unde-cided, thinking of going back to Daniel. I was getting the shaft, dumped by my girlfriend who was trying to take the child I had helped raise as my own. This was a lovers' tiff. Nothing more. Silly lesbians.

I saw too that this narrative garnered their sympathy. It ex-plained why the boy would be mine but not mine, why I would consider him my son even though I lacked a birth certificate to prove it, why I lied, and why Jill was so angry, and it clearly put me in the wronged-and-harmless-victim box. I was loath to give up this advantage. But though it wasn't too far from the truth, it wasn't quite there either.

"Jill and I are best friends," I confessed. "She got pregnant. The father left. We're in grad school so we don't have much money. Our other friend Katie and I moved in with her, and we all raise the baby together. Our friend Jason, who brought At-las in to the hospital, also helps. We take shifts on the child-care thing and also bathing, feeding, whatever else needs to be done. I was there when he was born and nearly every day since.

I have taken care of him like he's my own. Jill and Katie have both been pretty distracted lately, so I've taken up the slack. It's a joint arrangement. I didn't birth him, but essentially, he's my son."

A little paragraph that, a short, simple, entirely true explanation. To my ears, it sounded perfectly reasonable. To my ears, it put me totally in the right. How could anyone who loved him have the heart to leave him alone in an emergency room? And how could anyone doubt I loved him? And then how could anyone blame me for this?

They looked convinced. But not moved. Not one way or the other. "Wait here," said one or the other. I'm not sure which. I was looking at the table by then, the floor. I had become very small, sad, and darkly. Worried scared angry and waiting.

Thirty-two

"WHAT THE FUCK did you tell them?"

The door banged open sometime later, and there was Jill, red-faced, furious, yelling already, with Daniel Davison in tow and corner cop who closed the door with a pointed look—at whom I wasn't sure—behind us all.

"What the fuck did *you* tell them?" I said wearily, exhausted already.

"I told them the truth. I told them you were lying and trying to keep us from our baby." At first I took this "our" to mean our, hers and mine, but then I realized she meant "our," hers and Daniel's. She was ranting in paragraphs. It was hard to keep up.

"They said would Janey want to kidnap the baby, and I said you might. They said would she have given him something to make him sick, and I said you might. They said were you acting strange lately, and I said you were. They said could I think of any reason you would want to keep us from our baby, and I said yes, I could think of lots of reasons. I told them you were experiencing unnatural attachment and maternal delusions and you were angry at the father and you wanted to hurt me. They said were you alone with the baby in the last twenty-four hours, and I said you were. They said did I think you would poison Atlas or give him something to make him sick on purpose like to get attention or control or something, and I said yes I thought you might."

"Is that because you're insane or just evil?" I asked, mock-mild, but unable to pull it off so hard was I shaking. I couldn't even meet her gaze let alone stand.

"I don't know, Janey. Which are you? What was I supposed to say? Jason called me and said he'd been trying for hours. Atlas is in the ER; he won't wake up; no one knows why. We rush over there, but they won't let us back there to see him because it's immediate family only, and his mother's already with him. I said *I'm his mother*, and they wouldn't believe me. Even Jason vouched for me, but they wouldn't let me back there. When I went home and got the birth certificate, that's when they started asking questions. And I'm thinking when I left he was fine, and now he's in the ER with you. What was I supposed to think?"

"We didn't bring up poison or purposely making him sick," Daniel put in more gently, half embarrassed, half scolding me, "but once they did, it scared us. We don't understand how he could have gotten so sick so quickly. You promise to take good care of him, but then all of a sudden he's in the hospital, and we can't even see him." There was a pause during which I imagined backwards cop and corner cop behind the two-way glass calling for backup from the irony cops under whose jurisdiction this clearly fell. "If you gave him something, Janey, please, please tell us now so we'll have more time. The tox screens will save him anyway, but it would be better—for everyone—if you told us right away."

It was hard to know where to start. I lacked enough energy for screaming anger and bred-in-the-bone fury and caustic silence and quiet freezing truth all, so I had to choose among them. I do not like yelling. I do not like confrontation. I tried to choke back everything. And what came out instead was tears. It was either going to be tears or laughter I guess. The latter secures dignity and the aura of high ground. But there was already too much lost there.

"You actually think I would try to make him sick?" I spat. I just wanted to be clear.

"We don't know."

"I didn't poison Atlas, you assholes."

"Why is he sick then?"

"I don't know. And neither do you. And neither do the doctors at the hospital. They did an initial tox screen that turned up nothing. They're running more tests. No one there seemed to think he was poisoned."

"Then why did we get a panicked call from Jason that Atlas is in the hospital and had a seizure?"

"Well, he tried me, but there's no cell reception in the stacks. Katie's in Portland. So I guess that left you, a poor choice at best, but you are his parents as you keep pointing out. I imagine he was desperate because he'd been trying you for hours, but no one was picking up. Where were you guys? You both have cell phones. Truly concerned parents keep their cell phones on when they leave their kid with a babysitter."

"You were supposed to be with him. Not Jason. We thought we could trust you," said Daniel.

"Well, Dan, that's not actually true." I tried to keep my voice steady. "You didn't think anything. You left before this child was even born. You didn't make arrangements for his care or for anything else. You have no idea who was supposed to be with Atlas this morning. You just assumed someone was doing it. You've never laid eyes on this child. You only decided to give a crap at all about twenty minutes ago. So in your case, this isn't a matter of thinking or a matter of trust.

"And as for you, Jill, no, I wasn't supposed to be with him. You were. I teach in the morning, every morning, since the end of May. Katie's in Portland, not that she's scheduled for weekday mornings either, so we had to call Jason to stay with Atlas this morning when you didn't show up. I said sure I would take Atlas yesterday, even though it wasn't my day, and Jason said sure he would cancel his appointment this morning, even though he needed to meet with his advisor. Even though I'm completely wasted because I've spent the last week in Vancouver with my sick grandmother. Even though I am totally exhausted and totally behind. Even though Jason and Lucas have a million things to do to get ready for their baby. But you wouldn't know about any of that. Because you don't know anything about taking care of a baby—other people do it for you. And because you don't know anything about anyone else's life because it doesn't matter because it isn't yours."

"We have a babysitting schedule. That doesn't mean Atlas is yours."

"Right, I can see where you need a babysitter. I was teaching; Katie's getting married; Jason is having his own child. Where were you?"

"That doesn't matter."

"Where were you?"

"She stayed overnight at my place. And I took the day off,"

said Daniel. "We have a lot to work out, a lot to talk about, a lot of catching up to do." His tone was serious—very serious actually, like their needing time to talk was the most important thing in the world—but I caught the twitch of a flicker of a suppressed smile that told me why they weren't answering the phone for so long this afternoon.

"Why did you say you were his mother?" asked Jill.

"I didn't want him to be alone," I said. "And otherwise they wouldn't let me back."

"There's a reason for that," she said.

"Really? What is it?"

"We know you love him, Janey. We let you take care of him. We let you be with him. We're grateful for your help, but he's not yours." Jill had toned it down a little, moved from furious-yelling to furious-condescending. She was just as angry but far, far more frustrating this way. In my mind, I picked up one of the chairs and threw it across the room at her, perhaps through the two-way window. I saw shatterproof glass rain down all over the irony cops who would surely conclude, having witnessed this scene, that I was free to take Atlas home and leave, just the two of us, for whatever faraway place I preferred.

"Jill," I said, sighing, "I am not your babysitter. I am not your nanny. I am not your maid or your cook or your housekeeper. I am your family and I am your friend, but you aren't being mine. I have taken care of Atlas like a son, and you know it. I have been there more than you have. I have rearranged my life to make this work just as much as you have. I have not complained that I put in more time and more care and more money than his parents. I stood by when Daniel left, and I stand here while he tries to decide whether or not he wants to come back. I have been the responsible one here. So I don't care who this boy came out of—he's mine." At this point, I would have walked out of the room—it was a good exit line, and besides, I was done having this conversation—except I was still under arrest, so I couldn't do anything but sit there.

Backwards and corner cop came in then.

"The hospital called. You should get over there." You? Who?

"They determined there's no foul play. You're all free to go."

"What is it?" I said.

"I'm not a doctor, ma'am. They can answer all your questions when you get there. We appreciate your cooperation, and we're sorry for the inconvenience."

Thirty-three

As I'd gotten a ride over to the police station, I had to ride back to the hospital with Jill and Daniel. Out in the parking lot, they piled into her car, and I stood around looking stupid and lost. "Oh just get in," said Jill, annoyed but apparently willing to share a car ride with me. I wondered at how I'd been released so quickly with no lawyer, no paperwork, no phone call even, and Daniel guessed I wasn't really under arrest but just in for questioning. He allowed as how if I became more unemployed and more depressed, I too could watch three episodes of *Law & Order,* sometimes four, a day, and then I would be clear on such distinctions. He was being cute. As if our, all our, lives didn't hang by spider thread. As if our, all our, son didn't suffer from no-one-knew-what in the ER without us. As if they hadn't just had me arrested—or brought in for questioning—for poisoning and/or kidnapping their, my, our baby boy.

•   •   •

At the hospital, Jason was waiting, head in his hands, more or less where I'd left him except he'd called in reinforcements. Lucas was there. And Ethan. They all three stood up as soon as we walked in.

"They know something, but they won't tell us," Jason blurted.

"Are you okay?" Ethan asked. Me. Ethan asked me.

I avoided eye contact and gave him a half nod and said a firm and unequivocal no to the screaming that threatened to come and come and never stop.

Lucas went over to the nurses' station calmly. Then he came back to us. Then we waited. Jason wanted to ask what happened, what happened after I was arrested by the police, after Jill produced a father and a birth certificate, after she screamed stolen baby in the ER waiting room. But even Jason couldn't think of a way to bring this up in polite conversation. Finally, a doctor came over. He clearly had been briefed because he looked from one to the other to the other of us and said, "Why don't we find a room where we can all talk."

We all followed him down the hall to the same empty room where I'd waited before. He closed the door behind him and took a deep breath.

"Atlas has bacterial meningitis." I registered at first only that he hadn't said cancer, willed my ears open, my attention focused . . .

". . . very smart, very lucky you brought him in when you did. It's treatable but it's a very, very serious disease, and children die from it . . ."

Very smart and very lucky. Very lucky. Very lucky . . .

". . . intravenous antibiotics for a few days and IV fluids because of the vomiting and diarrhea. It's very contagious, so we'll prescribe anyone who's been in close contact with him in the last few days a course of rifampin to be on the safe side. There's a good chance he'll recover completely though he'll be quite weak for a while yet—"

"A good chance?" I interrupted.

"Sometimes children suffer long-term side effects—heart problems, brain damage, deafness. You can't worry about that right now because we won't know any time soon. We're doing the best we can for him right now."

"Can we see him?" I asked.

"Not tonight. Come back tomorrow and—"

"But if he needs his mother—" Jill began.

"Not tonight," the doctor said firmly. "Tomorrow you can sort all this out."

Sort all this out. He didn't mean the meningitis, about which everything there was to be done was already being done. He meant us, this family, who was his mother and who wasn't, who got to see him and who didn't, who was blameless and who was at fault. For a while, no one said anything. Then Jill said, "I'm staying with Dan tonight," and, nodding in my direction, "Someone else drive her home." She turned and walked out, Daniel on her heels.

"I'll take you home," said Jason and Ethan together.

"My car is here actually. I just needed a ride back to the hospital after she had me arrested."

"Drink?" Lucas concluded.

"Thanks, I just want to go home."

"Maybe leave your car here anyway," said Ethan. "I'll drive you home and pick you up and bring you back here first thing in the morning before class. We could stop on the way home and get something to eat."

"I should go home."

"Gonna be awfully quiet at home. No one there but you."

This had not occurred to me. I accepted the ride, tabled the rest, grateful to put at least something in someone else's hands. Said goodbye to Jason and Lucas. Jason hugged me and said it wasn't my fault. I hugged him and thanked him for being so smart and lucky.

"If you had waited . . ." I said.

"Don't even think it," he said.

In Ethan's car, he didn't even get the ignition switched on before I was sobbing in the passenger seat, panicked heaving soaking the front of my shirt hands in fists over my eyes gasping for air rocking back and forth shaking like to break apart sobbing. Ethan got out of the car, came around to my side, opened the door, crouched down on the ground in front of me, and pulled me into his arms. We stayed like that till I was done, me leaning out of the passenger seat, folded in half, trembling and soaked, Ethan reaching up, crouching down, air and ground, sky and earth, all directions at once, his hands in my hair, on my neck, his whispers, indiscernible, in my ear. Finally, I was all out.

"I don't think I can go out to dinner," I said.

"Let's eat at your place."

"I don't think I'm up to cooking."

"I'll cook."

"You'll cook?"

"Other people besides you can cook. I manage to feed myself nearly every day actually. Sometimes you have to let someone else make dinner," he said. And then, "Janey, it's going to be okay." I didn't believe him, but it was sweet of him to say so.

•   •   •

When we got in, the light on the machine was blinking.

Katie.

"Hey, it's me. Couldn't get you on your cell, but I wanted to check in, let you know we got here okay. Tried about fifty billion hors d'oeuvres. More tomorrow. It's pretty crazy. We're having a great time though. I also wanted to mention that Atlas had some diarrhea late last night and this morning. He seemed fine otherwise. I'm sure it's nothing. Just wanted to make sure everything's cool there. Oh well. See you tomorrow. Call me. Bye."

Thirty-four

THE NEXT MORNING, Ethan and I went back to the hospital early—we both had to teach at ten. No one else was there yet. The doctor from the day before had left a note with a list of names. We were to be allowed back, any of us, whenever we came. Atlas still seemed too small, warm, and lethargic, with half closed lids and a slack little mouth but, the nurse told us, "not worse," which evidently counts as "responding."

I was skeptical. Regardless, I went to class anyway. The thing about teaching is you just go and do it somehow, and while you do, there's nothing else. You find yourself in front of the classroom performing the role of a sane, held-together adult, and so you become one, at least for the duration of the period. No matter what else is going on in your life, if you have to get up in front of a group of people and say something, you are likely to think of something to say.

Since I had genre on the brain, we started there. As my grandmother pointed out, just because a story is sad doesn't make it a tragedy. All stories are sad, at least a little bit. I told my students to think about all the tears shed during the happiest moments of people's lives—graduating from school, falling in love, getting married, having babies—not all of those tears are tears of joy. All stories have sad; tragedy is something else altogether. Stories exist on their own, outside of everything. The business of their telling is searching for a genre to call home.

So how do we find home?

"It depends on what happens in them," Sarah Iverson guessed.

Brent Haddon echoed, "When sad things happen, it's a tragedy. When funny things happen, it's a comedy."

"When there's lots of sex, it's a romance," Pete Fansom piped in from the back.

By the fourth week of summer term, engaged, creative insight is a lot to ask. But I pressed them. The vast majority of stories are none of the above I insisted. Endings are ambiguous. Mostly we see how quick bright things come to confusion. So often, characters go from a state of being settled, where they more or less feel they understand and have a handle on things, to being sadder, more confused, more at sea, more unsure. And then it ends. Obviously, literature is like this because life is too.

With film, it's easier. In most genres, we know how movies will end. The joy is watching those ends play out. The joy is we know when we watch movies that all the angst, indecision, misery, heartache, injustice, and torture will turn out okay. Most movies aren't tragedies. Most movies are redemptive. We see their characters going through the hard parts knowing that it will turn out well for them, that they will learn from their pain what they wouldn't without it. And it is nice to see this play out and to live vicariously, for a few hours, a life where, unlike yours, this is the case. My hip, savvy students named exceptions—there are lots, of course—but we noted they were exceptions indeed. So my gripe was that it seemed unfair that though my life was very filmic (dying relatives, rare diseases, blood feuds, warrantless arrests), my ending wouldn't be.

"Maybe it will be," said Ethan on the way back to the hospital after class.

"No it won't. It can't."

"Why not?"

"Because I can't even imagine it. That all this mess, this heartbreak, this anger and fear could mean something good and useful? No way. Even in my fantasy, I can't write this so it all works out. There's too many pieces. It's too big. That's my point—it's only in the movies that it all comes together in the end, and you realize it was worth it, and you learn important somethings and become a better person. I don't see how that could happen here."

"Of course you don't," said Ethan. "Not now. But it's not over yet. You won't know until the end."

"I don't get to see the end. I'm not an omniscient narrator. This is first person all the way."

"Clearly."

"At the end, I'll be dead."

"This is not a tragedy, Janey," Ethan said, suddenly serious.

"How do you know?" I whispered.

"It has none of the markings. It doesn't feel like tragedy. It feels like trial, but not tragedy."

"Life doesn't work like that. Literature doesn't even work like that."

"In this case," he promised, "it does. It will."

·   ·   ·

When I got home after the hospital, Katie was standing in the middle of our living room, looking lost.

"Hey."

"Hey."

"How was your trip?"

"Great. How's Atlas?"

"Responding evidently. You can go visit anytime."

"How's your grandma?"

"Also better, thanks."

"I'm on my way to the hospital in just a sec."

"Good. Atlas could use more company. I'll join you again later."

"Yeah, for sure. We should get a pizza and a movie or something tonight."

"Sounds good."

"Uh, Janey?"

"Yeah?"

"Where's our furniture?"

There was a note of course. There usually is in the movies. No loose ends here. In fairness though, I knew the contents before I even found the letter, and though it offered explanation, it lacked reasons or even reason. Worst of all, it was from Daniel. Even via letter, evidently, Jill wasn't speaking to me. To us.

Dear K&J,

Don't worry—everything's fine. But this arrangement, if it was
ever working, isn't anymore. Jill is moving in with me. We belong

*together—we know that now. As you can see, we have already
moved most of her stuff. We know much of the furniture was
shared, but we feel that Atlas should have as many remnants of
home as possible to ease the transition. Of course, Atlas will be
with us, and I know you would want him to be as comfortable as
possible. We will be in touch soon and let you know where we are
and how to contact us but not yet. I think we all agree we could
all use some space. I have learned, more than you can know but
as you will observe, what problems time and distance can mend.*

See you soon,
Dan (and Jill)

"What an asshole," said Katie.

Then the blessed phone rang. We both leapt for it, afraid it
was the hospital and things had turned for the worse again,
afraid it was Jill calling to regret, apologize, make amends, afraid
it was the police and they had decided to arrest me after all. But
instead it was my father calling to tell me that my grandmother
had died.

Thirty-five

JEWS BURY THEIR dead almost immediately—in the ground within twenty-four hours if possible—no doubt a very reasonable practice in a hot climate in a time before full body refrigerators but something of a hardship now. The business of funeral, food, and forum are welcome distractions I guess, but really, honestly, who has the energy, the will, the focus at that point? My grandmother wouldn't have cared I told myself. I didn't care. It was too much to deal with, to process, to matter. And it left almost no time at all to say goodbye. My mother's argument though was that my grandmother would have wanted things done the proper way and that someday I would cherish a week's worth of sitting around listening to people reminisce about a woman I did not yet acknowledge as gone.

Over protestations, Katie drove me home. She did not judge me fit to drive or to be alone and reasoned that she was going to have to come up the next day for the funeral anyway. For mile after mile, we talked over and over and around Atlas and

Jill and Daniel and us and not about my grandmother at all. Hours later, at my parents' middle-of-the-night kitchen table, the four of us sat around eating chocolate cake, talking wedding plans, and indulging in more distraction and denial. Later still, towards morning, I rolled over from a not quite sleep into a not quite dawn and realized, sinkingly, that I hadn't gotten anyone to cover my class in the morning. I called Ethan, full of apologies for waking him up, and asked if he could combine it with his again or at least tell them what was going on. "I can't," he said, full of sleep. "I've got a funeral to go to tomorrow."

He drove up with Jason and Lucas and Peter. Nico was there too, without Caroline, and at one point when I looked up, I saw Diane alone in the back. My mother looked back at them all and whispered into my hair, "You've got quite a group of people who love you back there." I didn't respond because opening my mouth would have released howling that would not have stopped. And because it was rude to admit that my friends didn't matter to me without my family—without my grandmother and without Atlas.

I cannot tell about the ceremony because I do not remember it at all, so hard was I squeezing shut my eyes and reining in my head. Graveside was short and garish with sun, blooming things, and fiercely good weather insistent on lightening the proceedings. Someone passed around the Mourners' Kaddish in phonetic Hebrew so that we all could say it, but I did not. Everyone was supposed to throw dirt on the coffin, but I declined that too. Then we were meant to watch as they lowered it into the ground though I looked carefully at my feet in the grass instead. I did hear my mother wailing, surrounded by her friends. I did notice when Ethan came over and put his arms around me from behind, but I pretended not to and held very still and tried not to move or even acknowledge him at all, but he didn't seem to care about my show of apathy. I also noticed as we were walking away that the guys in overalls, who couldn't possibly still be called gravediggers but could not have looked more the part had they the RSC costume shop at their disposal, were already, already!, shoveling the rest of the dirt over, filling the hole left by my grandmother. As if that were possible. And finally, as I got in the car, they were using a strange dolly and strap and pulley apparatus to lower an enormous lid over the entire grave. Dropped only the last inches into new dirt, its thud shook the ground even from thirty feet away. It was that heavy. To keep her in I guess so that even if she became a vampire she couldn't escape. Then I was sick on the floor of the car.

At my parents' house, deli platters had mysteriously appeared. And, as Nick Carraway puts it, amid the welcome confusion of cups and cakes a certain physical decency established itself. People moved on. They thought: at least that's over with. They thought: lovely ceremony, I wonder what's for dessert. They turned to each other and said: how sad for the family, now what's new with you. This is how it is. It didn't make me mad. In fact, if someone had asked me to reminisce or tell stories about my grandmother, I might have been sick again. So I was grateful. Sitting alone out back in the sun, my strategy was, if I'm very quiet, maybe no one will want to talk to me.

Katie came out and sat down next to me, handed me some kind of soda, a sandwich, and a cookie, and showed me her phone. Two missed calls from Jill. Atlas! I panicked, retched again.

"Okay fine," she said, "you don't have to eat anything. But at least drink the soda."

"Did you call her back? Maybe it's Atlas."

"I tried but she's not picking up. If it were bad though, she'd have left a message."

I was unconvinced but accepted this because, really, what else could I do.

"You should go inside," I told Katie. "Eat something."

"I'm fine here with you."

"I just want to be alone," I said.

"No one will find us back here."

"No, I mean alone."

"We are alone," said Katie.

I accepted this too. Same reason.

We sat for a while in the sun. I ripped out fistfuls of grass and made a little pile. Katie inspected the tan she was getting around her sandals that made her toes look dirty. Then the back door opened, and I didn't even look up because there really was no one I wanted to see, but it was even worse than that.

"How is neither one of you answering your phone?" Jill began.

"You came!" Katie observed.

"Which I would have told you had you answered your phone."

"I had it off for the ceremony. Why didn't you text me?"

"I was driving."

"You could have pulled over."

"I was in a hurry. I was late."

"You missed the service."

"There was a long line at the border."

"You could have texted me then."

"In line?"

"Yeah."

"I didn't think of it. I was distracted."

"I called you back."

"Really? I didn't hear the phone ring."

"Did you have music on really loud?"

"Not that loud. I was—"

"How is Atlas?" I interrupted.

Jill looked at me like she'd forgotten I was there. Jill looked at me like she'd forgotten if she were talking to me or not. "Seems the same to me. But they say they're satisfied with his response to the drugs so far."

"He's by himself?" We were all here.

"Daniel's with him."

"Alone?" Katie and I shrieked together.

"Not alone. With a whole hospital staff. Besides, he has to get to know his son."

I accepted this too. Same reason.

"I'm really sorry," Jill said finally. Finally.

"It's about time," I said.

"No, not about that," she snapped and then softened. "I'm really sorry about your grandmother. She was an amazing woman. An amazing grandmother. An amazing great-grandmother."

"Oh," I said. Then, "Thanks." Then, slowly, "Thank you for coming up. It's good you're here. She'd have wanted you here."

"Don't be ridiculous," said Jill. "Of course I came; of course I'm here."

•   •   •

Towards dusk, we were between waves. Jill went home to be with Atlas and check on Daniel. It was nice of her, I supposed, to drive all the way up just to turn around and drive all the way back. Lots of people who had been over all day went home finally. And the folks who had been at work all day—come home, had dinner, and put their kids to bed—were on their way over. My parents had a lot of friends. My grandmother had a lot of friends. The presence of all these people maybe should have been comforting. But it wasn't.

My mother called me up to her room.

"I found this at the house." *The house.* My grandmother's apartment. How had it become *the house* so quickly? She held out a wooden box tied tightly with a white ribbon, beautiful, but with a Post-it note on the top with my name scrawled on it in my grandmother's absent handwriting.

"What is it?"

"I don't know. You have to open it."

I turned it over and over. Shook it. Turned it over again. "Maybe not yet."

My mother shrugged. Understood. Was too tired to care. Something.

"This is what she left me?"

"There are a thousand things at the house. You're welcome to anything. I know there was some jewelry, some china, some silver she wanted you to have. We'll have to go through everything eventually. Sort it out."

"But this must have been the thing she most wanted me to have."

"Maybe it was just on her mind. It's probably a note to herself to remember to give it to you the next time she saw you."

"Maybe."

Is death always sudden? By definition?

Ethan and I took advantage of the lull and went for a quick run. So I didn't explode. The sun was thinking about setting. It was nearly cool with a nice breeze, good summer smells, a whole world out there that kept on spinning evidently. We ran by people living normal lives—grilling, gardening, playing with kids, standing by mailboxes talking to neighbors, reading books on porches—and above all I envied them their normalcy. Their grandmothers had not died; their babies had not nearly died as well, had not been stolen away by their best friends.

"It's comforting, all these normal people with their normal lives," I said, breathing hard, on our cool-down walk home.

"What do you mean?"

I explained about how their grandmothers were alive, their babies not taken from them.

"Their grandmothers probably aren't alive," said Ethan.

"What do you mean? Look at them. They're very happy."

"Who?"

"Them." I waved absently at the people. At that moment, they included only an elderly woman on a porch swing doing what looked like the crossword.

"I am pretty certain her grandmother is dead," said Ethan.

"Then why is she so happy?"

"What makes you think she is?"

"She's whistling."

"Maybe it's just a thing she does."

"I guess."

"Also, it probably didn't happen yesterday."

"And wasn't so sudden."

"What do you mean?"

"I mean I think it wouldn't be so hard if we had had more warning. If it wasn't so out of the blue. She was totally fine in the morning and then by afternoon she was dead."

Ethan had stopped walking and was looking at me, hands on hips, like I was crazy.

"Janey," he said slowly, "I told my class last week there was a good chance I would have to miss some of this week for a funeral. I gave them their final assignment early and everything."

"How did you know?"

"Sweetie . . ." He had never called me that before, so I knew this wasn't going to be good. "She was eighty-seven. She had lung cancer. She talked about dying and told you her final wishes and everything. You seemed so . . . broken when you came home. I just figured . . . it wouldn't be long."

I was shocked, stunned. "But they said she'd be fine."

"Who did?"

And suddenly I couldn't remember. "But I wasn't by her bedside. She hadn't taken a turn for the worse. She hadn't slipped into a coma. She didn't get rushed back to the hospital."

"Sometimes it doesn't work like that."

"I didn't get to say goodbye."

"You did," said Ethan, but I wasn't convinced. "In lots of ways, she was lucky. It was fast. She was sleeping. She didn't suffer much. She missed the misery of watching her family watch her die. I can't imagine it wasn't better this way."

"So . . . what? She was old. She died in her sleep. This is a blessing? I should feel grateful?"

"It's very sad and very terrible for you, Janey. You will miss her. Her absence will be huge. But she didn't have to linger in pain. She knew it was coming but didn't have to live with that knowledge very long. And that is a kind of blessing."

I couldn't look at him. "She didn't know it was coming. She wrote herself a note to give me a package the next time she saw me."

"What was it?"

"I don't know."

We walked in silence the rest of the way. Just as I was going into the house, he grabbed my arm and pulled me back.

"Janey, I'm sorry. I was trying to make you feel better, not worse. I don't know what I'm saying. I didn't mean anything by it. I'm just talking."

"It's fine," I said.

"I only meant— You said you envied how happy everyone else seemed, and I only meant everyone's lost someone they loved and recovered from it. You will too. Atlas and your grandmother."

"I haven't lost Atlas," I said.

"That's not what I meant. Look, I'm just making things worse. I'm sorry. That's all I wanted to say."

He tried to hug me, but I pulled away and went inside to take a shower.

Late that night, I took my grandmother's box into the bathroom. Katie and I were together in the double bed in the guest room. I didn't want to disturb her. But also, suddenly, I had to know. I closed the toilet lid, sat down on it, and tried to hold in my hands the last present she'd ever give me, her last intention on my behalf, but it kept slipping away—not the box itself, just my head around the moment. I put the Post-it note carefully into the pocket of my robe. I untied the ribbon and put it away as well. The lid was on a hinge. I rocked it gently gently slowly carefully back and looked inside. There was another note. It was in its own tiny envelope, like a gift card. It had my name again on the outside. Inside was a small square of green and white paper, folded neatly in half. It looked like it used to be wrapping paper. On it, in my grandmother's scrawling hand, it said cheerfully, "See? I told you so. You'll have to pass these on for me. Miss you, honey! Guess who?"

Under the tiny envelope were my grandfather's cufflinks and his everyday watch.

Thirty-six

I SNUCK INTO my own bedroom where Ethan was sleeping in the twin bed I'd grown up in. Sneaking into your childhood room feels wrong in every way. First, you are only used to sneaking out of it. Second, it has the unsettling suggestion of trying to climb back into the womb or at least back into your childhood. Being five again certainly held some appeal at that moment. I coveted my own past life. So simple. I looked around the room and remembered my mother and grandmother laughing at me while I looked, painstakingly, through every wallpaper sample in the wallpaper store. Then I remembered when they stopped thinking it was cute and went across the street to have lunch and leave me to my own miserable indecision. It had paid off in the end though. Red and purple tulips on a cream background were still cute now. The little girl next to me who had insisted on her first instinct, despite her mother's protestations, was presumably stuck with pink and green My Little Ponies on her wall forever. Or maybe her parents wallpapered more often than mine did.

My very own room. And my very own bed. One of my first memories is of my parents bringing that bed home to me, trading me for my crib. I had been reluctant to give up the crib, thinking my stuffed animals, who lived there, would disappear with it. Then my father demonstrated that I could get in and out of this bed on my own whenever I wanted like a big girl. My parents must have quickly regretted this point as I spent many of the wee hours of the next three years in their bedroom, but I loved the bed straightaway. Always, coming home from vacations, coming back from college, even from school now, the best part was climbing back into this bed.

Now with a boy in it. This was unsettling. I am only five! I shook him awake.

He shot upright in bed. "Janey?" he whispered, frantic.

"Obviously."

"You scared the crap out of me."

"Sorry. Scoot over."

"Over where?"

"Just over."

"I'm pretty over. It's a really small bed."

I shoved him more over anyway, took off my robe, climbed in next to him in the T-shirt I was wearing underneath.

"This is what my grandmother left me," I whispered, sitting up against the headboard and holding the box out in front of us.

"What is it?"

"Well, it's cufflinks for Atlas and something for you."

"For me?"

"Something she thought you'd like. You will."

"Why me?"

"She thinks we're getting married."

"Right, I forgot." Then Ethan said nothing, processing this

I guess or trying to decide what to say in response. "Well," he said finally, "I guess I should look."

He opened the box, took out the watch, held it up to the light coming in off the street. "Wow," he said. "I do love it. She was absolutely right."

"She wanted me to hold on to it because she didn't think she'd be around anymore when you were ready to have it." I shrugged. "She was right. So were you."

"How was I right?"

"It wasn't sudden. She knew." I showed him the note.

"I'm sorry, Janey," he said.

"Why? I was the one who was angry and mean and wrong. You were kind and nice and right."

"Well, I'm sorry for being right."

We sat like that for a while in the dark, saying nothing, sort of floating.

"We should go to bed," he whispered, startling me. I had almost forgotten he was there. Maybe I even fell asleep sitting up against the headboard.

"Okay," I said, but I didn't go anywhere. I was already in my bed after all.

He put his hands on either side of my face and rested his forehead against mine.

"You have not had a good week," he said.

"No," I agreed.

"Next week might not be much better."

"No," I said again.

"Maybe the one after that."

"Let's hope so."

And then he kissed me. Soft a very little bit at first just barely so at first I wasn't even sure it was kissing and then a little more and a little more and it definitely was. And then the part where he opened his mouth and I opened mine and then we closed them again right away like we changed our minds about saying something we shouldn't and then open again to explore that way a little bit and see what happened next. And then little small tastes of kisses and sideways ones and ones where he moved his hands from my face to my neck and back again. And then where he paused for a bit and drew away and put his hand on my hair and looked at me for a long time and touched me again softly and a little bit sad and looked and looked. And where we smiled at each other. And then the part where we started kissing again, like kiss number two, like this time we know about it before-hand and we mean it and it didn't just happen. And that way for a while, for a long while, because you never get to do the first night over again, and secret whispered middle of the night kisses don't happen often enough to rush. And waiting and breathing and breathing and listening, aware of my heartbeat (too fast) and my breath (too shallow) and not thinking of any-thing at all. Nothing at all.

Eventually, what can you do? More. Or less. Leave or stay.

"I know I said this before but . . . we should really go to bed," he suggested. "The sun's coming up."

"I am not allowed to have boys in my bed," I said.

"Okay," he said. And lay down on his back, and I lay down on his front (it really is a very small bed) and slept for the first time in days.

Not very many hours later, I snuck back into bed with Katie while Ethan—and everyone else—was still asleep. I tried very hard to stay in my half-sleep place, lightly buzzed from predawn kissing and its swirling implications, lightly numb as well and so holding my grandmother, Jill, Atlas at bay, ready to slip back into that bright sleep you find on summer mornings when it's already fully light and yet still entirely too early to be up. Having finally slept, my body remembered what it was like and wanted more. It was not to be. I slipped into bed, laid my head on the pillow, closed my eyes, and would have been asleep again within moments except Katie was having none of it. Up on one elbow, she whisper-hissed over my gratefully closing eyes, "Janey, *what* is going on with you and Ethan?"

I lay perfectly still and would not open my eyes, feigning the very edges of sleep, trying still to keep them with me. "What brought that up at this hour of the morning?"

"You did when you snuck into bed like I wouldn't notice at five A.M. Where else would you be?"

"Really?"

"Yeah really."

"I could have been in the garden crying. I could have been downstairs watching TV, unable to sleep. I could have been in the kitchen having a snack."

"You don't eat when you're upset. The window's open so I would have heard you crying in the garden. Lucas and Jason are on the sofa in the TV room downstairs. Also, clearly something is going on between you and Ethan."

I kept my eyes clamped shut. But I couldn't help giggling. "What makes you think so?"

She flung herself back against the pillows, also giggling. "The last month of my life. Looking at him looking at you. Looking at you looking at him. Living in the house with you. Being alive in the world."

I explained to her about my grandmother's box, about

opening it in the middle of the night, about the watch and my sudden need to deliver it right away. "Then he kissed me."

Katie squealed. Loudly. I clamped a hand over her mouth.

"How was it?"

"You know. You kissed him."

"I forget," she said. "Tell me everything."

"No." Then, "It was nice." Then, "He is very nice."

"What does this mean?"

"It doesn't mean anything." Then, "I don't know what it means." Then, "I'm sorry, Katie."

"Why?"

"I kissed your ex-boyfriend. That's the number one rule of dating. Don't kiss your friends' ex-boyfriends."

"That's *your* number one rule, not mine. I believe in vetting my friends' boyfriends first."

"Still."

"If it weren't for not dating Ethan, I would never have gotten to date Peter."

"Still."

"I think it's great. I'm really happy for you." Then she added, "Both!"

"If it makes you uncomfortable, I'll stop right away. I don't have to do it again." She looked at me skeptically like I was an addict who claimed to be able to stop anytime. "I can't lose another friend. You're my best friend too. Nothing's worth losing you too."

"You haven't lost Jill," Katie said. Then she added, "We."

"Then why has she taken Atlas we don't know where?"

"She's freaking out," said Katie. "But it's not because we've lost her. And you could never lose me. Definitely not over a boy." She was quiet. I thought we might go back to sleep then, but instead she asked, "Why did your grandmother leave him a watch?"

"It has a baseball on it." Then, "It was my grandfather's." Then, "She thinks we're getting married."

Katie squealed again. "We could have a double wedding!"

"Katie, you are actually insane," I said.

There was a soft knock on our door. Jason stuck his head in.

"I heard squealing," he said. "I came up to get the dirt." He climbed in bed with us.

"Go away," I said. "There is no dirt. We're trying to sleep."

"You hooked up with Ethan," he guessed.

"No!" I said. Then, "We kissed." Then, "How did you know?"

"Oh Janey, it's so obvious." He rolled his eyes. "Even Lucas knew. Tell me everything."

There was a soft knock on our door. Ethan stuck his head in, eyes blurry, hair sticking up in a thousand directions, squinting at us. "What's going on? Why are you guys so loud? It's five o'clock in the morning."

Thirty-seven

Not very many hours later, Ethan went home to meet with his students. Katie and Peter and Jason and Lucas went home as well—to work, to cook, to plan a wedding, to cover my class, to otherwise get back to their lives. Though Katie was missing Atlas and promised to talk to Jill and demand . . . something, I could also already see him, us, ebbing from her life. She was getting married in a week, beginning a new life, starting to think about having children of her own. Since getting married—to a man and not her roommates—had never been in doubt for her, since having babies of her own—and not her roommate's—hadn't either, maybe she was more willing to let all of this go. She loved Atlas like a babysitter? She loved me and Jill like roommates? She could put all this behind her for a guy she'd known for a month? It seemed unthinkable to me.

Unthinkable like impossible. But also unthinkable like I couldn't think about it. I had another life to pack up as well. Though my dad argued for renting my grandmother's apartment for another month to give us time before we had to either find a place for or toss everything my grandmother had owned, my mother wanted to get it done right away, not drag it out, add searing pain to searing pain rather than what would be, in a month or so, searing pain to miserable absence, numb resignation, and regret. It was horrible.

Things don't seem like novels, but they are. If I'd been at school, I'd have been explaining this to my students. Since I wasn't, I distracted myself with these ruminations while I packed. Things don't exist on their own. They don't exist at all without being owned. And in being owned, they have a story. Some are remarkable of course. "My father brought these candlesticks back for her from Paris when he was stationed there during the war," my mother told me as she packed them up in bubble wrap. "He used to remember, laughing, how everyone else bought perfume or jewelry for their girls and they teased him, but he told them how beautiful my mother looked by candlelight, and even though they were big and heavy, he carried them throughout his time there, picturing how they would light her face when he got them finally home."

But other things, endlessly everyday and mundane, have stories worth telling in them too. "Are we really saving these hideous things?" I asked, pulling puke green velvet curtains with huge orange flowers embroidered over them off her windows.

"Ugh, no, toss them," said my mother. "She found them in the remainder bin at an outlet store and liked the price. You know your grandmother. I told her they were ugly, but she said she was an old lady and wouldn't live long enough for it to be worth paying for expensive curtains."

"When was that?" I asked.

"Must have been more than fifteen years ago," said my mother, laughing. But then she dissolved in tears, regretting that she hadn't bought her prettier curtains for a birthday present or something in between.

"What about the card table?" asked my dad.

"Bring it across the hall," said my mother. "Mary and Mabel always played over here. They probably don't have a card table of their own." And we thought about my grandmother playing bridge—and hostess—into her final week on earth. "Give them the chip and dip plate too," added my mother. "They'll need it." See? Like a novel. Card table as character development. Candlesticks as memory.

In between sorting and packing sessions, we went back to our house, and people came and ate and remembered and forgot. Jews do this, sit shiva, spend a week sitting around hosting well-wishers and reminiscers, plying everyone with food. In some ways, it's very nice—this insistence that no, not yet, we aren't ready to move on. But it's also a long time to sit and look at the same sad faces and hear the same stories and eat bagels. I spent most of the week at home helping my parents, visiting with their friends and distant relatives, packing food out of and then back into Tupperware containers more or less hourly, and trying to talk myself into my new world. Nico came over one night, and we went for a long walk.

"What will I do without her?" I said.

"You won't be without her. You'll have your memories of her, her wisdom. Whenever I cook for a holiday or special occasion, I put a photo up on my fridge of my grandmother in an apron holding me on her hip with one hand and waving a huge spoon in the other."

"When did she die?" I had never met any of Nico's grandparents. By the time I met him, they were already gone.

"I was in middle school. But taking that picture, cooking with her that day, it's one of my earliest memories. She gave me the best cooking advice I ever received that day. It was because I wanted to add an entire bag of chocolate chips to the Rice Krispies treats we were making. She told me, 'You can always add more, but you can never add less.'"

"So that's where that came from," I laughed. "I think about that all the time when I cook." Then I admitted, "I guess I'm lucky really. I got to keep my grandmother for such a long time. I didn't lose her like you did so early."

"Yeah, but maybe that's bullshit," said Nico. "It sucks. You had more time. But you also have to feel it harder. All those years we didn't get are sad for me and my grandmother, but on the other hand, I was twelve. I was sad but also I just wanted to run around with my cousins in the backyard and forget about it. And I did. So it was easier for me in that way."

We thought about that for a bit. Then right before we got back to the house, Nico took my hand.

"I have one more thing to tell you," he said. "Caroline's pregnant."

I hugged him. I said I am so happy for you both. I said you will be a great father. He would be. But my heart wasn't in it. I was feeling anti-baby. I was feeling anti-family.

"We want you to be the godmother," said Nico.

"I'm not Catholic," I said.

"It's more ceremonial than that for us obviously. We aren't even married, so I'm not sure the church's biggest hang-up here is going to be that the godmother is a Jew. Really, there are only two criteria. It should be the person who's your favorite friend. And it should be the person who you'd want to take care of your child if you both die somehow. That's you."

"Why me?"

"Because you're my favorite friend. And you're a very good mother."

"I'm not a mother," I said quietly.

"But you've been being a mother. And someday you will be." I snorted. "What makes you think so?"

"Because you're my favorite friend. And you're a very good mother," said Nico.

Late that night, Ethan called. To see how I was doing. To update me on things at home. And to tell me this:

"I don't want to alarm you or anything, but we made out."

"I noticed," I whispered so as not to wake my folks. "I was there." Then, "It was nice."

"I thought so too." He was also whispering for no apparent reason. "But also kind of crazy."

"How so?"

"I don't know."

"I agree but me neither."

"What would you like to do about it?" he asked.

"I think I'd like to do it some more."

"This sounds like a good plan," he said. "You come home and we'll put it into action." Then we didn't say anything for quite a long time, just sat and felt the heart swell that came with the echo of our whispers, the memory of the kissing, and the promise we'd just made of there being more. Finally he whispered, "Do you want me to come up? Just for company? Support?"

"No, I'll be home tomorrow. It's a little crazy up here. But thanks."

"One more thing, Janey. I have this wedding to go to this weekend—an ex of mine is getting married—and I wondered if you'd be my date."

"I'm in," I said.

Thirty-eight

B Y THE TIME I got home, we had only two days left to start and finish the novel unit in my class. Katie had introduced it, and she and Ethan had tag-teamed the discussion, but there was still so much to cover. It had not been a good Summer One for me. But I had Summer Two to make up for it. In exchange for teaching so much of my class, I was taking the first week of Katie's so that she could honeymoon. Who would have imagined in October when we signed up for summer session classes that my grandmother would die in the middle of mine, that Katie would get married the weekend before hers? When I posed this rhetorical question to Ethan, he mused that actually both would have been pretty good bets. True, maybe, but not my point.

My point, as I discussed with my students, was that of course what happens in a novel is going to be momentous because that's why we're getting this story. Every day, every moment has its own story, but most of them are boring. The novel has culled all those cloudy moments into one crystal narrative worth telling. When I was a kid, I thought it so improbable that the poor boy I'd met in chapter one turned out to be the one kid in a million who unwrapped his chocolate bar and found the last golden ticket. But of course that was missing the point. A story where a kid unwraps a chocolate bar, finds no ticket, eats it, and goes home is not a narrative worth telling. And so we never find it in novel form. Maybe that kid goes home and finds, instead, a purple rabbit eating strappy sandals in his armoire; that would be remarkable indeed and then we would get that story instead.

My students thought this was obvious, but it's also somehow a sticking point to getting our heads entirely around the novel. We are, so often, lured in with the promise of a story about us, and indeed we meet people like us, only their lives are so exciting, so devastating and improbable, so full of intrigue and significance and coincidence that we cannot relate anymore. We know though that the narrator isn't going to tell about the summer when nothing happened; the narrator is going to tell about the summer when everything happened, when everything changed. In the end, maybe it's that one word—change—that is the point of the novel. Not what happened, maybe not even why so much, but what changed and what we learn as a result. And that "we" is so big. It's the major characters; it's the narrator; it's the minor characters too and the bit parts; it's the author; and, maybe most important of all, it's the reader as well because the reader has been on a journey too. But the journey itself is only half the battle. The other half—the take-home half—is figuring out what you learned along the way.

My students welcomed me back like old friends, and I don't mean that as metaphor alone. They were sorry about my grandmother, asked how my folks were doing, asked how I was doing. They were worried about Atlas. They asked about Katie's wedding plans (about which they knew a startling amount). For people with whom my relationship was pretty clearly not friendship (they work; I give them grades), for people I had met, en masse, just a few weeks ago, they knew an awful lot about my life. That happens sometimes, in some classrooms, with some groups. It happens especially during summer sessions—brief, intimate, intense—and especially, evidently, during summer sessions with crises. You'd think having three teachers—any one of whom could appear on any given day—would have unsettled them, but instead it had drawn them in. Just as we were dispensing with details for last days—portfolio requirements, when to turn in what, how to get final grades—Eliza Alford, speaking for the group, raised her hand, giggling, and said, "Can I ask one more thing? What's going on with you and Ethan?"

I tried but couldn't quite suppress the smile. I did, however, decline to answer the question.

At home, Katie, Jason, and Peter were packing Katie's stuff because of course when she got married, she wasn't going to keep living with me, a fact I should have realized long before I finally did. They were also packing what remained of Jill's and Atlas's stuff. I made them stop. I felt they could throw Jill's stuff out the window. And I maintained that Atlas might come back—would come back—and would need blankets and toys and books when he did. Jill and Daniel had missed the point entirely when they concluded that bringing Atlas's furniture to a new place with new people would be familiar to him, as if we weren't the home, as if home weren't where Katie and I were too. But he'd still need his things when he came back, and I refused to wrap them up and cram them into a box. I had done that once already this week, and I wasn't about to do it again. Instead, I went upstairs to grade.

Later, we rented movies about weddings and ordered pizza and sat on the floor in the living room, since there was no furniture there anymore, and tied birdseed and lavender into miniature squares of tulle with tiny green and purple ribbons that would have delighted Atlas had he been there to try to eat them. Lucas came by later, and he and Jason wanted to take Peter out somewhere ("Tying tulle is the lamest bachelor party ever," said Jason), but no one seemed much interested. Ethan had to grade and couldn't come over either. It was very quiet in the house. There was no Jill to yell or fight or slam doors. There was no Atlas screaming or crying or laughing. We did not have a house full of people. We didn't even have any furniture. And even though Atlas would have been sleeping, his quiet was always very loud, holding as it did the threat of waking and screaming or waking and wanting to be held or sleeping through the night and waking beaming and laughing at some ridiculous hour of the morning. The lack of Atlas's quiet was deafening.

Katie and I left the boys downstairs and went to try on her dress with various combinations of hair up/hair down, pearls/diamonds, veil/no veil. And then hair up, diamonds, no veil. Or hair down, diamonds, veil. Or no, what about hair up, pearls, no veil. Et cetera. It was fun, but it also felt like faking it, like it was supposed to be the happiest day of her life and mine, as her best friend, by extension, except it was dampened to the point of saturation.

The phone rang, but for the first time in weeks, my heart didn't pause when it did. I didn't even care. The bad news had already happened. It couldn't get any worse. It could only be mundane. "I'm coming over," said the telephone without pre-amble or pleasantry. "Get rid of everybody else." Jill. Of course. We told the boys they didn't have to leave, but there was no convincing them to stay.

Jill walked in without knocking about forty minutes later. (A clue to where she was living? Or had she stalled for time to throw us off her trail? Stopped for a snack? No way to know.) Katie and I were standing in the middle of our empty living room walking down the aisle to see whether we preferred with bouquet/empty-handed in combination with hair up/hair down and veil/no veil. The door banged open, and in walked Jill, hands on hips.

"Katie, you look ridiculous," she said.

"So . . . no bouquet then?"

"Why are you wearing that?"

"I'm getting married?"

"Not tonight."

"We're trying to figure out what to do with my hair and jew-elry and stuff."

This was getting off to an unfortunate start. It was also, of course, entirely missing the point.

"You didn't bring Atlas," I said.

"He's asleep," said Jill, angry, like I should have known that, but that wasn't my question. She figured this out. "He's at home with his father."

"His home is here," I said.

"There isn't even any furniture here," said Jill, like that was why she wouldn't bring him over. Like the reason we had no furniture was because we were unfit parents rather than because Atlas's own unfit parents had stolen it all. No one knew what to say to that. Jill softened a little bit.

"You look really beautiful, Katie. I was just surprised to see you dressed already," she said. "I've always liked your hair up."

"Thank you," said Katie. "Could you try to be a little nicer?"

Jill considered whether or not she could. Finally she said, "Do you guys have any food? I'm starved."

I offered her the tub of birdseed and lavender. Katie went to warm up the rest of the pizza. I suggested that she change first, but she said she'd be careful. Katie liked being in a wedding dress.

"I'm sorry about taking the furniture," said Jill. Like we cared about the furniture.

"Like we care about the furniture, Jill," I said.

"Look, Janey, I'm trying here. But you scared me. You were way too attached. I thought you might actually try to take Atlas away from me. I couldn't figure out why you'd lie. I couldn't figure out why you'd be back there with him trying to keep me away."

"Janey wouldn't do that," Katie broke in. "Janey was never trying to take the baby away. *You* took the baby away—"

"He's my baby," Jill interrupted.

"Yeah, now he is. Now that you have someone else to baby-sit—"

"Dan isn't babysitting. He's the father."

"Now that you have someone else to pick up the slack and support your nervous breakdowns and your mood swings, someone else to rearrange his life to take care of your responsibilities, someone else to do diapers and go to Atlas when he wakes up in the middle of the night and pick him up when he wakes up in the morning before dawn."

"You're getting married the day after tomorrow," said Jill. "You weren't sticking around anyway."

"You are deluding yourself," said Katie, "if you think that we wouldn't have rented a house right in the neighborhood, taken late shifts and early shifts, continued to arrange our lives around all of our schedules so we could keep taking care of Atlas."

"He's our baby too, Jill," I added. "Just because we didn't give birth to him doesn't mean that isn't true. You know this. I wasn't trying to keep him from you. He was sick. He needed his mother. I was the mother that was there. It wasn't even a lie. That's good parenting, not bad parenting. It's what he needed so it's what I did."

"The only person thinking about taking a baby," Katie said to Jill, "was you."

Jill said nothing. She looked dark. Then she said very, very quietly, "I had a chance to get Daniel back." And then, even more quietly, "We have a chance to be a real family."

"We were a real family," Katie and I said simultaneously. And Katie added, "You're the only one who seems not to have noticed."

Thirty-nine

SUMMER ONE'S FINAL project is a creative assignment. During regular term, everyone's brains are fried with final exams and the ends of four or five classes and a zillion other worries, none of them conducive to creativity. But during summer session, students aren't also taking calculus and chemistry and Latin American history, so they can dedicate all of their brain power to making meaning of their own. And Seattle summer is enchanting, inspiring; there's something magic about all that sun, all that long daylight. It enkindles creativity. I give them lots of choices—a few poems, a short story, a one-act, an essay, the start of a screenplay or novel. But mostly I get memoir, sometimes cloaked as something else but their own stories nonetheless. They think their lives are epic—and maybe they are, maybe all our lives are—and so they take the opportunity to get it all down.

I had missed a lot of time with these students. In recompense, whether in the spirit of guilt or solidarity, I have tried as well. Hence this story—my Summer One final exam. Somewhere between memoir, autobiography, literary theory, and pedagogical treatise, but isn't everything?

Last days are always a little bit sad. They are mostly joyful—I was about to have almost two months off—but even in the worst of classes, there are a few students you will miss. In this case, I was going to miss the whole bunch of them. Everyone shared snippets of their writing projects—read a poem or a chapter, an excerpt of an in-progress memoir or part of a short story. A couple of them cajoled classmates into performing part of a screenplay or one-act. It was amazing, not because they were all brilliant—they were varying levels of decent and not, rough drafts all of course—but because they were all so personal and heartfelt and dramatic. My students were right; their lives—or the lives they imagined—*were* epic, full of drama, full of plot. It wasn't just me. Many of them had had a crazy five weeks.

Last days also, of course, inspire reflection. I looked back with them on the five weeks we'd spent together and wondered at all that had changed, wondered, in fact, at how little had stayed the same.

I met Ethan on the steps outside, after all the goodbyes, just as we had on the first day of class.

"How'd it go?" I asked.

"Fine. I gave a lecture on the import of the study of history, reflected on what we learned in the course of human progress through the five hundred or so years we covered. You know, big-picture stuff. How about you?"

"Same."

"Really?"

"Everyone read excerpts from their creative writing projects."

"How is that the same?"

"It's the point of literature. What's changed. What we've learned."

"Interesting," mused Ethan. "Well, I can't give you five hundred years, but I can give you five weeks. What have you learned?"

"Me?"

"Everyone."

I thought about this. "Katie learned how to plan a last-minute wedding, a skill I'm sure she'll use again and again."

"Jason and Lucas learned crisis parenting," Ethan offered. "A skill they probably *will* use again and again."

"My grandmother learned to predict the future."

Ethan smiled. "Peter learned what he's in for."

"You too," I said.

"Yeah, me too."

"Jill learned she's mean and insane. She learned she doesn't care about me or trust me or even really like me."

"I don't think that's quite it."

"What about you?" I asked.

"I learned I do care about you and trust you. I even really like you," said Ethan. We sat quietly, eyes closed against the sun, legs leaning lightly against one another's, hands touching but not holding. "You?" he asked quietly after a long time.

"That," I said. "And, in the last thirty seconds or so, that it's warranted." He smiled again. "And some other stuff I haven't quite figured out yet."

"Atlas?" he asked.

I laughed and also teared up a little. "Atlas learned to make bubbles with his spit. He learned he likes wedding cake. He learned to chew blocks. He learned to bang on things with other things. He met his father. His lost his great-grandmother. He lost me and Katie. It's been quite a five weeks for Atlas."

"For Atlas," Ethan agreed, "it's only the beginning."

Ethan walked me home. Then Katie and I spent the afternoon on the phone making last-minute arrangements, answering questions for friends, giving relatives directions, reminding caterers about various dietary restrictions, and finding something blue. At some point, we realized we were starved.

"We should just carry out of somewhere," I said.

"No," said Katie, suddenly horrified. "You have to teach me how to cook. Before I get married."

"I tried," I reminded her. "You weren't really interested."

"I didn't really want to learn how to cook back then. I just said I did. Really, I just wanted to be friends with you and Jill."

"Seriously?"

"Of course."

"Can Peter cook?"

"I have no idea," she said blankly. And then under her breath, a little giggly, "I've only known him for a few weeks."

"You're not going far, and you're only getting married, not turning into a new person. I'll teach you how to cook next week."

The door opened suddenly, and it was Jill with a peace offering—pizza—having forgotten, evidently, that we'd had pizza last night for dinner. She also had Atlas.

"I want to come to the wedding tomorrow. I can't imagine you could get married and I wouldn't be there. I gave my blessing after all. Well, I *can* imagine that you could get married and I wouldn't be there, but I don't like it."

I walked directly over and took Atlas from her. He let out a squeal of delight. I turned around and walked straight up to his room, still mostly set up, slammed the door, and collapsed in the corner sobbing, rocking and rocking and rocking him in my lap. I expected Jill on my heels, but she had evidently concluded this was a cost of doing business or had forgiven me or chose just to let this one go. In any case, we had some time alone. "I love you and will always love you," I whispered to his hair. "I will never let you go. It may seem like I'm not there, but I am there. I will always be there. I am always there. You are mine. You are always mine. We are always family, you and I." Atlas did not seem to mind my hysteria or his newly sodden shirt. Atlas was entirely distracted by his yellow rabbit whom he'd evidently missed. Atlas seemed wholly healthy and well, happy, eating, repaired, and well. Atlas seemed home, but I knew he couldn't stay for long.

After a while, Jill and Katie came in and joined us on the floor. Jill had a speech. She delivered it while playing with the blocks, stacking and unstacking and restacking, but never looking at any of the three of us. We looked at the blocks too. "I'm sorry but not entirely sorry. I'm sorry I yelled, but I was angry. I'm sorry I had you arrested, but I was scared. I'm sorry I overreacted, but I was angry and scared. I'm sorry I took all the furniture—I was feeling vindictive. I'm sorry I wouldn't tell you where we were—I was being dramatic. Those are the things I am sorry for but not entirely. I also had a right to be scared and angry. And I have a right to do whatever I want with Atlas even if you don't agree with it, even if it's crazy.

"I also agree you have some right to Atlas but not entirely. I'll still need help with childcare, especially during Summer Two, plus I might be getting a full-time job, and since you two will both still be in school, you'll have a lot more flexible time than I will. I still want you to be a part of his life—a big part. I always want you to be a part of his life. But I don't want to live with you two for the rest of mine. I want to live with Dan. Dan and I are going to try again. We already loved each other. And who wouldn't love Atlas? I want to share but not entirely."

This seemed to be her theme—some but not entirely. And I figured I could live with that because I had to live with that. She still wanted to consider us babysitters rather than family and, at that, at her convenience rather than ours. She was being condescending and selfish, and she still wasn't getting it. But she was trying. And I was holding Atlas. And I figured I could live with that.

"We never thought we would all live together forever," said Katie.

"No," I agreed.

"We aren't babysitters," said Katie.

"No," I agreed again.

"And furthermore," said Katie, "we're your friends. Forget family. Forget what you owe us. We're your best friends. We have been for a long time. We only want what's best for you and anyone you love. We can talk about stuff. We're not mean and we're not idiots. And we're not characters. We're friends. We treat you like that. You should treat us like that."

"Yeah," I agreed. And then added, "I'm keeping the dog."

Because Jill is like this, after we all smiled gamely, exchanged hugs all around, and agreed to try, whatever that might entail, she asked if we would babysit so she and Dan could have an evening alone together. "We so totally need it," she said con-spiratorially. I swallowed my annoyance because it meant I got Atlas. Katie went over to Peter's for a last not-married-yet eve-ning together. I called Ethan and asked him to come over but didn't tell him why. While we waited, I told Atlas all about what he'd missed—how sick he'd been, how worried I was, how his parents had had me arrested, how much better he was now, how his great-grandmother had died, how Ethan had kissed me on the mouth and apparently wanted to do it again. I knew he couldn't understand. I just wanted him to know. I gave him his great-grandfather's cufflinks to suck on for a while. Then I put them back in their box and put them away for him for a few more years until he was ready as my grandmother had in-structed. "You can suck on them whenever you come over to visit me," I promised him, and he seemed satisfied.

"There's my baby," said Ethan, delighted, when he walked in and found Atlas on the floor playing with the stacking cups. He scooped him up. More squeals of delight. Atlas thought ev-eryone loved him because everyone he met did. "What hap-pened here? Janey, you have made some very good progress. Unless you really did kidnap him this time. You didn't kidnap him, did you?"

"Jill came over. She wants to go to the wedding tomorrow. She apologized but not entirely. She said she'd share but not entirely. She said she needs lots of babysitting help. She was really annoying but not entirely. Then she said she and Dan needed some alone time."

"Ballsy," said Ethan.

"Indeed."

"So we get Atlas."

"Indeed," I said happily. We settled in with Atlas between us on the floor to watch the ballgame and eat yet more pizza because that was what there was.

"Jill learned to share," offered Ethan during one of the commercials.

"I guess so. Or learned that she has no other choice."

"You learned to forgive," he somewhere between stated and asked and reached over Atlas as he did so and cupped the back of my head with his hand.

"Working on it," I said.

"You learned you can never lose this child—"

"Maybe."

"Because he will always be in your life—"

"Maybe."

"Because that's what family means—"

"Maybe."

"And because you are a very good mother and a very good friend and a very, very good person."

"Are you trying to make me cry?" I said.

"Maybe," he said.

Ethan begged off early. Wedding setup (the guys' job) started earlier than getting Katie dressed (ours). Katie came home, fairly floating, and then Jill, less so. It used to be that we sat on the floor together when we were having silly evenings or intimate ones or when we were watching Atlas play. Now we did it because Jill had taken all our furniture, but it conjured those evenings nonetheless. I couldn't decide whether this recollection made me feel happy in the memory of it or sad in the vast gap that had opened up between then and now. Both I suppose. Sort of like the night before your best friend gets married—I was so happy for her, but also, I was pretty sad for me. There were so many ways in which this wedding was also loss.

"So are you nervous?" Jill asked Katie.

"No, actually."

"You should be. You hardly know him. Marriage is long." Jill, indelicate as ever, but I checked my annoyance because, the farthest reaches of my memory insisted, this was what we'd always loved about Jill, her bluntness and honesty.

"I know this is meant to be. I know it's what God intends. I know Peter loves me, and I love him. I know he's the perfect person for me and I for him."

"And you know sex hurts a lot, right?" said Jill.

"Really?"

"A lot. Your first time? It's going to hurt like hell."

"It's not that bad," I put in. "It doesn't hurt that much. You'll use lots of lubricant. I already stashed some in the side pocket of your suitcase. Wedding present. You'll be fine."

"Gross," said Katie.

"You better get used to this pretty quickly," said Jill. "You only have about sixteen hours. You know how, right?"

"Yes. I'm not stupid. I do read."

"You're a Victorianist," Jill pointed out. "It's more fun than they let on, you know. But not the first time."

"Be on top," I advised. "It's easier."

"Don't be nervous," said Jill gravely. "Being nervous will make it harder."

"He's a sweet guy, Katie." I tried to sound reassuring. "You'll figure it out together."

"You could have heavy petting," suggested Jill, getting giggly. "You haven't ever even touched an adult penis. And the man hasn't had a nipple in his mouth since his mother's. It took me three years to get from second base all the way home. You're thinking of doing it in twenty minutes. Maybe you should delay actual sex for a night or two."

"That's not a bad idea," I said. "Give you something to look forward to, give you a goal for your honeymoon."

"You have to have sex the night you get married," Katie insisted.

"According to God?" Jill asked.

"According to everyone. Everyone knows you have sex the night you get married. I'm sure it will be great. Stop freaking me out. What about you? Are you nervous?"

"Me? Why?"

"Because all of a sudden you're not just back together but living with a guy who dumped you when he found out you were pregnant."

"He didn't dump me," said Jill, going dark again.

"No, he didn't even do you the courtesy of dumping you. He just disappeared and then reappeared without apology or explanation," said Katie, whose near wifely status had evidently conferred on her some of Jill's bluntness.

"He's given me both apology and explanation," said Jill, but she didn't seem sure. "He was scared and angry and felt manipulated. He needed to get away and finish being a kid, a college student. He thought he had years more of that freedom coming to him. But then he got a job, lived alone, realized he was lonely. It wasn't a baby that was encroaching on his freedom; it was adulthood that was doing that. What, was I supposed to never forgive him and ruin all of our lives over some confusion and fear?"

"But don't you feel settled for?" said Katie. "He's lonely, so he'll come back to you. He has to be responsible anyway, so he might as well have a kid."

I thought Jill would explode or try to have everyone arrested again. But instead she just talked to us and got more and more sullen, so much so that soon we switched tactics and started reassuring.

"I'm sure he loves you and Atlas, or he would have stayed gone," said Katie.

"If living with him doesn't work out, you can always try living alone for a while or with your mom. You can always move back in with me," I tried.

She looked up. "You would still do that?"

"What?"

"Let me live with you again?"

I shrugged and admitted it. It was embarrassing maybe. But it was also true.

"Because you love Atlas?" said Jill.

"Yes. And because I love you."

Then, finally, Jill apologized—entirely. "Weddings suck," she said. Maybe this didn't sound like an apology at first, but that's what it was. "Dry cake, bad outfits, creepy relatives. That stupid chicken dance. Sappy, empty vows—honor, obey, forsake all others—what is that crap? No offense, Katie, but I've always thought it was such a load of shit.

"Now, though, I don't know. Things change. Love's unstable. I would never obey anyone, obviously. But I do know we'll always be together—that we're stuck with each other—because you are Atlas's family. My family," said Jill. "This will never not be true. Other things will change. Everything else might change. But for better or for worse, this will never change."

Then it was late, and we had a big day tomorrow, and Jill claimed not to want to drive back to Daniel's so late, but really I think she was just coming home, and since mine was the only bed left in the house, we all climbed into it and went to sleep.

Forty

THE NEXT DAY we had a wedding in the backyard. I stood at the front next to Katie and Jill and felt the sun and the wind and considered, because the bishop asked us to, what it all meant. This story ends with a death and a wedding. Does that make it tragedy or comedy? It ends with the dissolution of our little family, though not entirely, and the forming and re-forming instead of two couples, possibly three. Does that mean it reifies traditional conceptions of family? Of narrative? It couldn't possibly because none of us believe it. Because Jill and Katie and I are all moving, not in together anymore, but near each other like before. Because Jason and Lucas are having a baby. Because Ethan promises me that Atlas will always be my family and not, I think, just to make me feel better. Because we are all too in love with each other to be just friends. Because sometimes I hate them, but it doesn't matter. Because who else would you forgive for having you arrested but family?

But it's also because this journey is not to death; this journey is not to marriage, and it's not to couplehood or even parenthood. This journey begins with friendship and comes back to it again. My grandmother thought it all started with the baby in the Waldorf-Astoria, but that's because for my grandmother, the story was all about me. I know better though. It's the cracker aisle, meeting Jill, teaching Katie how to cook. The beginning of this story, Atlas's story, is the three of us. And here, at the end, at the end of this part anyway, I looked out over how much bigger we'd become. Atlas was sitting on Jason's lap, for the moment anyway more comfortable with him than with Daniel, and holding Lucas's index finger in his tiny fist. Diane sat next to Lucas, trying to watch the wedding but having a hard time taking her eyes off her beautiful grandson. Dan sat next to her, sneaking occasional nervous glances at her beautiful grandson but having a hard time taking his eyes off Jill. My parents were there, happy for the first time in weeks, trying to keep Uncle Claude from rushing the altar. Ethan was there, smiling at me from somewhere between awe and wonder. It was a combination that worked for me. But none of that suggested it wasn't a story from friendship and back again. In the beginning, in the end, it was our story, our wedding, we three.

Katie was happy. Truly happy. You had only to look at her. Peter seemed indeed like he must be her One. It wasn't based on the foundation of the years of friendship they shared, but maybe it was all the trial and error. Maybe it was God. Jill I was less sure about. Jill seemed angry and depressed and insane. I didn't know that Dan would stay. I didn't know that she would forgive him. I wasn't sure she should. I wasn't sure she could handle Atlas without more live-in help. So that's a wash maybe? They cancel each other out? Katie's surety versus Jill's unknown? Katie's joy versus Jill's crazy?

And me? I was what an unreliable narrator should be. Sadder but wiser and happier too. More skeptical, more injured, more in love. More tied in. Neither tragic nor comic. Not a happy ending exactly and certainly not a sad one. Ambiguous. With an emphasis on the why rather than the what, the what having been fairly clear all along. With an emphasis on the love rather than the anger, there being hefty helpings of both, this being family after all, but with love winning out in the end because that's what it means to end. That's how you know you've come to a close for the moment—because you've found the love again. You've reclaimed it, or it has—they have—you. This is why, finally, there are so many weddings at the ends of books. Not because the weddings are so much ends themselves but because it's hard to go forward with the story after that much love. It's too trite to use words to talk about it. It's too momentous and extraordinary to return from to the mundane and the everyday. It is astonishing that after all the evidence and warnings to the contrary, such a leap of faith is possible. It asks us all what if you could love and be loved this much? In words, in spirit, in person even, it's almost hard to believe. But believe it we must, we do, and so in the end, with our family, with our friends, with the ones who are both, with the ones we parent and choose to parent, with the ones we kiss on the mouth, with the ones we take in, with the ones who leave us, with the ones who come back, with the ones we remember, we make the leap. In the end, we leap; we always do.

Acknowledgments

One of the ways writing a book is better than winning an Academy Award is your thank-yous can go on as long as you like, and no one can play cheesy music to make you stop before you're ready. My thanks are many and large and from my heart of hearts, so this might take a while.

Thank you to Molly Friedrich, worker of miracles, whose phone call was the best I've ever received and whose guidance feels always absolutely right.

Thank you to my editor, Lindsay Sagnette, whose work on behalf of this book has been tremendous and whose enthusiasm for it has rivaled my own mother's, which is saying something.

Thank you to the lovely Lucy Carson for her guidance and patience and kindness, and to Paul Cirone for all his support and hard work.

Thank you to early readers and cheerleaders Paul Mariz, Susan Frankel, David Frankel, Erin Trendler, Lisa Corr, Sam Chambers,.Rebecca Brown, Alicia Goodwin, Jennifer Crouch, Helen Heffer, Paul Capobianco, and especially, Lil Maughan.

Thanks to Barbara Catlin for permission to use her story, to Adrienne Grau-Cooper and Alicia Goodwin for medical advice, and to Mike Everton, with apologies, for the *Moby-Dick* bit.

Thank you to Daniel for finally coming home.

Thanks to my parents, Susan and David Frankel, whose support of this book started before I could even read books and has never waned. They have been—they have *always* been—more loving, more warm, more generous, more supportive parents than I can even imagine, and hence Janey's folks pale in comparison to my own.

About Paul Mariz, I can say only this: 6.8 billion people in the world, and he is the very best one. So much of this book is his—in spirit, in creation, in idea, in will, in love and support, in all the practical ways and all the gushy ones. He read and reread and discussed endlessly, fixed what was broken, cheered up what flagged, and believed from the beginning. I am very very lucky.

And last, I wish there were a way to say thank you to my grandmothers, Doris Hess and Reba Frankel, both of whom are all over this book and both of whom would have been beside themselves with joy to see it in print.

1. Which of the three main characters do you identify with most? Who do you identify with least? Do these three seem too different to be such close friends? Do you have friends with whom you don't have much in common, but you love them to death anyway? What holds friendships like these together?

2. Janey talks a lot about family versus friendship. What other kinds of families are there in this book besides Janey's very traditional one with her parents and her grandmother? Which of the relationships in this book feel like family and which like friendship? What's the difference between a group of friends and a group of friends who become family?

3. When Dan finds out Jill is pregnant, he argues that he should have the right to choose an abortion, that the decision to have the baby or not shouldn't be Jill's alone just because she's the woman. Are you sympathetic to his argument? Do you think he's right here?

4. What does Atlas lose and what does he gain from his nontraditional upbringing?

5. Janey keeps comparing life to literature and literature to life. How do life and literature overlap in this book? And how do life and literature or books overlap in your life?

6. Janey forgives Jill at the end of the book. Do you? What has Jill done that seems unforgivable? Why might she have done it? To what extent are her actions understandable and her fears well founded?

7. All three of the main characters seem more or less paired up by the end of the novel. Which of these relationships seem like they'll last and which seem like they might be headed for breakups? Do you like the guys?

8. What has Janey learned from her grandmother by the end of the book? What are the most important lessons you've learned from loved ones you've lost?

9. Janey argues that the wedding at the end is really for the three of them—herself, Jill, and Katie. For better and for worse. In what ways is their relationship like a marriage?

10. Where do you see these characters in five years? Janey? Katie? Jill? Atlas?

Discussion Questions

St. Martin's Griffin